NO SHOES, NO SHIRT, NO SPELLS
by Rose Pressey

Praise for Me and My Ghoulfriends by Rose Pressey

"Rose Pressey spins a delightful tale with misfits and romance that makes me cheer loudly."
Coffee Time Romance

"Her characters are alive and full of quick witted charm and will make you laugh. The plot twists keep you turning the pages non-stop."
ParaNormalRomance

"I absolutely loved this book! It had me chuckling from the beginning."
Fallen Angel Reviews

Rose Pressey's Complete Bookshelf (click title to preview/buy)

A Maggie P.I. Mystery: Book 1 – Crime Wave

The Halloween LaVeau Series:
Book 1 – Forever Charmed
Book 2 – Charmed Again

The Rylie Cruz Series:
Book 1 – How to Date a Werewolf
Book 2 – How to Date a Vampire
Book 3 – How to Date a Demon

The Larue Donovan Series:
Book 1 – Me and My Ghoulfriends
Book 2 – Ghouls Night Out
Book 3 – The Ghoul Next Door

The Mystic Café Series:
Book 1 – No Shoes, No Shirt, No Spells
Book 2 – Pies and Potions

The Veronica Mason Series:
Book 1 – Rock 'n' Roll is Undead

D0366417

A Trash to Treasure Crafting Mystery:
Book 1 – Murder at Honeysuckle Hotel

The Haunted Renovation Mystery Series:
Book 1 – Flip that Haunted House
Book 2 – The Haunted Fixer Upper

Table of Contents

Dedication
This is to you and you know who you are.

Acknowledgements
To my son, who brings me joy every single day. To my mother, who introduced me to the love of books. To my husband, who encourages me and always has faith in me.

Chapter One

"This town would fall apart without magic." Grandma Imelda plopped the big leather-bound book onto the café's kitchen counter. "The people of Mystic Hollow needed me...and now they need you."

"You want me to add magic to the food? Me? You do remember that incident with the grilled cheese and the fire department, right?" Sure, I'd been fourteen at the time. Fourteen years later, and my clumsiness hadn't changed much. I took in a deep breath, catching a whiff of fresh-from-the-oven biscuits and wild blueberry muffins. In spite of the aroma, my insides churned and bubbled, forming a big ball of anxiety in the pit of my stomach.

Grandma Imelda nodded. Her expression remained impervious at the reminder of the house fire episode. The mass of white hair whirled high on top of her head like a giant ice cream cone didn't budge an inch as she pushed the massive aged book toward me—the thing took up half the counter space. Across the front of the book, the words *Mystic Magic* stared back at me, revealing the gravity of the situation. I traced the gold embossed letters with my index finger.

"Don't gawk at it, honey, open it up," she nudged with a tap of her crimson-red painted fingernail against the counter.

"Why didn't you tell me about this before now?" I looked at her, then back at the mysterious tome.

Out of nowhere, she had hit me with this magic business. I didn't know if she'd lost her mind, or if I had, and I was only imagining this whole peculiar state of affairs.

"It wasn't the right time to hand over the controls. You weren't ready to handle the steering wheel."

"What makes you think I'm ready now? I got a speeding ticket just last week."

She chuckled. "You'll be fine."

Wafts of cinnamon, vanilla and nutmeg tickled my nostrils when I flipped open the cover. The pages were made of thick, cream-colored paper with romantic black font. Each one had its own unique symbol placed in the center at the top. A book of magic spells; I expected sparkles to pop out with each turned page.

Grandma Imelda had announced her retirement two days before and insisted that her little café was now mine. Imagine. Me running a café. Of all the career options out there, this was the last one I'd have selected for myself. I wasn't sure my experience as an administrative assistant qualified me for restaurant management. But she didn't seem concerned. Now I had to figure out how to run the whole operation, magic and all. Pronto.

"Running this place is one thing, but magic? How is that possible?" I fingered the pages of the book.

"Follow my recipes and it'll be as if I'm still here." She reached across the counter and squeezed my hand.

Magic was make-believe, part of fairy tales and their promises of happily ever after. But regardless of how hard this was for me to accept, by taking the book I'd promised to follow her recipes exactly as she'd specified, and I never liked to break a promise.

"How will I know what kind of spells to use?" I asked. "People can't ask for specific help if they don't know they're receiving it."

"You'll know what spells are needed. You'll feel it." She pointed toward my heart. "Right there."

So far, I felt nothing other than the burning desire to run away from this situation as fast as my legs would carry me. Unfortunately, it wouldn't be nearly as quick as needed. Days ago, I'd been in my tiny Brooklyn apartment, eating a peanut butter and jelly sandwich. After a long day working too many hours for too little pay for a boss who thought it was her world and everyone else was living in it, I wanted nothing more than to relax and watch a few down-home cookin' TV shows. I loved Southern cooking, even if low fat meant three sticks of butter per recipe instead of six. My cooking might not be the best, but that didn't mean I couldn't fantasize about giving the chefs on TV a run for their money.

That night, as if Grandma Imelda sensed my misery, she called. The next thing I knew, I was on a plane headed back to Kentucky for a 'family emergency', which turned out to be nothing more than Grandma Imelda wanting to retire, effective immediately. When she got an idea in her head, she didn't stop until she'd accomplished her goal. Her goal this time: walk along the sandy Atlantic shore and read a good book.

Grandma Imelda had insisted I arrive at the butt-crack of dawn to pick up the keys, churn out biscuits, prepare batter for pancakes, and have a crash course in magic spell preparation before she took off for oranges and Disney World.

Mystic Café served good ol' southern food for breakfast and lunch, plus mouthwatering desserts. Grandma's pies and cakes ranked at the top of my favorite indulgences list—even above white chocolate. I know it's not real chocolate, but it's oh-so-creamy. My mouth watered just thinking of the intense flavor of grandma's juicy blueberry pie. For the love of all things deep-fried, how was I going to live up to her talent? How would I fill her apron strings?

"Grandma, you know I can't cook like you." Like I said, I'd never been the best cook, even though I'd always loved to bake. But baking was a far cry from serving breakfast and lunch every day.

"You'll be fine, Elly. You know how many years I worked to make the café a success. If I had any doubts, I wouldn't hand this place over to you."

No pressure. No pressure, at all. I'd worked in the café every day after high school, but that was years ago. Back then, grandma had allowed me more and more opportunities to handle the cooking, but baking was always my favorite—my specialty: red velvet cake. When she'd hovered over my shoulder, telling me which ingredients to add, I'd thought she was only checking my work, now I knew she had been adding her magic.

"At least I finally got you back here. It was hard to get the magic to you when you lived so far away. Why do you think I sent you those cookies all the time?"

"I thought you were being grandmotherly."

"From the looks of your skinny self, I can tell you didn't eat any." She squeezed my arm.

"Pshaw. Look at my hips. I'm well within the healthy range for my height, thank you very much."

Grandma pinched off a piece of warm biscuit. When I parted my lips to speak again, she popped the morsel into my mouth. I coughed, then chewed in order to prevent choking.

She winked and broke off another piece and dropped it into her mouth. When grandma finished chewing, she said, "When I make customers' individual meals, I add the spell meant for them, but some of the desserts have general spells attached to them. The general spells are a piece of cake."

Easy for her to say.

Chapter Two

"General spells?" I rubbed my temples, feeling a throbbing pain begin its steady pounding in my head.

"Yes, for things like health, love... Everyone can use those things." She smiled.

"I suppose that's true." When I finished the rest of her biscuit, I asked, "Am I a witch?" Next thing I knew, I'd grow warts and cackle.

"I can't answer that question, dear, only you can know that," she said with a wink and a twinkle in her eyes. The same twinkle she had when, at the age of six, I asked her if Santa Claus was real.

"You're not telling me everything," I pressed.

"This is a lot to understand, Elly, I know that, but everything will fall into place. You'll see. I have faith in you." Just because she had faith in me didn't mean I had faith in myself. "Everything you need to know is in the book. And remember, focus is the most important part. You can't be thinking 'bout your grocery list."

How would I focus on something I didn't understand? I wasn't convinced I believed in her magic. Grandma wouldn't lie to me, but still...magic?

She glanced at the delicate gold watch on her wrist. "It's time to open, why don't you go flip the sign."

We'd prepped the café for the breakfast crowd, but I wasn't sure I was prepped. I did as I was told though, and flipped the sign in the window to *Open* and unlocked the door. The first customer didn't waste any time marching in once we'd opened for business.

"Did Mom know about this? Is that why she didn't want to run the café?" I watched as a man slipped into a booth by the front window. He pulled out his newspaper and began reading.

"No, she doesn't know. She'd rather clean toilets than cook a meal. You should know that by now." She patted me on the back. "Go tend to the customer, dear. Why don't you give the magic a try?"

My mouth felt as if I'd devoured a package of saltines. "How will I know what magic to use on whom?"

"It's part of the magic. Intuitive. You'll know and feel it. Use the book and follow the spells."

This was getting weirder by the minute.

"I don't know what to do." My hands tingled and my heart thumped. "I can't do this." I shook my head.

She held my arm. "You can do this. Just give it a try. Now concentrate. Go over and tell me what you feel from him. Does he send off any vibes to you?"

I took in a deep breath and studied the customer. A middle-aged man who wore jeans a little too short for him, or maybe they were pulled up a little too far. He wore a yellow polo shirt tucked in with a tight belt around his middle. His salt-and-pepper hair was combed over to the left side.

After taking another deep breath and releasing it, I said, "Okay, I'll just go over with a glass of water and see if the vibe comes off him when I'm closer. But remember, I'm only doing this because I love you so much." Water splashed over the counter as I tried to steady my shaking hand. I poured the glass of water and moved toward him, focusing on feeling a vibe the entire time. *Feel the vibe. Feel the vibe.* This was crazy. There was no way I'd sense anything.

When I was a few steps away, the electric-like charge hit me. The energy surrounded him and glided toward me, circling me like an invisible dust storm. It seemed so real, I expected sparks to fly. With heavy legs and forced steps, I moved closer until I'd reached the edge of the table. A dab of water splashed over the side of the glass as I placed it in front of him.

"Welcome to Mystic Café." My voice wavered.

When he peered up at me, his energy slapped me in the face. The shock from this feeling made me suck in a sharp breath. The stress came off him in waves. He needed to relax in the worst way.

I handed him the menu. "I'll be back in a second to get your order."

He waved a hand. "No need. I already know what I'd like."

"Oh, okay. What can I get you?" I tried to sound more confident.

He handed back the menu. "I'll have the biscuits and gravy, and a cup of coffee."

"Coming right up." I spun around and hurried back toward the kitchen, almost giddy from the adrenaline of feeling his emotions.

Grandma watched from the kitchen window with a smile plastered on her face.

"Well?" she asked when I pushed through the swinging door.

"I felt something. I actually felt something." I attempted to catch my breath. "I can't believe it. You may be right about this magic stuff."

"May be? Honey, I know I'm right. So tell me what you felt."

"Stress. I felt lots of stress, as if he needs a breather...and a vacation." She slid the book in front of me. "Okay, so look in the book for a little somethin' to reduce stress."

I flipped through the pages until I found a spell that might fit. Large calligraphy print covered the space with a scrolled symbol at the top. I studied the yellow-tinged page.

"This doesn't add up. The book looks old, but the wording is modern." I looked at grandma.

"They update it periodically."

"Of course they do." I clicked my tongue. "But who are *they*?"

"The overseers of magic...but we won't get into that just now. That's a conversation for another day."

It seemed as if that was kind of an important detail to leave for a later discussion, but I didn't press the issue.

"This whole thing makes my head swim."

"It confused me at first, too, but you have to do this for me. I need a break from cooking. You don't want your dear grandma to work herself to death, do you?"

She knew my weakness. The guilt of saying no would cause me a slow, agonizing death. "Okay, Grandma, I'll do it. Don't worry about a thing." I knew she had doubts in spite of her upbeat attitude to the contrary. I had doubts too, but my protestations would be fruitless. I might as well start flippin' pancakes and fryin' chicken legs.

"Okay, this one says *Vacation in a Jiffy*. That's a real spell? It sure beats the heck out of a Carnival Cruise, if it is," I deadpanned.

She winked. "It's in the book, isn't it?"

"Well, I can't believe my eyes, but yes, it sure is." I nodded. "So what do I do now?"

She pointed at the book. "What does it say to do?"

"It lists magic spices."

Grandma's many bracelets jingled as she moved to the other side of the kitchen. "I have all the spices in the cabinet over here. I take out what I need and apply them to the food the customer orders. What did he order?" She placed her hands on her hips.

"Biscuits and gravy," I murmured.

Her eyes lit up. "Makes my mouth water. You know, the biscuits recipe came from my great-grandmother."

"Did she perform magic?"

"Yes, she did, and from what I've heard, she was darn good at it. Okay…" She clapped her hands together. "Put the biscuits on the plate and cover 'em with a healthy dose of gravy, then sprinkle the appropriate spices on top."

"Just like that? That's all I do?" I placed biscuits around the plate and covered them until it looked like nothing but a plate of thick white gravy.

"Just like that," she said.

My mouth watered, too. Grandma's gravy had always been one of my favorites—with little bits of sausage and pepper, seasoned to perfection. Yum. Okay, so I had a ton of food favorites, but that's what they made treadmills and gym memberships for, right?

"Okay." She clapped her hands. "Do you have the right spices? Always make sure you double check. You wouldn't want the wrong person to get the wrong magic."

"Would it hurt? I mean, everyone can use less stress in their life, right?"

"You'd be surprised. Sure, everyone can use less stress, but it may not always have the best outcome. What if the person is all worked up because of financial problems and you give them magic for stress for love reasons, that would make the person still stressed, but in love with money. Does that make sense?"

"I think so…" Not really, but I didn't want to worry her further.

"It's always best to leave the magic for the intended receiver, unless it's just one of the general spells."

I nodded. "Okay, general spell, but for the person it's meant for." Would that still make it a general spell? Never mind, I didn't ask. It would only make my head hurt worse.

"So put spices on top," she nudged with a touch of her hand.

My hands shook as I stretched my arm forward. The bottle slipped from my grasp, bouncing off the stovetop and tumbling to the floor. It landed with a thud. Spices littered the ground. I let out a breathy little gasp.

"Grandma," I said as I picked the bottle from the floor.

"Yes, sweetheart." She reached for the broom and began sweeping without saying a word about my clumsiness.

I inhaled a sharp breath and nearly dropped the bottle again.

"I was going to ask what happens when the spices run out...but I think I got my answer." Almost the entire bottle's contents had spattered onto the floor, but as I held the little glass container, they reappeared before my eyes.

"They don't run out. They're magic."

"Right. Of course. Magic."

"When they get low, they just replenish." She clicked her tongue.

"I see that."

Tightening my grip, I reached forward and sprinkled the spices across the food. The gravy popped, crackled, and sparked. It sounded like the pop rock candy I ate as a child, except the sizzling sound wasn't just in my head. Blue and red lights flashed in a spectacular mini light show. Grandma grabbed my arm and stuck my hand over the top of the food. Tiny zaps of electricity poked at my palm.

I jumped back and clutched my chest. "Oh my gosh. I wasn't expecting that."

Grandma chuckled.

"Can the customers hear or see that?" I looked toward the dining area.

"They can't hear or see what's going on back here, don't worry about it. Don't forget to recite the words from the spell."

"Right." I cleared my throat and studied the page. This had better work, or he'd end up in some vacation hell somewhere. Like a no-carbs-allowed retreat or an antiquing weekend getaway with his wife—every man's worst nightmare.

"Time for rest, time for play, take him from this stress into a place of hope and quietude. So mote it be."

"Excellent, Elly." She draped her arm around my shoulders and squeezed.

"Is that all I do?" My expression must have shown my confusion. "Seems kind of simple. I thought there would be more to it than that."

"For that particular spell, yes, but some spells have words to recite, while others allow you to speak from the heart, adding your own words. Trust your grandmother, dear. You'll get the hang of things in no time. Oh, and one more thing, always stir clockwise to ensure the spell works. Because that's the direction the sun moves and you'll want to use the earth's energy."

No offense to my grandmother, but she should have started these magical lessons a long time ago. I hesitated before picking up the plate, afraid that I'd be electrocuted or disappear into a puff of smoke.

"It won't hurt you. Pick it up." She nudged my elbow.

Why couldn't the spell casting be as easy as a twitch of my nose complete with a cute little tinkle sound? I grabbed the plate and marched through the kitchen door with the man's food stretched way out in front of me as if it was a dirty diaper of contaminated poo-poo. I placed it on the counter in order to grab a mug for the coffee. I prayed I'd make it to the table without dumping the contents on the man's lap. My hands shook and my heart thumped loudly in my ears. Guilt must have been written all over my face as if I'd committed the most heinous crime.

"I'll get the coffee. You get the biscuits over to the customer and see the reaction on his face when he takes a bite."

I let out a deep breath, full of anticipation. "If you say so."

"I'll bet he looks ten years younger after one bite. Hmm. Now that I look at him, he's not a half bad looking man."

"Focus, Grandma."

"I got the coffee." She grinned. "You go ahead."

I picked up the plate holding the magic biscuits and forced my feet to move forward, back to the table where the man was still engrossed in the business section. He didn't look up until I placed the dish in front of him.

Chapter Three

"Oh, thanks. It looks delicious." The man placed his paper down.
Grandma set the mug on the table and poured the hot liquid, giving him
a little wink and a smile. I rolled my eyes. Now was not the time for
flirting, although she'd always lived by the personal philosophy that
there was always time for flirting.
"Thanks." He smiled back.
We moved back to the counter for a better view of the show. I was
convinced we wouldn't notice any difference in this man. Maybe a look of
delight when he realized how good the gravy was, but I wasn't expecting
much else. He lifted his fork and I held my breath in anticipation.
"Get ready. Just watch," she said.
Staring at him while he ate was a bit weird. The man relished the first
bite and didn't slow down, taking the next shovelful in his mouth. The
more he ate, the more he grinned and a glint appeared in his eyes. The
air of anxiety around him seemed to fade like a deflating balloon.
"You did it." Grandma beamed.
"You think?" I looked from grandma to the man and back to her.
"I don't think, I know. You can feel it, don't forget to feel. You'll sense
everything you need to know."
"How many people know about this magic?" I lowered my voice so the
man wouldn't hear.
"Not many, and we have to keep it that way."
"Isn't it a little hard? Won't word get out?"
"Not if you don't tell them." She raised a brow. "It's been a secret for
many years."
"Is that why this town's called Mystic Hollow?"
She winked. "You catch on quick."
"Apparently not quick enough, if it took me all these years to find out
about this. You were doing this right under my nose."
I had always wondered about that big mysterious book placed
awkwardly among the other normal-looking cookbooks. But the few
times I made up my mind to snoop at the contents, it would be gone.
"Does Mom have the ability to perform this magic?"
Grandma shook her head. "I wish she did, but she doesn't. Only a few
do, and you're one of the lucky ones. It skips a generation most of the
time. Your daughter…." She looked toward the sky and placed her hands
in a prayer gesture. "Heaven hope that you eventually make me a great-
grandmother."
I rolled my eyes.
"Your daughters may or may not have this talent."
"Talent? Is that what you call it? I don't know about that. Curse,
maybe." I poured myself a glass of water. "So, where does this magic
come from?"
"It comes from all around you. It comes from nature." She gestured
around the room. "It just is. Like the sky is blue and the sun rises and
sets every day. It's part of the magic. Intuitive. You'll know and feel it."

I took a big gulp from the glass. "There has to be more to it than that."

"That's it." She shrugged with a chuckle.

"I like definitive answers."

"You can't always have answers, my dear, sometimes you have to go with the flow."

I finished off the water. "I think I'm going with the flow now, don't you?"

She smiled. "Well, you're certainly giving it your best shot, I'll give you that."

"Thanks...I think. What if something goes wrong?"

She frowned. "Nothing will go wrong. And if it does...well, no..." She shook her head. "I know you'll be perfect."

"Grandma, I know you let me bake before, but I had the strange feeling you never trusted me with more than refilling coffee cups. Now you leave the running of the café to me. I'm expected to cook? What made you change your mind?"

"I trusted you with the baking, didn't I? I sensed the magic. It usually doesn't appear until the mid-twenties, so I had no idea if you'd be a terrible cook and awful with magic like your mother or if you'd take after your dear, old grandmother." She batted her eyelashes.

I shook my head. "Are we the only people who do this 'magic'?"

"No."

I swallowed hard. "There are others?"

"Yes, ma'am."

"Like who?" I asked.

"That's a story for another day. Let's just say this town wouldn't be so cozy and charming without the help of a few magic spells here and there."

"Come on, Grandma, I can't believe you're not going to tell me. Give me a hint. One name?"

"Harry at the barbershop gives magical haircuts." She blurted out with a mischievous twinkle in her eye. "Oops." She covered her mouth with her hand.

"Haircuts? Magical?" I snorted.

"His scissors are special." She glanced over her shoulder as if someone might hear her secret.

"From the looks of the haircuts I've seen around here, I wouldn't call that magic. Tragic, maybe."

She laughed. "It's not about the haircut. It's about the way the person feels when he leaves Harry's place."

I stared for a beat. "This is a lot to take in, you know?"

"I know, and it'll be more real to you once you get the hang of things."

When my magical experiment paid and bounced out the door, Grandma Imelda walked around the counter. "If you need help, just give me a jingle on my cell phone." She held her hand up to her ear, mimicking a phone.

Next thing I knew, she'd be sending text messages with smiley faces and following me on Twitter. "If I'm on the golf course, leave a message and I'll call you back. Don't worry about a thing. Remember, Mary Jane is always here to help you, too."

Mary Jane had worked at Mystic Café for quite a while, but my grandmother never let her near the stove. She didn't know how to cook or cast a magic spell and these things were currently at the top of my priorities list. How much help she'd provide was up for debate.

Grandma Imelda handed me the keys to the café and headed toward the front door. "And remember, Elly, the spells won't work for selfish reasons. Don't try one on yourself, it won't work."

"Do you have any idea how many times I've wanted to be like Samantha on *Bewitched*?" I asked.

Being able to turn someone into a frog alone would be worth putting up with Endora. Of course, I wouldn't leave someone as a frog for long...just long enough to hear a few croaks and have them eat several flies. I'd start with Beth Higgins. She was the ultimate mean girl in high school. I'd heard she hadn't changed much since, either.

"I'm afraid it doesn't work that way, sorry." She draped her arm around my shoulders and squeezed.

"Bummer."

"Magic does have its limitations. It can't give you everything you want. I'd have found me one hunk of a man by now if that were the case. You have to rely on fate for that." She moved out the front door.

My sneakers squeaked across the hardwood floor as I hurried to follow her outside.

When I reached the sidewalk, she turned and cupped my chin in her hands. "I wish I could stay longer and help you, but you know I believe in allowing you to figure things out on your own. It builds character."

"Just like the time you made me drive your manual-engine car across town."

"Honey, you were an expert with that clutch by the time you got back."

"I cursed every time I had to stop on a hill."

Grandma chuckled, then embraced me in a gigantic hug. "I love you, sweetheart."

The familiar scent of her favorite White Shoulders perfume encircled me. "I love you, too, Grandma." I squeezed back. "What about the magical people? What if they don't like me?"

"You'll be fine, just like your grandma. They don't call me the magical Dear Abby for nothing, you know?"

Would they call *me* the magical Dear Abby now?

My grandmother had been helping solve people's problems one delicious meal at a time, only they didn't know it. And neither did I, until now. She'd owned Mystic Café for thirty years, and not once in all my twenty-eight years had she mentioned adding magic to the food. Customers used words like delightful, enchanting, and captivating to describe her dishes, but I thought they meant my grandmother's exceptional cooking skills. Never did I imagine it was *real* magic.

She backed away and marched over to her little red roadster like a spring chicken. Grandma slid behind the wheel, putting on her rhinestone-encrusted sunglasses and revving the engine.

"You remember the name of the retirement village?" she yelled over the roar of the car.

I nodded. "Sunny Acres in Ocala, Florida, I remember. I wrote the information down. Are you sure you want to leave us?" My voice broke and I gave her my best sad-eyed look. "This is your hometown."

"We talked about this, honey. I always said I'd retire to Florida and that's what I'm doing. Now you have fun with the café and don't do anything I wouldn't do. Oh, and mashed potatoes make the best base for magic. I learned by trial and error over the past thirty years, so take my word for it. And one more thing...don't let anything happen to the book or the spices." She waved as she drove off, the wind whipping the wisps of her white-coifed head.

Chapter Four

When I couldn't see the back of her car any longer, I wiped the tears from my cheeks and moved back inside the café. A cool blast from the air-conditioning slapped me in the face as if saying: what the heck are you thinking?

No new customers had entered the café yet and, in spite of being nervous at the thought of having zero customers, I was thankful not to have any right at that moment. How would I do this on my own?

I stood in the middle of the room, taking in the whole space. My heart thumped, afraid I'd screw this up. But forget about running a business on my own...that was the least of my worries. People in this town relied on magic performed by me. Me. It's a good thing they didn't know their fate was in my hands. Shivers covered my skin and it wasn't because of the cool air.

Apparently, my hometown of Mystic Hollow, Kentucky, was more mystical and magical than I'd ever known. How the heck had that one gotten past me? I'd grown up in this town and never suspected for a minute what was right under my nose the whole time.

To an outsider, Mystic Hollow looked like Mayberry—a quiet, innocent little town. The population in Mystic Hollow barely broke the three thousand mark. No way to hide many details of your life in a town that size, but grandma had somehow managed.

Grandma Imelda always said they didn't name it Mystic Hollow for nothing. She claimed the limestone under the soil made it a special place. It didn't make sense to me at the time, and I still wasn't sure it did now.

Grandma also claimed a special energy moved with force around town. On every blade of grass that swayed with the wind and every leaf that cascaded to the ground. Now I knew what she meant—even if it didn't make sense.

As I peered around the café, I realized it was now or never. Sink or swim in the big pot of grits cooking in the back. What was the worst that could happen? I'd follow the magic book and cook the best darn food I could; everything would fall into place. Maybe.

Keeping busy would be the best medicine, so I slipped into the back and mixed batter for muffins. As I put the pan into the oven, the bell on the door jingled.

Mary Jane O'Donnell bounced through the door. "I'm here. I'm here." She rushed behind the counter and stashed her purse, then grabbed an apron.

Her penny-colored ponytail peeked out from the back of her baseball cap. She had a voice loud enough to break the sound barrier and a penchant for hats. All kinds of hats: baseball caps, cowboy hats, fedoras, just to name a few. She claimed the hats distracted from her round cheeks. I hadn't seen her without one since high school. She probably slept in a hat. Today she wore a white baseball cap with little pink flowers across the front.

Grandma Imelda was right: at least I had Mary Jane. She may not cook or know magic, but I trusted her and knew she wouldn't let me down. Mary Jane was my best friend from high school and had been working at the café for several years now after an ugly divorce. No way would I make it without her help. She was a darn good waitress and smarter than anyone I knew. When Mary Jane wasn't in the café, she was studying for her bachelor's degree; she wanted to teach math.

"Thank goodness you're here." I stretched my arms up and hugged her. She stood a good five inches taller than my five-foot-two frame.

"You know I'll show up." She patted me on the back. "I always show up."

"Oh my gosh." Panic set in. "I forgot about the muffins. I gotta get them out, come with me."

Mary Jane followed on my heels as I raced into the kitchen and toward the oven. Snatching the oven mitts and shoving my hands into them, I yanked the door open.

"You know I love you, Elly, but you also know I tell it like I see it. You're in over your head here." She leaned against the refrigerator door.

"What? No." A plume of smoke circled my head and I fanned the air.

"Honey, do you have any experience cooking? I know you worked here waiting tables, but cooking is a whole different ball game. I never saw you cook before." She coughed and covered her nose with one hand.

"I cooked all the time when I lived in New York. I couldn't afford to eat out much so I really had no choice. Cook or don't eat. I guess I could have eaten frozen pizzas and Pop Tarts every meal." I picked at the edge of a black muffin. It looked more like a hockey puck. "I'll have you know Grandma Imelda says I have the natural talent for it."

"Cooking at home is a lot different from this, sweetie. But if Imelda trusts you with this place, then I have no choice but to trust you, too." She shrugged her shoulders, then shook her head.

"Thanks for the vote of confidence." I dumped the muffins in the trash.

"Like I said, I call it like I see it. I'm going to get the front ready."

"Yeah, okay. I'm going to make more muffins." I let out a sigh.

Brushing the hair out of my eyes and letting out a deep breath, I mixed up the batter for more muffins. With no clue what I was doing, I tossed grandma's 'special herbs' into the mix, then added some to the grits too, waiting for something magical to happen. A spark, a sound, some kind of sign to let me know it worked.

With a pinch of this and a dash of that, I waited, but nothing. I picked up the magical spices and studied the labels. The words were etched on the front of the bottles with the same extravagant lettering as on the *Mystic Magic* book. Cinnamon, vanilla, allspice, ginger, and rosemary were a few of the magic ingredients I recognized, which at least would make the food taste good. It was better than eye of newt and toad legs. But some I'd never heard of, like mace—which sounded as if it should be sprayed on the face of a deranged attacker—and galangal. That one sounded like it needed a special ointment to cure it.

I intended to take this new endeavor seriously. Just because I didn't know my magic didn't mean I couldn't make the café just as successful as Grandma Imelda. First thing on my agenda for Mystic Café was to make healthy southern dishes—an oxymoron, but substitutes could be made for the worst fattening offenders.

The way I saw it was I could panic, or realize this was the first day of the rest of my life and make the most of it. My mama didn't raise a quitter. In sixth grade, I wanted to win the gold medal at the school's annual field day. I was born with the athletic ability of a snail. Nevertheless, I set my sights on winning the race in my age group. Classmates told me there was no way I'd win, and they had a right to believe that. I wasn't a weakling, but short legs meant a short stride, so running was the worst of the worst for me. But when that beautiful spring day arrived, and the horn sounded for the race to begin, I worked my legs and lungs harder than I ever had. There was nothing going to stop me from wearing that fake gold medal around my neck. Something inside me came to life that day, a spark that wouldn't be defeated and my short legs easily crossed the finish line a full second before the other girls. Some said it was a fluke, but I knew it wasn't. Somewhere deep down, there was still that spark in me. Now if only I could ignite it, I'd be set. Ultimately, I may be defeated, but I'd give it my best shot before I waved the white flag.

Stepping away from the grill, I peeped out into the dining room. A few men slipped into a couple booths at the front of the café, waiting to place their orders. Did I dare attempt magic on my own? I had to do it eventually, right? No, it was too soon.

As if she read my mind, Mary Jane ambled over next to me. "When are you doing the magic?" She tucked a pencil behind her ear and slipped a thick order pad in her apron pocket. "You told her you'd do it the first day. Things will start getting wonky around here if you don't."

"I didn't know you were my magical warden. Are you going to tattle on me if I don't?" I avoided her stare, but the longer she glared, the more I couldn't avoid her.

She placed a hand on her hip. "Yes, I will tattle."

I let out a deep breath. "Okay, okay. I'll do it at lunch. Lunchtime, I'll do some magic." I crossed my heart with my right index finger. "Promise."

Chapter Five

I sprinkled a dash of spice across the pot, stirring them into the potatoes. Mashed potatoes made the best base, she'd said. We'll see about that. Allowing grandma to take off for a sunny retirement village had been a mistake. I should have chased her down and forced her to stay. Thinking I could handle this was insane—the craziest thing I'd ever done by far. With a large spoon, I scooped out a hefty serving of potatoes and plopped them on the plate. I'd started with the general magic as grandma called it. The bottle of spice just had Health written on it, so I figured I'd take a chance on it. With mashed potatoes like these, customers would need a good dose of health.

"Order up!" I tapped the bell and set the plate on the ledge of the food window.

"The lunch crowd is growing bigger than Miss Janice's hairdo." Mary Jane placed another ticket on the silver wheel and gave it a whirl.

"They sure do eat a lot in this town." I wiped my hands on my apron.

"That's a good thing. More eating equals more money." Mary Jane left the window, slipped through the swinging door and into the kitchen area. "I think you need to take a look at one customer in particular."

I wiped drizzled cheese off the counter with a towel. "If I don't finish these orders, the customers will be coming back here looking for me. No need to go to them."

"But this one is different. He's so handsome." She clutched her chest, mimicking a swoon. "He's been in a couple times before. I can't remember his name, but he's so gorgeous, what difference does it make?"

My eyebrow quirked. "Well, maybe I should take a quick peek. It's good for the owner to interact with customers, right?"

I made my way across the kitchen and hurried over to the little window on the door. "Which one am I looking at?"

"Do I have to point him out, really?" She gaped at me with astonishment on her face.

I peeked out the window again and followed her pointing index finger. "Hmm."

"Hmm is right." Mary Jane nudged me for a better view.

"He's certainly eye candy, huh," I said. "I bet he's nothing but a ladies' man. He's got bad news written all over him like a neon sign." I shook my head.

The hot air from our breath was steaming up the window. I reached up and wiped it with the dish towel I'd had draped over my shoulder.

"You can tell all that by one look?" She snorted.

I lifted an eyebrow. "I shouldn't look anyway because I'm done with men. Completely and utterly finished. They're nothing but trouble. After I broke things off with Ray, I said no more."

"Oh, stop. How could a man that good-looking be trouble?" Mary Jane clucked her tongue. "The only trouble I'd have with him is forcing myself to leave his bed."

"Mary Jane!" I chuckled.

She wiggled her eyebrows, then moved back out into the dining area. I slipped out the door for a better view. My stomach took a dive as he crossed the café floor. He slid into a booth on the right side of the room, never noticing four eyes staring at him. Another man was with him, but I couldn't take my gaze off the hunk long enough to tell you what the other guy looked like. But I sure knew what Mr. Tall, Blond and Handsome looked like. He wore jeans and a red T-shirt. Short mussed hair and a strong jaw. Light green eyes, maybe? A closer inspection was in order to answer that question. Yes, I needed to see him up close and personal.

I hurried away from the door where I'd been hiding and grabbed a menu. But before I made it to his table, Mary Jane had approached with a huge smile spread across her face and handed him a lunch menu. She was the one who had suggested I take a look at him, now she was ruining my chances.

The gorgeous customer smiled and laughed while he engaged in conversation with the other man.

"I want to make sure the horse goes to a good home," Eye Candy told the other man.

I inched away and shoved the menu back in the rack before anyone caught me staring like the fool I was. But my gaze remained fixed on my new customer. Who was this man and what was he doing in Mystic Hollow? Did he live here? I'd never seen anyone who looked like him around here before.

I needed answers. But I couldn't exactly go up to him and play a game of twenty questions. There was still a little bit of introverted teenager left in me; the better looking the guy, the more the shyness made an unwelcome visit. Mary Jane loved being nosy, maybe she could question him for me. She prided herself on her gossiping abilities. I think she was the reigning gossip champ for the entire tri-county area. I didn't have the nerve to do it myself. She said he'd been in before, so why hadn't she discovered the scoop then? Her crown may have to be revoked.

Mary Jane ambled back over with that same sly grin.

I raised an eyebrow. "Did you take his order yet?"

"No. I was too busy staring at him." She gave me a doe-eyed look.

"Well, don't you think you'd better get his order? I need to finish the eggs for table one. Now scoot before he leaves, and you can't stare at him while he eats." I placed my hands on her shoulders and turned her body in the direction of his table.

"Yeah, cause I'm the only one who was lookin'." She laughed and marched toward his table again.

I took one last glance and shook off the tingling feeling in my stomach. No more time for gawking. There was work to be done. Magic to be made. If only the spells worked for me, but grandma said not to be selfish and use them for myself. But if I could...

Chapter Six

Mary Jane tapped the bell to get my attention. "Okay, I have the order for Mr. Gorgeous and the order for table four." She stared at me for a beat. "I think table four needs your help. If you know what I mean." She winked.

"Table four?" I frowned.

She gestured with her thumb toward the table. "Oscar Harrisburg. His girlfriend just dumped him for his best friend. Or should I say ex-best friend?"

"That's terrible."

She nodded while tucking her pencil back behind her ear.

"Poor, poor Oscar." I shook my head. "Which one is he?" I walked closer to Mary Jane.

"See the young man with the flannel shirt and overalls?" She gestured with a tilt of her head.

"Half the room has overalls on." I quirked an eyebrow.

"Short blond hair and round face. Right over there." She pointed with her index finger.

"Oh, okay, yes, I see him. He looks so sweet and innocent with those rosy cheeks."

"He's been heartbroken ever since that Sue Ellen Martin dumped him. I wish he'd just move on, but I guess that's easier said than done. She was no good for him, anyway. But he seems convinced she's the only woman he'll ever want in his life. She started running with Luke Taylor the same day she broke it off with him. She told everyone what a loser Oscar is. Now you tell me, does he look like he deserves something like that?"

"No, well, no, not at all. Poor Oscar," I repeated.

She grinned and tilted her head toward the grill. "He wants the cheeseburger lunch special. Maybe you could give him a little extra cheese."

"You're not very subtle, Mary Jane. Why don't you just go tell him I'm mixing up a special elixir for him?" I placed my hands on my hips.

"I never said I was subtle. Fix him up a little something special, okay?" She gave a pleading look.

This magic thing wasn't going to be easy.

"I haven't gotten the hang of it yet." I picked at the edge of my apron while avoiding her stare.

"You haven't even tried yet. How do you know you don't have the hang of it?"

"I'm afraid I'll mess it up." I shook my head.

"How do you think you'll learn if you don't try? How bad could you possibly mess things up? It's only magic."

"Only magic? Only magic, she says." I glanced around as if I spoke to a crowded room. "What if I turn him into a bat or something?"

She snorted. "Don't be silly. Look at the poor guy. Give him a chance at happiness."

I sighed. "Well, I guess if I mess things up he'll never know it was me that did it anyway, huh?"

"Exactly. He's already miserable. How much worse could it be?"

I snorted. "Probably a lot. But I'll do it anyway."

"So you think you can do something to make him feel better?" She bit her bottom lip.

The knot in the pit of my stomach twisted tighter.

"Sure," I squeaked, then let out an audible gulp. I pulled the big book from the shelf and placed it on the counter next to me. "What's his order again?" I grabbed the two tickets. "Cheeseburgers and fries for table two and four. Okay, I can handle this. I can do this." I let out a deep breath and wiggled my hands to get myself psyched up.

I drudged back to the grill and threw on a few hamburger patties, then grabbed a couple plates, setting them on the counter. Looking at Mary Jane again, I let out a big sigh.

"You can do it," she encouraged. "Give those Five Guys a run for their money."

Mary Jane hovered over me, her breath loud in my ear.

"You're making me nervous." I swatted at her with the spatula.

"Sorry," she said, backing up a few steps.

I fidgeted from one foot to the other. "Okay, I can do this."

"Will you quit saying that and do it already?"

After flipping the front cover open, I scanned the index. Thank goodness everything was in alphabetical order, or I'd have been searching all day. The directory had everything from charmed cheeses and enchanted eggs to spiritual soups, along with spells for everything in the love department from finding a mate, mending heartbreak, to general flirting. When I discovered the spell for patching up a broken heart, I knew I had the right one, plus it allowed for personalization. Turning my attention back to the grill, I tossed the burgers over, then turned to the page listed. The spell required mixing the potion myself, since this was a specific spell and not a general love spell. I retrieved my special fried potatoes from the fryer and placed some on one side of the plate, then added a dash of rosemary and sprinkled the love potion on top. The words came to me as if I'd always known just what to say. It was as natural as smiling, laughing, or crying.

As I continued adding the spices, I said the words aloud:

"Let love find him and may his lost love want him in return." I sprinkled more spices over the burger.

Just like something from the movies, it sizzled on the grill, steam flying upward in a mini-tornado-like cylinder, whirling and churning like mad. It bubbled and sparked, growing faster as I murmured the words. The sound of magic in progress rippled through the kitchen, bouncing off the walls, floor, and the door. Above the island, pots and pans hanging from the ceiling rack swayed back and forth. As quickly as it started, the bubbling waned, settling to a simmer, then coming to a stop.

"She'll be jealous, and it serves her right," I added to the spell. "So mote it be."

"Wow, you mean business. That was some spell work. And you said you didn't know what you're doing." She squeezed me. "Your grandmother would be proud."

"Was it too much?" I frowned. "I just figured a little jealousy wouldn't hurt her after the way she's treated him."

"I bet he gets a date in no time, and he'll have to fight the women off with a stick."

"If you say so." I shrugged.

She grabbed the plates and headed for the dining area. As I watched through the tiny window in the door, the knot in my stomach churned as if I'd eaten one of my burnt muffins. Mary Jane stopped next to my gorgeous customer's table and began chatting with another patron. She always had been a talker. She may be a good waitress, but when she got to talking...

Mary Jane yakked away and the more I watched the hot food, the more I was sure it had turned cold. What good would cold food do? Oscar wouldn't eat it or he'd possibly want to leave after taking one bite before getting any of the magic into his system.

But with one little movement, cold food was the least of my worries.

Chapter Seven

To my horror, Mary Jane set the plate with the magic-laced food down on *his* table. Not Oscar's table, but the magnificent-looking man we'd been ogling from the kitchen since Mary Jane had not so subtly pointed him out.

He looked up and thanked her. She waved off his comment and continued talking with the other customer, not even realizing she'd set the plate in front of the wrong person. A person who now thought he was getting his meal, the food he'd ordered, not someone else's spell-spiked cheeseburger.

What could I do? I frantically waved toward Mary Jane, but she didn't as much as bat an eyelash in my direction. I'd kill her for this. With sweat forming on my brow and my heart thumping, I had to do something before it was too late. The handsome customer grabbed the burger and moved it toward his mouth. It was now or never. I couldn't let him take someone else's spell. What consequences would the wrong magic bring? I didn't want to find out.

I peeked out from around the swinging door. The hamburger moved to his lips, then he took a bite from the sandwich. One big chunk was already missing and ketchup oozed from the side.

The pathway leading to his booth seemed as if it stretched on forever. In spite of the dread in the pit of my stomach, I finally made my feet move forward. It was as if I was on a conveyor belt, walking and walking, but making no progress. Each step seemed to carry me further away.

Finally, I lunged from behind the counter, making a dash for his booth. It was as if everything played frame by frame. Glasses no longer clanked and conversations stopped as all eyes no doubt focused on me—the lunatic owner flying across the café floor.

As my eyes met his confused and alarmed stare, I reached for his burger. My hand made contact with the bun and I swatted, making the bun and meat fly from his hands, before they landed in the middle of the hardwood floor.

My arms flung out as I stumbled and grabbed the air, trying to save myself. The moment seemed as if it moved in slow motion, frozen in time. Gasps echoed around me—probably Mary Jane and the nosy women at table six. The surroundings appeared fuzzy, as if my eyes couldn't focus, yet I made out every detail around me. My arms and legs felt as if they were weighted down with cement.

I put out my hands to stop myself from falling. He reached down to grab me, but missed. My lips parted to gasp in air and a high-pitched yelp escaped my mouth. My face met with the floor as I fell at the edge of the booth, my mouth practically coming to rest on his work boot. The smell of Lysol from the freshly mopped floor made my stomach turn, as if I weren't already sick enough. My cheeks burned as if I'd been caught making out in the backseat of my parents' car.

I grunted and turned my head to the side only to see his green eyes peering down at me. Okay, I'd wanted a closer inspection of him, but I hadn't wanted to make an ass of myself in the process. The heat from his gaze ran through my body.

Silence filled the space except for a stifled snicker from the other side of the room. I shot an evil glare in the direction of the young dark-haired girl. She darted behind her menu. I stared around the room at the frowning expectant faces. The old ladies gave me a disapproving shake of their heads.

He didn't ask what the heck I was doing, or call for the men with the white jackets...at least not yet. Instead, he leaned over me with his mouth agape and stared for a beat. Finally, he grabbed my arm as I shuffled up from the floor, brushing off my pants to allow time for my face to return to a shade lighter than fire-engine red. My mind raced a million miles a minute, trying to conjure up a logical explanation as to why I had knocked the food from his hand like a deranged freak. I had none. Not one logical thought. I might as well just tell him I was crazy, it sounded much better than the truth.

"Are you all right?" His brows drew together in a puzzled frown as he continued to hold my arm. With his gorgeous green eyes fixed on me, he waited for an answer.

"I--I—I'm sorry about that. I gave you the wrong order," I muttered, like a complete fool.

I looked to his friend who sat staring at me with the same confused and astonished look on his face.

His eyebrows rose. "No, I ordered a cheeseburger and I'm pretty sure that's what I was eating." He placed emphasis on the word *was*. He gently released his hand from my arm.

"Oh, well, um, I'm sorry about that. My bad." I held my hands up in surrender.

Yes, yes, it certainly was my bad. If only I could have melted into the hardwood floors, then I'd escape the mortification. I limped over and reached down, grabbed the burger and bun, then scooped up the pickles one by one.

"Are you okay? Did you hurt your leg?" he asked with a concerned look on his face.

"I'll be fine. I'll walk it off." I gently placed the bun and meat back on his plate. "Let me get you another one. It'll just take a minute." I wiped the mustard and ketchup from my fingers onto my apron, then took the plate from his table. What a way to make a great first impression. I had one chance, and I blew it.

He waved his hand as he studied me, no doubt taking in my messy appearance. "No, that's not necessary, I don't have the time. I'll take my check."

I'd never get his business again. He knew a crazy person when he saw one. His friend would never come back, either. Heck, within thirty minutes probably everyone in town would hear about me knocking the food from his hand. I'd be out of business before the end of the day.

He stood and reached in his pocket for his wallet.

"Are you sure?" I asked. "It's no trouble."

He gave a half grin. Obviously, he felt pity for me. "It's fine, really. How much do I owe you?" He opened his wallet.

"Nothing, of course. I can't charge you for a half-eaten burger that I knocked out of your hand and proceeded to mop the floor with." I blushed.

I wanted to tell him the truth and have him understand, but that was impossible. The truth was worse than the embarrassing lie I'd just come up with.

"Are you sure?" he asked.

"I'm positive. Again, I'm really sorry. I hope you'll come back."

He eyed me up and down with a look I interpreted as full of mercy. "I'll be back."

The odds of him returning were about as good as the odds of me taking that scum-sucking ex of mine back.

As the thought entered my head, he smiled at me. And this time I didn't think it was a you're-so-pitiful-I-have-to-be-polite smile, either. My stomach tingled as I watched the dimples on his face slide up into a full-on smile. His friend stood beside him, drawing my attention away from his gorgeous face, no easy task.

"How much do I owe you?"

I looked to him. "Nothing, of course. I'm really sorry."

I'd lose my business one way or another if I had to keep dishing out complimentary meals. He smiled again and I watched as they walked out of the café. I hoped he wasn't walking out of my life for good. I may have resolved to be done with men until the end of time, but I could use a regular customer like him.

"What in heaven's name is wrong with you?" Mary Jane rushed over.

"What's wrong with me?" I pointed toward my chest, then turned it around on her. "You're the one not paying attention."

Her face turned red. She opened her mouth, closed it again, her jaw tightening as she swallowed down whatever she was going to say.

Guilt clasped its strangling grip around me for calling her out on the catastrophe. Perhaps catastrophe was a strong word, but it was darn close to accurate. Mary Jane always had been a good waitress, though. Well, by the way Grandma Imelda raved, I figured she had to be fantastic. Plus, she'd never do anything to hurt me on purpose. Everyone makes mistakes. Heaven knows I had made more than my share.

I decided to break the silence. "I thought I could stop him."

Her lower lip softened. "Once he's had one bite, it's too late. You're going to have to practice that magic, or it's going to be chaos in this town." Mary Jane stacked dirty dishes in the tub behind the counter. She blew her bangs out of her eyes, and faced me again.

"Thanks for the advice." I folded my arms in front of my chest. "I didn't want this magic in the first place."

"Too late for that now. Besides, the way I hear it, you don't have any choice in the matter. It's written in the stars." She gestured toward the sky with an overly dramatic wave of her arms.

"Written in the stars, huh?" We stopped talking long enough for me to take a customer's cash and hand them their change. When they were out of audible range, I continued, "Where do you get your magical information from?"

"Your grandmother, of course." She didn't glance up as she wiped water off the counter.

"Of course." I rolled my eyes. "Right from the source."

More customers approached. After ringing up the inquisitive women and waiting for their departure, I continued the conversation with Mary Jane. "Why don't you finish telling me how the heck you found out about the magic in the first place?"

She shrugged her shoulders. "One night I'd had a little too much..." She mimicked drinking with her right hand. "Anyway, I walked in on one of your grandmother's spell-casting sessions. She could have led me to believe I'd imagined it, but she didn't. The next morning she told me the truth and cast a spell to cure my hangover."

"I still don't understand why didn't you tell me this earlier?" I sat on a stool next to the register.

"It's some kind of magical oath. You know?"

"Right." Silly me. How could I forget about the oath?

"I had my suspicions before that. Once she had a picnic over by Mystic Hollow Baptist Church. I saw sparks next to her and a tub of potato salad. Little Willie McDaniel thought it was fireworks. You know, sometimes I think she wanted me to know, that's why she let me see it."

"Why do I miss all the excitement? Who'd have thought a church picnic could be so much fun?" I rearranged the sugar packets.

"All good questions, but I'll never understand the mystery that is your Grandma Imelda. She's an enigma." She laughed.

I shook my head. "I don't know if I'll ever get used to this new talent."

"It's only been a day, it'll grow on you."

"That's what I'm afraid of." I chuckled.

Since I'd gotten back to town, Mary Jane and I hadn't had a chance to catch up and spend time eating chocolate and watching silly movies like we used to; I missed that.

"So, you still haven't heard from Steve?" I asked.

"Not a word. Next week it'll be two years since our divorce." Mary Jane stared straight-ahead, as if she was watching the bad memory play out in her head. "It's as if he fell off the face of the earth, which is fine by me. Last I heard he was in Louisiana."

"What about the guy you were seeing? What was his name? Frank?

"Yeah, I should have known he was a loser when he said he could tell I was good in bed because my hair was wild, as if I'd just woken up. Too bad *he* was terrible in bed. If his theory were correct, then I should have known his bedroom prowess was less-than-stellar by his lack of hair. I mean, really, what twenty-five-year-old has a comb-over? Just shave it bald for heaven's sake, and be done with it, that's much sexier."

My lips curved down into a grimace. "He said you'd be good in bed based on your 'wild hair'?"

"Word for word." She held up her right hand. "Cross my heart."

"Listen, I want to apologize for not having much time to chat over the past few weeks and since I got back to Mystic Hollow. I'll be the first to admit I was wallowing in self-pity for quite a while."

"I know what you were doing, and I was about to come to New York and drag you out of your hole of self-despair when your grandma saved the day. By the way, you hear from Ray since you left New York?" Mary Jane asked, while twisting her ponytail with one hand. She always had to move her hands. Sometimes she got that ponytail moving so fast I thought it would spin on its own like a propeller.

"He left a voice mail and threatened to come back for the Mustang. I told him he could have it over my dead body. I'd rather torch the thing. It was a gift. I own it now. Oh, I also told him I drove it through one of those automatic car washes. I thought he might cry."

"It serves him right. Good riddance. You're better off without him. Anyone who'd cheat on you is nothing but a dirty rotten, scum-sucking pig. He'll soon realize that floozy is nothing but a gold digger. When she discovers he doesn't have a penny to his name, she'll dump him."

"Yeah, well, I don't care what he does." I grabbed a couple dirty dishes and headed for the kitchen. "I gotta get back to work. There's food to cook, a kitchen to clean and magic to cast." I clucked my tongue.

"Did you drive the shiny red car so you can show off?" Mary Jane readjusted her ponytail. Her copper-colored hair shone like a penny in the sunlight. Her tan skin from weekends at the lake blended with her hair and made her white shorts and blue shirt appear even brighter. I should make a trip to the lake. Relaxation time would do my soul some good.

"I sure did, although I should probably start walking to work. I'll need to burn all the calories I can with all this temptation around me all day." My ex had moved to New York first, leaving me his prized Mustang. He'd restored the car from nothing more than a rusted-out shell. Now that I thought about it, he'd probably given it to me out of guilt. When Ray asked me to move to New York, I knew I wouldn't need the car, so I'd kept it at my mom's house, not realizing that I'd soon be back in Mystic Hollow. My stay in The Big Apple had been short-lived.

Before I made it to the kitchen door, the sensation smacked me in the face. The feeling that hits you when someone is watching you washed over me. A lump formed in my throat. Something was definitely out of sync in Mystic Hollow.

Chapter Eight

The odd feeling stayed with me for the rest of the day. The next morning wasn't any different, if anything, the sensation had grown. Something strange brewed in the distance. I felt it in my bones, coursing through my veins, like an infection antibiotics just couldn't shake. Dark clouds had formed, rolling in quickly from the south. The wind whipped against the window, whistling and hissing through the cracks in the jambs—a storm would be here soon. The neon sign blinked *Open* in a steady rhythm.

"How 'bout a refill on my coffee? I got a chill I can't seem to shake. Storms do that to my arthritis," the man at the end of the counter said, breaking my reverie.

"Sorry, coming right up." I hurried over and took the pot off the heating element, watching the door as if waiting for something to happen. "I got it," I told Mary Jane. She couldn't take her eyes off the door, either.

"Your cherry pie seems about the only thing that helps ease my aching joints," the man offered, then chuckled. I barely noticed his compliment until the thought hit me: my magic must be working.

My stomach rumbled when I noticed the stray crumbs on his plate, but my thoughts were too consumed with watching the door to worry about my hunger. I poured the hot liquid into his awaiting mug. I hadn't eaten since the night before and should get a slice for myself before it was all gone. But before another thought of cherries or flaky crusts could run through my mind, the door to the café flew open, allowing the rain to surge in, bringing a stranger with it.

He shook his umbrella, then ambled over to the counter, his gaze intent on me the entire time. I stiffened and glanced over at Mary Jane.

This man looked like he had a bone to pick with me. The last thing I needed was trouble. What could he possibly want from me?

"Whoa. Come to mama," Mary Jane muttered. "He's a tall glass of water."

Mary Jane moved closer. In spite of her apparent awareness of his magnetism, I knew she had a short fuse sometimes, and if he said one cross word, she'd give him a verbal tongue-lashing. She didn't like rude people as much as she didn't like not wearing a hat. Of course she couldn't hurt a fly—she was all talk, but he didn't know that. With any luck, her sharp words would make him uncomfortable. Although, I needed to remember: the customer was always right. Right?

The stranger plopped down on the stool in front of me, placed his briefcase down, then removed his black fedora, and positioned it on the counter beside him. He wore khaki pants and a white button-up shirt. I gave a halfhearted smile and nodded in return.

"Hi," I said weakly, handing him a menu. "Would you like a cup of coffee?"

Somehow, I knew he wanted more than coffee, and it wasn't the cherry pie he wanted, either.

"Sure. I'll take sugar and cream, please."

My hand wobbled slightly as I placed a mug in front of him and poured. He studied the menu and I studied him. It was hard not to—he was good-looking. Dark hair, tall, and well-built. He wasn't from around here, I knew by his accent. Was he lost? Not a lot of tourists in these parts. Mary Jane watched from over my shoulder, being her inquisitive self, as usual. By the look on her face, I knew she was dying for me to ask the stranger why he was in town. I suppose it was my job to make small talk with customers, so what harm could it do?

"So, you're not from around here?" I'm not known for my subtlety. Better to get right to the point.

"No." His voice had a laugh in it. "How'd you guess?"

"I know everyone in this town and I don't know you." Okay, so I didn't know everyone, but he didn't know that. I wiped off the counter—better than staring.

He nodded. "Good point."

"Plus, you talk like a Yankee." I grinned.

"A Yankee?" He unsuccessfully attempted to hide a smile behind his coffee mug.

I'd gotten used to the accent, but now that I'd returned home, it stood out like a veggie burger with low-fat cheese on Mystic Café's menu.

I nodded. "Yes, you know, from up north."

"Maybe you should be a detective or a reporter," he said.

"Is that what you are?" I asked.

He sipped his coffee and eyed me for a minute. "Not exactly, but I am from New York."

"I knew you were a Yankee!" I chuckled.

"You got me—guilty as charged." He held his hands up in surrender.

He had a teasing tone in his voice, but I knew he was there for something more than witty banter.

The customer at the end of the counter approached the register, handing me cash for his cherry pie and coffee. His movements appeared less stiff. The spell really had improved his arthritis pain.

When the customer had walked away, the stranger continued his questioning, "So, what's going on in Mystic Hollow, Kentucky?"

I shot a look to Mary Jane and she shrugged. "I don't know. Why don't you tell me?"

He took a sip of coffee, then placed his mug down, never taking his eyes off me.

I glanced down at my apron and fidgeted with a loose thread, avoiding his stare. "Nothing goes on in this town," I said.

With his gaze still fixed on me, his grin faded and he said, "Someone told me otherwise."

"Someone did?" I bet my gulp was audible from across the room.

"Let's not worry about how I know yet." He wrapped his hands around his mug.

How he knew what? What did he know?

"It seems you've had an out of the ordinary few days."

"There were moments." I swallowed hard.

"One moment in particular?" He regarded me with purpose, waiting for an answer.

"Right. Well… I'm not sure what you're talking about. I wish something went on in this town, it can be boring. But sorry, there's nothing to report." I wiped the countertop again, brushing off invisible crumbs.

He opened his briefcase and pulled out a card, then handed it to me. The card read:

National Organization of Magic

Tom Owenton, Lead Investigator

Uh-oh.

Chapter Nine

"Our records indicate that we haven't had a problem with Mystic Café or your grandmother since..." He shuffled his papers, then peered up at me. "Since never."

"You keep records?" My mouth dropped. The fact that they kept files and already had one on me was disconcerting. Had they been spying on me?

"Yes, we do." His expression was stern, the teasing tone had vanished.

I leaned over to get a closer look and he slapped the file closed.

"Was that my picture stapled to the inside? How did you get that photo?" The picture was of Grandma Imelda and me last Christmas, smiling for the camera, both of us wearing reindeer antlers. Of all the pictures, they had to pick one where I looked like Rudolph?

"Your grandmother had to send it in when she applied for you to take over."

"There's an application process?" My mouth hung open. What I wouldn't do to get my hands on that file.

He nodded. "You look just like your grandmother, by the way, minus the gray hair, of course. Your hair is beautiful, though. Did your grandmother have dark hair like you?"

"Why don't you look it up in your file?" I placed my hands on my hips.

"The antlers are a nice touch." He smiled cheekily.

"It was Christmas and Grandma Imelda thought they were cute," I retorted.

"I'm sure Santa would approve." He flipped through the file pages again.

"What does the file say about me?" I demanded.

"Other than this little snafu, not much yet, and I'm hoping it'll remain that way." He scrubbed his hand over his face.

"I didn't mean to mess up the magic, it was a slip up." I crossed my arms in front of my chest.

I couldn't tell him it wasn't actually my mistake. I mean, technically, I guess I was responsible for the magic until it reached its rightful recipient. It would be mean of me to rat Mary Jane out. No, I'd take whatever punishment I was handed. It was time to put on my big girl panties.

"So what happens now?" I asked.

He shifted on the stool as he hesitated with the answer. "It's been recommended that your café be closed until we can determine this won't happen again."

A paralyzing anxiety smacked me in the stomach. "Closed? As in, not open? But I just took over. There has to be something else. My grandmother ran this place for thirty years, I have it for two days, and it's shut down? I can't do that to her. Isn't there something I can do to make this up to...to whoever is in charge at whatever the name of the place is you work for?" I took a glass from under the counter, filled it with water, and took a big gulp. I wiped my forehead with my sleeve.

"I'll make some calls and see what I can do." His tone softened a bit.

Finally, a sign of compassion appeared on his face in the form of a half-smile. A small dimple appeared as if by magic on his right cheek. He certainly was good-looking, no denying that. But a good-looking stranger ready to close my café, nonetheless. If he thought a handsome face would stop me from running this place, he had another think coming.

"Can you please explain what happened? Slowly. I want to hear your account of the event." Tom leaned forward, propping his arms on the counter, waiting for a play-by-play of my stupidity.

Mary Jane still stood behind me, her breath hot on my neck.

"I made the food for Oscar Harrison. He'd had some problems with a woman." I fidgeted my fingers against the counter.

"Uh-huh, that's right," Mary Jane chimed in.

"Ah, it's always the women." Tom smirked.

I scowled and placed my hands on my hips. "It's not always the women."

"Yeah," Mary Jane said.

He held up his hands. "Okay, sorry, I can see I'm outnumbered here. Go on, please."

"Thank you. Now where was I? Oh yeah, I accidentally placed the food down on the wrong table." I cast a glance in Mary Jane's direction. She had a huge frown spread across her face as she studied her shoes. "It was an honest mistake."

"You didn't remember that the spell was intended for someone else. The food had magic specifically for that person. You can't give out magic meant for someone else," he scolded.

"I'm aware of that...now. I only learned about this stuff a couple days ago, can't you give me some slack?"

"You're right, you're right." He nodded. "We should cut you some slack. We should speak with your Grandmother Imelda and ask her why she left a novice in charge of something that is obviously out of her control." He gave a sardonic lift of his brow.

"No! I can't let Grandma Imelda get in trouble for this." What kind of trouble she may get into, I had no idea. Did they have a jail for magical mess-ups?

"What would be her punishment?" I licked my lips. My mouth had become as dry as if I'd eaten an entire package of saltines.

"For starters, she'd never be able to perform magic again."

"Well, maybe that isn't such a bad thing. Fate should be in control, and I wasn't so sure we should be messing with fate."

"We make the fate, gorgeous. That's why fate is fate. And you would lose the café for good. We'd close it down."

"Close the café?" I gripped the counter.

What would I do then? I wouldn't have anything else. Food was going to be my life from now on. Sure it had only been a few days, but I'd already become attached.

"I'll let you know what I find out tomorrow. Until then, maybe you should close the café for the evening?" Tom observed me, searching my eyes.

"Okay, yeah, I guess that would be a good idea." Good idea for him, but I didn't like the sound of it.

He finished off his coffee and placed the mug back on the counter.

I didn't ask if he wanted a refill. No need to encourage him to stay longer than he had to.

"I'll do all I can, but I can't make any promises." He touched my arm.

"Of course not." I shook my head.

"Oh, and one more thing, they want me to watch you for a while, report back with my findings, they'll make a decision based on that. I'll be overseeing the café, you know, to make sure you don't have any more goof-ups."

Oh, great, a magical babysitter. "So you'll be following my every move?" I exhaled through pursed lips.

"Not every move." The tense little lines around his mouth disappeared as his lips twitched into a smile.

"I don't like the sound of this."

"Well, the only other alternative is to close the café, which one would you prefer?"

I took a deep breath. "To have you follow me."

I knew when I'd been defeated. I had to get rid of this guy as quickly as possible, even if he was good-looking. What would my grandma say? I couldn't believe this was happening. Just a short time ago, everything had seemed so normal, now nothing made sense.

"I need to get back to the kitchen. Customers will be after me with pitchforks soon if I don't make their food. Are you going to follow me there, too?"

He nodded. "I'm afraid, yes. I need to see what you're doing."

What I was doing wrong, he meant. How could I perform magic with him watching? It's like trying to pee when you know someone's listening, it just won't happen. It was bad enough when I tried cooking with Mary Jane or grandma watching. Tom followed on my heels as I passed through the door and into the kitchen. My magical escort. He smelled like mango with a touch of leather.

When I passed Mary Jane, she mouthed, "I'm sorry."

As well she should be. If it wasn't for her gossiping, I wouldn't be in this mess. But I couldn't dwell on it. I'd make the best of the situation and move on from this nightmare. She'd taken a couple of orders for pancakes, eggs, and bacon. Easy enough. I'd noticed the customers were Mr. and Mrs. Stevens, Grandma Imelda's neighbors. I'd known them since I was a little girl.

Mr. Stevens had a bad case of arthritis, so I'd do a spell to help him with the pain. I wished the magic could take away the pain permanently, but apparently it didn't work that way. Grandma Imelda would have taken away every ailment in Mystic Hollow if it did. I'd do a spell for Mrs. Stevens' garden. She had beautiful roses and they made her feel good, a cathartic affect. Making the colors on her rosebushes a little brighter would put a smile on her face regardless of whether she needed it or not. I had to admit, uplifting people's spirits sure gave me a good feeling. So the magic wasn't all bad, though I suppose that could be considered selfish on my part.

Tom studied the kitchen, writing notes on his clipboard. This was worse than the health inspector. I grabbed eggs from the refrigerator and a stainless steel bowl. After cracking open a few against the bowl, I reached for a whisk. I selected my spices and sprinkled them on top of the liquid. Yes, I had no idea what I was doing. I leafed through the *Mystic Magic* book until I found what I thought would work best.

"You're pretty good with that whisk." Tom leaned over my shoulder, watching my every move.

Chapter Ten

"So this is how it's going to be, huh?" I felt his breath against my neck.
"Please, do continue. Pretend I'm not even here."
I snorted. "Yeah, sure thing."
Within seconds, the kitchen door swung open and Mary Jane hurried over, allowing the door to swing back and forth wildly. She panted and clutched her chest.
"My gosh, Mary Jane, what the heck? Are you all right?" I asked.
"I need you out front," she said between pants.
"Do you need a drink of water? Can you breathe?"
"No, no water. I'm fine." She waved off my concern.
Mary Jane leaned down, attempting to catch her breath. "Just come help me with something, okay?" She gestured with her hand.
"Okay, calm down, it can't be that bad." Or could it? Maybe the dining room was full of Magical Investigators, as if they were multiplying like bunnies.
"Excuse me for a second," I gestured for one minute with my index finger.
Tom frowned and a tiny crease formed between his brows. I didn't wait for him to complain.
Mary Jane went first and I followed close behind. When she stopped in front of me, I stumbled through the door, tripping over my feet and landing on the floor again. I needed some non-skid shoes or something. This was the craziest few days I'd ever experienced, and I'd had crazy ones when I moved to New York City. But nothing compared to my day o' magic at *Mystic Café*.
A lady, round as she was tall, with very blonde hair tied up high in a bun, watched me. Her bright red lipstick bled into the wrinkles around her mouth. Her fingernails coordinated with the lip color. She shook her head in disapproval at our antics and scolded us with a wave of her crimson fingernail.
A couple of old ladies sat in the corner. Both had the same fine, gray pouffed-up hairstyle and ghostly white skin. These women must have been eight hundred years old, if they were a day. Their slender frames made them appear as if fragile dolls, but the scowls on their faces made them look more like pit bulls. One wore a light blue pantsuit, while the other sported a peach sweatshirt and beige polyester pants. They stared, beginning at my toes and finally stopping at my hair. One whispered to the other, their gazes glued to me all the while. I watched them as I picked myself up. Hadn't they seen a girl fall flat on her face before?
A bit dazed from my collision with the floor, I gave a halfhearted smile and glanced over my shoulder at the blue-hairs perched in the corner. They stared back.
"Don't pay attention to those old hens. They never get any excitement in their lives." Mary Jane grabbed my arm.
"Oh. That would explain it then." I nodded and turned for another look. Their gaze didn't falter. I waved and they jerked their attention away.

"So sorry, please continue with your meals. I'm fine," I said to my audience. As if they cared whether I was hurt or not. The old ladies started up their surveillance again.

They raised their snooty brows and whispered.

"Oh, miss, can I get some more butter?" the one in the peach asked.

"I need more coffee," her BFF demanded.

Mary Jane tugged on my arm again. "I'll tend to them, you tend to him." She pointed at the door, then straightened her shirt and smoothed down her hair. "Fix your hair."

Chapter Eleven

My eyes may have been deceiving me, but the man I'd humiliated myself in front of was walking toward me. Was it a mirage? I needed to pinch myself and find out. As he neared, I soon realized I wasn't dreaming. He was a lot taller than I was but at five-two, most people were. He grinned down at me, his green eyes sparkling. Sharp features and short blond hair made him look like a cover model, but he had a clean-cut boy-next-door quality that was surely irresistible to any woman. How had he managed to become better looking in just a few hours?

"How's your leg? Are you doing okay after your stumble?" He sat at the counter, placing his baseball cap next to him.

My heart thumped a little harder. In spite of my nerves, I couldn't help but smile. "Didn't expect to see you here after my craziness."

"We all have our moments, I suppose." He chuckled, revealing dimples on each cheek.

Yes, we all had our moments. Some more than others, though, and I was almost positive I was in the 'more' category. I grabbed a menu, dropped it, then quickly scooped it off the floor and placed it in front of him. "What can I get for you?" No way could he possibly want to eat here again, could he?

"How about a cup of coffee and a piece of that cherry pie?" He pointed. "It looks really good."

"I think it's delicious. Of course, I made it, so I might be a little biased." Butterflies fluttered in my stomach as I turned and retrieved a plate. While I sliced the pie, I felt his gaze on me. Please don't let me do anything stupid in front of him again. Or at least, let it be only mildly stupid. Nothing like sweeping the floor with my body and taking out his burger in the process.

"So, are you going to tell me what was really going on yesterday?" He took a sip of coffee.

"What do you mean?" I placed the pie in front of him. "Whipped cream?"

"Sure."

I gave the can a good shake, ready to spray the top of his slice with the yummy cream, but I had no way of knowing the container would malfunction. Whipped cream spewed from the can like kids' Silly String. I sucked in a breath of surprise. The sticky mess landed in his hair, on his face and shirt. I may have stopped breathing for several seconds, the wind was knocked out of me as if a football player had tackled me to the ground. I'd always been a klutz, but this topped the time I fell in the school cafeteria, landing face-first in my mashed potatoes.

My mouth hung open and my eyes probably looked like saucers. I cast a glance to Mary Jane and she had the same expression featured on her face, as if she were mimicking me. The cream dripped down the side of his cheek. He grabbed a napkin and wiped his face.

"I am so sorry," I finally managed. "I don't know what happened to the can." I tossed the container in the trashcan. "It must be defective." Or I was defective.

He smiled. A bit of cream still lingered on his upper lip. "Don't worry about it. I asked for whipped cream." He chuckled, then licked the remnants from his finger.

"Yeah, but not in the face." I grabbed more napkins and handed them to him.

Mary Jane approached and offered him a wet towel. "Here this should help with the stickiness."

"Thanks."

I wanted to crawl underneath the counter and never come out. Maybe if I hid, time would reverse and this would never have happened. But that was impossible, and there was no taking it back.

"You have a little left in your hair." I pointed.

He swiped the towel across his head. "Did I get it?"

I reached for a napkin and rubbed the front of his head. "There, it's all gone now. Your hair will be a little sticky, though."

First, I ruined his lunch, and now I'd covered him in food. Not exactly my fantasy of how I'd like to cover him in whipped cream.

"Please let me know how much it is to clean your clothing. I'll pay for it."

"Are you kidding? This shirt has at least two holes in it. I need to toss it, but I hate to lose a shirt that's already broken in. There's no need to pay for anything," he said.

"If you're sure?"

"I'm positive. Forget it ever happened." He grabbed his fork.

Believe me, I'd love to forget. But I was sure something was written in my DNA making that completely impossible. It would be etched into my brain like ancient hieroglyphics carved into a cave wall, lingering for centuries.

After taking a bite of his pie, he asked, "What was really wrong with my burger? I expected to get sick after eating it, thankfully I never did."

Heat rose in my cheeks again. At least I'd never need blusher while around him. "I promise there was nothing wrong with it. I have a very clean kitchen, I pride myself on that."

He nodded. "You have a nice place here, I won't argue with that."

He chewed his bite while looking around, then without hesitation popped another piece of pie in his mouth. I stared like some kind of stalker as he swallowed. If I'd known he was coming, I'd have done a spell on the pie, but I didn't have the opportunity to slip back into the kitchen with it. Maybe there was something in the book that would undo the wrong spell he got lumbered with. Although, it didn't appear anything was wrong. My magic probably didn't work anyway, so I had no idea why this magic organization was worried. No harm, no foul.

After swallowing, he said, "This is really good. I could get used to this."

Yeah, well, I could get used to him.

"I might become a regular around here, just to warn you."

I smiled wide. The section of my brain controlling my smile had ceased to function. "I'd like that."

"I'm Rory Covington, by the way."

The gorgeous man stretched his muscular arm toward me. I took his hand in mine. His grip was firm, but his hand was oh-so-smooth. Yep, definitely eye candy, but did he know he was eye candy?

His touch produced a tingle in my body, almost like the electric charge I'd felt from the magic. "Nice to meet you. I'm Blair Elly." My face heated instantly. "I mean, my name is Elly Blair." Now I couldn't even get my name right. I needed to buy duct tape in bulk. Using it on my mouth was the only way to stop my stupid responses.

Mary Jane made a face behind Rory's back, pointing toward his backside. I pursed my lips and shook my head, hoping he wouldn't notice. Too late. He turned and Mary Jane pretended to stretch and yawn. She wasn't fooling anyone with that act. If only crawling under the counter really was an option.

In spite of the humiliation, I remained cool as a frosty December morning. I did what any girl would do: I pretended she hadn't been referencing Rory's hotness. Mary Jane inched further and further away from us. I wanted to grab her shirt and tell her not to leave me alone with him. She wouldn't have listened, though. After all, she'd gotten me into this mess. Even though today was the first time I'd ever met Rory, in a way I felt as if we'd met before. He seemed easygoing and relaxed, the exact opposite of my ex-fiancé.

"I own the café. I'm not normally this crazy person who knocks food out of my customers' hands, and douses them with whipped toppings, I promise."

"Well, it was nice meeting you, Elly."

"You, too. I'd better get back to the kitchen." I gestured with my thumb over my shoulder. "I'm getting some dirty looks. People get testy when they're hungry and waiting for food. If you need anything else, please let Mary Jane know."

"You have a beautiful smile, by the way." Tingling started at my feet and I swear it didn't stop until it reached the top of my head. Honest to goodness.

He smiled in return and our gazes locked. My stomach fluttered. Before I could continue the conversation which, by the way, was going wonderfully compared to the earlier event, what's-his-face stepped out from the kitchen.

Mary Jane tried to cut him off at the pass. I wasn't the panicky type, but the knot in the pit of my stomach grew and I didn't like it. Tom approached Mary Jane and they stood by the door, talking in a hushed tone. Her distraction tactic didn't work on my elixir examiner though, because within a second he stood beside me. Too close, as if he had appointed himself my bodyguard. His musky scent invaded my space.

Tom studied Rory. The smile slid off Rory's face. This situation was turning a dark corner quickly and I doubted I'd find the light switch in time to avoid the impending disaster. What if Rory thought something was going on between Tom and me? I didn't want to ruin my chances with Rory. Not that I had a chance, especially after yesterday, but the fact that Rory had returned was a good sign. And he'd just complimented my smile. That equaled flirting in my book. Rory stared at Tom while finishing off his pie. By the expression on his face, he had a message for him: he wasn't intimidated.

Chapter Twelve

"How's everything going out here?" Tom draped his arm around my shoulders.

I wanted to knock him on the ground. I shimmied out from under his arm.

"I think you have some customers waiting." Tom winked at me.

He acted as if he owned the place. I was still the owner and I planned to keep it that way.

"Everything is fine," I said through gritted teeth.

"Can I see you in the kitchen, Elly?" Tom asked.

"I'm busy right now, Tom." This didn't look good in front of Rory, and the puzzled look on his face let me know as much.

"Well, Elly, this is very important. Urgent, as a matter of fact." He stiffened up, then eased the tension from his jaw as his mouth twisted into a smile.

What could possibly be so urgent? Unless the kitchen was on fire. Oh no. I turned to look at the kitchen. Whew. No smoke, it appeared to be safe.

"I'll be right back." I held up my index finger.

"Sure." Rory flashed that perfect lop-sided grin of his as he lifted his coffee mug.

I stomped toward the kitchen with Tom following on my heels.

"This had better be good for dragging me away from a customer." I crossed my arms in front of my chest.

"Is that him?" Tom motioned with a tilt of his head. "I can't believe he came back after what you did." He smirked.

"I don't think I need any commentary out of you."

"So answer my question, is it him?"

"Yes, it is."

"And you said his name is Rory Covington?"

"I never said anything. Were you eavesdropping on our conversation? You were, weren't you?"

He ignored my question. "I'm going to need to talk with him."

"You aren't going to tell him about the magic, are you?"

"Of course not. But I do need to know if he suffered any effects from it. It's critical to whether you get to keep practicing magic and continue running this café."

I hadn't wanted to practice magic in the first place. Although, I admit I was starting to have fun with it. I didn't want to lose the café though, so what choice did I have?

With a shrug of my shoulders, I said, "I can't stop you from talking with him. But please, do you have to stand so close while *I'm* talking to him? He'll get the wrong idea about us."

"Are you interested in dating him?"

"What business is that of yours? He's a customer, I like talking with customers."

"Uh-huh. Don't get your feathers ruffled. I'm going to schedule a time to talk with him. If you'll excuse me." He brushed past.

"Gladly!" I followed him out of the kitchen.

To my disappointment, Rory was gone when we returned to the dining area. The plate only had a few crumbs left, the cup was empty, and money lay on the counter. Great. Tom had chased him away.

Tom snatched his briefcase and headed for the door. "I'll be back."

"I'm sure you will," I muttered in his wake.

Chapter Thirteen

Things had slowed down after I'd caught up with the customers I'd neglected while swooning over Rory and tending to my new pain-in-the-rear magical buttinsky.

Only a few patrons lingered over coffee, probably people who I'd soon reference as 'regulars.'

"You need to see this." Mary Jane beckoned me over to where she stood by the window.

"What is it?" I wiped my hands on my apron.

She motioned for me to hurry.

I walked around the counter, making my way over to the window. "What now?"

She tilted her head and my gaze followed her gesture until I spotted what the commotion was about. Rory stood across the street on the sidewalk, deep in conversation with a woman. But not just any woman. Nope. She was a gorgeous, leggy, supermodel woman.

"Who is he talking to?" I whispered as I nudged her out of the way for a better view.

"That's his ex-girlfriend," a voice said from behind me. It was Mrs. Perkins, one of my new regulars. I hadn't noticed her walk up behind us. "She dumped him for another man about a year ago. I reckon that boy was devastated. He was so in love."

Was in love? Or still in love?

Mrs. Perkins continued talking while we continued staring out the window, all huddled together for the best possible view. "She treated him somethin' awful. Told lies about him all over town. And just when he was maybe getting over her, here she is back in his life." She tsk-tsked. "She's an evil woman. Why, Rory is such a good man. I never knew what he saw in her in the first place."

I had my ideas about what he saw in her. Beautiful, long silky blonde hair. Long legs and big...well, never mind. I adjusted the apron across my chest. We watched as they chatted. Rory must have felt eyes on him because he glanced toward the café several times. Please, if there was any justice in the world, don't let him have seen us.

"There's one thing I've come to count on in this universe, and that's the Covington men being handsome and strappin'," Mrs. Perkins said over my shoulder. "They moved here about two years ago. He and his father bought a farm, unfortunately his father passed away not long after. Such a shame. Such a shame."

She gave up on the show and shuffled back to her table. I was about to return to my kitchen duties when the scene made an interesting turn. Another woman approached Rory. And then another. Within two minutes, he must have had twenty women around him, all laughing. The ladies' eyes seemed to have little hearts in them.

He started down the sidewalk and the gorgeous blonde hurried her footsteps to keep his pace. The rest of the women followed behind as if they were little ducklings following their mama. If I didn't speak the words, maybe it wouldn't be true. But Mary Jane knew just as I knew. The spell had worked. The ex-girlfriend had returned and she'd soon be furious with jealousy over Rory's newfound animal magnetism.

I bit my nail. Nothing short of a natural catastrophe could have forced my gaze from the sidewalk debacle.

"What do you make of that?" Mary Jane asked.

I was afraid to say it aloud. "It can't be, can it?" I grabbed Mary Jane and she faced me. "Say it isn't so, Mary Jane. It's the spell, isn't it?"

Her eyes widened and she nodded her head.

"What do I do now? I mean, I didn't think my magic would really work. This is not good."

"Calm down. We'll figure it out. The investigator can help."

"No. I don't think he should know about this." I tightened my grip on her arm.

"What do you mean? He already knows."

"He suspects that maybe the magic might have had an effect on Rory. He doesn't know for a fact."

"Somehow, I think he'll find out." She motioned over my shoulder. I groaned when I saw Tom approaching the café door.

We raced away from the window as if we weren't guilty of anything. Tom ambled up to the counter and casually leaned against it. "Well, I guess there's no time like the present. I need to interview Mr. Covington today. I haven't found him yet, but I have his address now."

I swallowed hard and didn't mention that Rory had just been across the street moments earlier. No need in helping to put the final nail in my coffin.

"Are you sure talking to him is one hundred percent necessary? You've told me about this mistake and I promise to never make it again."

"Oh, I'm positive. And promising won't cut it." He studied his fingernails. I had to admit, he had nice hands, and I was a sucker for nice hands.

I scowled. "And how do you plan on doing this? What makes you think he'll answer your questions? He doesn't know you, and from the looks he gave you earlier, I'd say he doesn't care for you all that much."

"I have my ways." He wiggled his eyebrows.

"What does that mean?" I stared, wide-eyed.

"You aren't planning to use violence?" Mary Jane asked.

He frowned, but his eyes twinkled with mischief. "Do I look like a violent man?"

I studied him. A gangster in Dockers and a button-down shirt? "No, I guess not."

"I'll use a little bit of magic. And you'll even get to be there to hear his response for yourself. So don't worry."

"Are you going to hypnotize him?" I placed my hands on my hips.

"No, I told you, it's magic. Just a little, to help him open up. It'll make him want to talk to me. It won't hurt him and it'll only last a few minutes."

I breathed a sigh of relief. "I don't like the sound of it. Not one bit." Tom seemed way too casual about all this. But I guess he knew what he was doing. I'd have to take his word for it.

"Well, no offense, but you don't have any say-so in the matter." He winked.

"I didn't think I would." I rolled my eyes.

Mary Jane rang up the last of the customers. The café was quiet for the first time all day. But the quiet didn't help, all it did was allow me time to focus on how messed up things really were. I'd walked out on my cheating fiancé, quit a job I hated, and moved back to my hometown. I should be happy, but I'd made a mess of my chance of a new life in less than twenty-four hours. That left me little reason to do a happy dance.

Tom slid into one of the booths and closed his eyes. He spoke words I didn't understand. It wasn't that he spoke a different language, it was just the words were so low, it was barely a whisper. It was more like chanting.

When he'd finished, he clapped his hands together and said, "That should do it. I'll be back with Rory." I wanted to grab him by the shirt, drag him to the back, and tie him up in the storage closet. But maybe this was a good thing. From the looks of what I saw earlier, I didn't know if I could handle watching women fawn all over Rory. If Tom discovered the spell had worked on him, maybe he could fix it, although I still stood the chance of losing the café. It was a lose-lose situation.

Chapter Fourteen

Within an hour, Tom had returned, and Rory came through the door with him. I said a silent prayer that a crowd of women hadn't followed him into the café. Maybe the spell had worn off. Could I be that lucky?

"I don't know what hit me, but I'm suddenly starving." Rory glanced from me to Mary Jane.

"Have a seat." I smiled, then cast a glance over at Tom.

He shrugged as if to say, "Yeah, I know I'm good at what I do."

Rory slid into a booth and I placed the menu in front of him. His smile made my body tingle all over, again.

He waved off the menu. "If you don't mind, I'd like another cheeseburger. I didn't get to finish the last one." He winked.

I blushed. "Sure, no problem."

As I moved away, Tom approached.

"I don't like this at all." I wiggled my index finger in his direction. "I only like the idea of doing magic that helps others, not something that would make them talk against their will."

"It won't make him talk against his will. He'll only tell me what he wants me to know. It'll come without him questioning my motives, though, so that makes things a lot easier."

"If you say so, but no funny business."

"Hey, I'm not the one mucking up my magic."

I stuck out my tongue.

When Tom slid into the booth across from my handsome magical mishap, I reluctantly walked away. Rory's burger couldn't cook fast enough. Now would have been a perfect time to try and find a reverse spell, but I wanted to hear every word exchanged between Tom and Rory. There was no time. Tom had said I'd get to hear it all for myself, and I was going to hold him to that. My only hope was Mary Jane listening in. Thank goodness she had busybody tendencies.

I hurried from the kitchen with plate in hand.

"Have a seat," Tom said when I approached their table. "We're just chatting. Since you don't have any other customers right now, why don't you join in?"

He had the smooth talk down pat. His demeanor bordered on used car salesman though, so he might want to tone it down a notch. I'd have to inform him later.

"I'd love to," I said through a forced smile. But I was faced with a dilemma: which side to sit on? If I picked Rory, I might overheat, but if I picked Tom, Rory would again think we were an item. I pulled a chair up to the end of the booth. Problem solved. Tom gave me a sideways glance and released a snicker. This all seemed so wrong and it kind of creeped me out.

"So, tell me Rory, how are things?" Tom picked up one of Rory's fries and popped it in his mouth.

"What do you mean?" Rory squirted ketchup on his burger, then replaced the top of the bun.

"I noticed you had a very beautiful woman hanging around earlier." Tom wiggled his brow.

My stomach churned when he mentioned the beautiful woman. Did she have to be a knockout?

"Is that your girlfriend?" Tom stared at Rory expectantly.

My throat tightened as if a boa constrictor had coiled around it. How had Tom found out? I didn't think he'd noticed. Please let Rory answer with a resounding no.

"No. She was my girlfriend." He glanced at me, then peered down at his plate. "We, um, broke up over a year ago."

"Still friends then, I see. Close friends," Tom said.

"No, not really." He took a bite from his burger and chewed.

This time I didn't knock it out of his hand.

Rory continued. "That's the thing. I don't know why she's back. I don't know why all these women are suddenly so interested in me, either. At first I thought it was just my imagination."

Tom quirked his brow at me. I swallowed hard. This was not going well.

"Don't take this the wrong way, I'm not hitting on you or anything, but you are a good-looking dude," Tom offered.

"They never acted this way before. Something doesn't seem right." Rory used his napkin to wipe ketchup off his hand.

The thought crossed my mind: were my feelings for Rory from my magic? My attraction to him had been instant, though. Before he ate the food. But what woman in her right mind wouldn't be attracted to Rory Covington? What I felt for him was pure, utter, out-and-out lust—exactly what the spell had called for. Plus, I'd gotten out of one bad relationship, what made me think dating someone else would be different?

Tom broke my reverie. "That is a dilemma, man. One that most men would love to have."

"I'm not must men." He took a drink of water. "I've been burned before and I don't need that headache in my life."

He looked at me as if saying he was sorry. Did he really mean what he said? If so, then there wasn't a chance for us. But if I didn't reverse the magic, there'd never be a chance for us anyway. Why did this have to happen? Why now?

Rory stood. "Thanks for the food. I'm glad I got a chance to finish it this time." He gave a flicker of a smile and pulled his wallet from his back pocket. "How much do I owe you?"

I stood and Tom followed behind me. "It's on me. I owe you for the other burger."

Rory frowned. "Are you sure?"

"I'm positive. Please, it would make me feel better."

Rory touched my hand, but the expression on his face appeared more confused than ever. "It was nice talking with you again, Elly. I'd stay longer, but I have to get back to work."

I nodded. "Sure, I understand. I have work, too. See ya later."

Rory looked as if he didn't know how or why he'd ended up in my restaurant, eating a burger and talking to a guy he probably didn't like. On his way out the door, Rory glanced back at me, then to Tom. No doubt he thought Tom and I were an item. I wanted the chance to tell him we weren't, but what could I say? Tom is just here on a magical intervention?

And Tom wasn't helping matters by standing so closely to me, either. I needed to have a little chat with him about personal space and boundaries.

"I'll see you," Rory said as he made his way out the door.

"Look what you've done," Tom said when the door had closed on Rory. "This is bad. Very bad."

Chapter Fifteen

After I'd closed the café, I remembered I hadn't eaten all day. I had been around food from sunup to sundown and never taken the time to eat anything other than a few nibbles here and there. I was now living at Grandma Imelda's cottage and she'd left the cupboards mostly bare. Mystic Hollow was like a ghost town. If tumbleweeds had bounced across the street, I wouldn't have been surprised. They rolled the sidewalks up when the first star twinkled. It was sad really, because the quaint little town had a lot to offer. More nightlife would do it good.

The only thing open was the supermarket, so I figured I'd grab a loaf of bread, peanut butter, and jelly for my usual meal of choice. As I passed by the window on my way toward the store's entrance, he caught my attention. Inside the store, Rory stood out like a beacon in the night. But he wasn't alone. Rory and his ex stood in the produce section in front of the apples, oblivious to the fact that someone was watching them. From the sidewalk, I gawked in the window, observing from afar, as if I was viewing a really bad movie.

I prayed no one would notice me gawking at them. They picked up a couple things, then moved to the next aisle. The ex-girlfriend had an exaggerated swing in her walk. It cascaded up from her feet to the top of her head, making her blonde hair swing with each sway of her hips. She slipped to his side and looped her arm through his, holding a grocery basket on the other arm. With a smile plastered on her face, she leaned in and kissed him on the cheek.

My stomach rolled. Suddenly, I wasn't hungry any more. At that moment, I wanted to be the one kissing him on the cheek, but I'd managed to make that impossible. I had screwed things up, and now I needed to take full responsibility for making sure my customers received the correct magic. Mama always said: when you fail miserably, be prepared to deal with the consequences.

She whispered in Rory's ear and he shook his head. If only I knew what she'd said. The guilt washed over me again for watching them. But in my defense, they were right out there in the open for anyone to witness their cozy tête-à-tête. No matter how much I wanted to, I couldn't force myself to look away.

"What are you doing?" The voice sounded from behind my right ear.

I jumped and spun around. "Oh, you scared me. Um, nothing."

Mary Jane stood next to me. "People don't usually window-shop at the grocery store. Are you going in, or not?"

"No, I think I'll come back later." I moved away from the window.

"But you're already here." Mary Jane peered through the window and I saw the realization in her eyes. "Oh," she said quietly. "How long you been watching them?"

I studied my shoes. "Just a minute or two."

She quirked a brow.

"Honest. I'm not some stalker." I held my hand up to my chest, covering my heart.

"What are they doing?" She moved closer to the window, cupping her hands around her eyes for a better view.

"I don't know. What do most people do at the grocery store?" I pulled my purse strap back up my shoulder, pretending to be unconcerned.

"Shopping, I guess."

"Well, you can't let her keep you from doing what you need to do."

"She's not keeping me from doing anything." I fidgeted from one foot to the other. "Do you think he's back with her? I mean, I know he said he wasn't, but they look very cozy."

"I don't think so. Look at him. He's leaning away while she moves closer." She pointed inside the store.

"But why doesn't he just walk away from her then?" My shoulders slumped a little farther.

"I don't have an answer for that, sweetie." She gave my shoulders a squeeze.

Deep down, I knew it was the magic. Not wanting to admit it didn't make it any less real. Women had begun to gather around the area. Wherever Rory went, they followed. The ladies smiled, waved, and giggled as they walked past him. I'd created the perfect storm without intending to, and I needed to find a way to fix this mess soon. Before something terrible happened. Rory said he didn't enjoy the attention. But what man wouldn't enjoy that much admiration from the opposite sex?

We stood in silence, watching the couple. The ex picked up a bag of what appeared to be rice cakes, or some other corkboard-like snack. Rory nodded, while scanning the store. Was he looking for a way out? As they moved down the aisle, a couple women headed in their direction. Their focus was on one thing, and it wasn't the food. When they walked past Rory, one grabbed his butt and the other reached up and ran her fingers through his hair. He darted to his left, escaping the clutches of the magic-entranced ladies who were only acting out the calls of my lust spell. His ex-girlfriend didn't seem to notice the unwanted advances Rory endured. She was too focused on the bag of Styrofoam disguised as food.

"There sure are a lot of women in there."

I frowned. "You're telling me. They're following him around like lost puppies."

"Gosh, they're so bold. Isn't that a friend of your mother?" Mary Jane asked.

"I'm afraid so. I'm so glad my mother's out of town. What if she was affected by the spell? I'd be so embarrassed."

"Luckily, you don't have to worry about it."

Without saying another word, Mary Jane reached out and tapped on the window. It rattled and I cringed.

"What are you doing?" I attempted to hide behind the line of shopping carts while glancing around for an escape route. I wanted to conceal my guilt-clenched face.

"I want Rory to see you."

"No! That's the last thing I want." I dashed away from the window and Mary Jane hurried beside me.

Before I made it all the way to my car, the sound of my name carried across the night air. Rory sprinted across the lot.

I froze as if I'd taken a tranquilizer dart right in the chest. When I finally forced my legs to move, I slowly turned around. "I'll get you for this, Mary Jane," I whispered through my forced smile.

"Only doing what needs to be done," she sing-songed.

"Hi." Rory smiled. "What are you doing?"

"I was just leaving." I clutched at my purse as if it was a life preserver. He looked down at my absence of groceries or cart.

"Well, it was nice seeing you. I gotta go." I waved.

As if the situation couldn't get any worse, before I made an escape, the gorgeous ex approached. She eyed me up and down, giving me the once-over. Her eyes judged me and I couldn't help but glance down at my food-covered clothing. I probably smelled like fried chicken and potato salad.

"You must be Elly Blair?" She knew my name? I didn't even know her name yet.

I moved closer to her and stretched out my hand. "Yes, that's right. Nice to meet you."

She ignored my offer of a handshake and gestured toward the store with her thumb so hard I thought she might have broken it. "What a coincidence that you're here. Rory was just talking about you in the store. He recognized you when you knocked on the window."

"I didn't knock." I looked at him, then to Mary Jane and back to Rory. "I didn't knock." I shook my head.

Her mouth dropped. When she regained her composure, she said, "I'm Kim Barnes, Rory's girlfriend."

Rory didn't correct her.

Kim stood ramrod straight. This whole scene creeped me out—standing in the Piggly Wiggly parking lot next to Rory, talking to his crazed maybe ex-girlfriend, who may or may not be willing me dead in her mind. I needed one of those eject buttons to get me out of there.

Rory shuffled his foot. "I thought I'd come by tomorrow for a slice of pie." Just like that? She made a statement like that and he segued into pie?

"Oh, that's a fabulous idea, Rory. I could really use a fix for my sweet tooth." She squeezed his arm. Yeah, right, it looked as if her sweet tooth never got a fix.

"I think we only have one piece of pie left," Mary Jane chimed in, sending a poisonous glare Kim's way.

I flashed a cross look in Mary Jane's direction. "We have plenty of pie and I'd love it if the two of you stopped by." I gave a fake smile.

Rory frowned and squinted at Kim. "Sure, okay yeah, we'll stop by."

Kim smiled a sweet, obviously phony, smile and looped an arm through his again. He slid to his left, gently pulling away from her. She scanned the length of my body before focusing on my face again as if waiting for a response. I shrugged. The last thing I needed was a feud with her. Judging by the scowl on her face, and the fact she hadn't shaken my outstretched hand, I was too late. She whirled around, stumbled on her wedge heels, and stomped off.

"I'll be waiting in the car," she huffed.

"Nice meeting you, Kim," I muttered in her wake.

"Okay, I'll see you for that pie," Rory said as I turned away.

"Go suck on a rice cake," Mary Jane said to Kim's back.

I hurried away, beating a hasty retreat, not giving him a chance to say another word, or offer an explanation. It was almost too painful to hear him speak.

Mary Jane shuffled along with me. "Why didn't you tell her to get lost?"

"I can't do that. She's done nothing to me. And I can't turn away customers."

"If they're lousy people, you can. She was lousy to Rory."

"Maybe she's changed. Maybe that's why she came back for him." I unlocked my car.

"Oh please, she hasn't changed and you know it. I can see right through her fake persona."

I nodded. "Yeah, she is pretty transparent, isn't she? What am I going to do?"

"I don't know, honey. But I'm sure you'll think of something. I have faith in you. You always were smart."

That was questionable. One thing wasn't questionable, though. I needed to work on the magic. There had to be something to reverse this. And I didn't want to wait around for Tom Owenton to tell me what that something was. If I did the magic right the first time, I had to be able to do it right again. At least I told myself that. It made it easier to deal with.

"I'm going in the store now that the showdown is over. Are you coming?" Mary Jane asked.

"I think I need nothing more than to bury myself under the covers. Tomorrow can't be any worse, right?"

She shook her head and waved over her shoulder.

I didn't look for Rory's car as I pulled out from the store parking lot. I didn't want to know if Kim had gotten into the same car as Rory. Thinking about the two of them together made me cringe. If they were a couple and in love once, it wouldn't be a stretch to think it could happen again.

Chapter Sixteen

Another thing I hadn't considered when agreeing to take on the café: the ungodly hour at which I would have to crawl out of bed. The sun was still sleeping when I went to work. By the time it became light outside, I'd already started serving customers. I'd arrived even earlier to prepare a pie for Rory. Part of my brain said: leave well enough alone. But the other part, the part I most often listened to when I shouldn't, said: give it a shot! So I did.

I measured off the flour and dumped it into the big stainless steel bowl. Then I added salt before cutting in my eggs, water, and vinegar. I'd make a couple pies for customers and a special one for Rory. Rolling out the dough put me in a slightly hypnotic state. It was therapeutic, and I needed that more than anything at that moment. After preparing the other pies and placing them in the oven, I was ready for Rory's special pie.

The back door rattled, and Mary Jane stepped into the kitchen.

"You're here early," I said.

"I thought I'd find you here. I came to help you."

"Help me with what?" I played dumb.

"The magic, of course." She gestured toward the book on the shelf. "There must be something I can do to help. I don't want to just stand around and do nothing. After all, it was my fault. You should have fired me because of it."

"Nonsense. I don't even want to hear it. It was a mistake. Anyone could have made it, and to be honest, I'm shocked I didn't do it before you did. We just have to keep it from happening again."

She wiped a tear from her cheek. I moved over and squeezed her in a big hug.

"Now stop that crying and help me, okay?" I lifted her chin with my index finger so she'd have to meet my gaze.

She grinned and nodded. "Okay."

"There has to be something in the book to tell me how to reverse this magic. My grandmother never had any problems with this. Maybe I'm just not cut out for this type of thing. I should go back to work for someone else, I can't be my own boss."

Mary Jane rushed over and helped me hoist it down from the shelf. I carried the book from its spot on the shelf over to the counter. The thing was almost as big as I was.

"Quit the silly talk. You and I both know how much you hated your job. Now set that hefty hardback down here and let's see what we can find." She pulled the book toward her and I joined her in front of the counter. I flipped open the cover and with my index finger went down the list of contents. "*Reversal of Spells and Magic Gone Awry*, page five-fifty-six. How many pages are in this thing?"

"I think over one thousand. Too many."

I quirked a brow and Mary Jane shrugged. Apparently, she'd taken a peek at the book before I had.

"I hope they don't expect me to memorize this thing," I said.

"I think as long as you have it around for reference, that's good enough. Like for when I screw up."

"Well, I wasn't going to say it, but yes, that's one instance." I laughed and she jabbed me in the side.

I flipped to the page. "All it says is see your National Organization of Magic representative." As if. "Can you believe it?"

Mary Jane leaned over my shoulder and read the page, then shook her head.

I scanned the page again. "No new information. No spells for reversal. Just that someone from the company would be by soon to tell me what to do. How the heck do they know when someone has screwed up, anyway?"

She shrugged, not offering an explanation.

I read on and got the answer to my question. "Magic is felt in the air and sent back to headquarters. When it goes wrong, it sends off a different wavelength and they can follow it back to its origins."

Good to know, like radar. I'd never get away with bad magic. Not that I intended to perform bad magic. I didn't want to perform magic at all, but suddenly I had no choice in the matter.

"Well that settles it, there's nothing I can do but wait and hear my fate. It's completely out of my hands." I wanted to cry.

"It'll be okay, your grandmother wouldn't have left you this place if she didn't think you could handle it.

"Oh, she just couldn't give it to anyone else. My mother has zero magical ability and grandma had to give it to someone. She couldn't leave the café closed. They need her to stay in business for the townspeople of Mystic Hollow. I just didn't know enough to say no. I didn't know what I was getting myself into." I let out a deep breath. "But enough about me, that isn't my biggest concern, my concern is for Rory."

"Well, you make really good pies, if that counts for anything."

"I don't think it counts for much."

Mary Jane tossed a towel at me and I ducked. She took my hands and stared into my eyes. "Ever since that first day in middle school when we met, I've looked up to you. You're smart, funny, and a sweet person. You can do anything you set your mind to. If you want to reverse the spell, I know you'll figure it out somehow." She waved her hands through the air, gesturing across the space. "Carpe diem."

Over the twenty-eight years of my life, I couldn't think of one moment, other than leaving Mystic Hollow, that I'd ever seized the day, and look what that had gotten me. "Thank you. I needed that little pep talk." Her chat may not have helped, but she didn't have to know.

"So what if there isn't a spell? You'll think of something. Google it if you have to." She patted me on the back and gave my shoulders a big squeeze. "I have to set up the dining area. What are you going to do?" She motioned with a tilt of her head toward the book.

"I guess I'll bake a special pie." I winked.

She smiled and moved toward the swinging door. "Good for you. Go get 'em."

The open *Mystic Magic* book lay beside the mixer. I refused to believe there wasn't a way to reverse the spell. I'd just improvise a little and cross my fingers I didn't make things worse. But how much worse could it be, right? Having this over my head was consuming my thoughts and making life unpleasant. And I thought it had been bad before.

An electrified energy whirled around me as I pinched off and sprinkled spices across the pie filling, up from my feet, traveling up my legs and flowing to my arms, stopping at my fingertips. My fingers vibrated as I sprinkled more spices across the pie. The flash of blue and red light whizzed around the pie, making a popping noise before disappearing into a blue-tinged puff of smoke.

"Reverse the spell gone awry, let the magic gone astray wait for another day. So mote it be." It surprised me how easily the words popped into my head. Maybe I had that natural talent, after all. Although, typically, natural talent doesn't screw up and let the wrong person receive a life-altering spell.

Grandma Imelda said to concentrate, and that's exactly what I did. Apprehension bubbled up inside me. I hadn't been sure what to expect this time, but the flashing lights and buzzing energy led me to believe I'd just added magic to the pie. What magic exactly, I had no idea.

I placed the pie in the oven. Now I'd wait until the opportunity came to give Rory a slice. That was, if there was an opportunity. Rory had said he'd come by for a piece. I prayed he wouldn't change his mind.

Chapter Seventeen

Tom was waiting by the door when I opened it for the day. Little did he know I'd already been practicing magic. With any luck, I'd slip Rory the pie, and Tom would be none the wiser. Tom wanted to watch all the magic performed at the café and apparently, he planned to be around every second of the day the café was open. Did the man never sleep? Didn't he have more important magical tragedies to investigate? Maybe I could slip him a sleeping spell in a pancake or something. That would probably be frowned upon, too. Too many magical rules and I probably only knew a fraction of them so far. Without Tom breathing down my neck, watching every move I made, maybe then I could reverse Rory's spell.

"Good morning, gorgeous." Tom waved.

Whether the day would be good or not was yet to be determined.

"How about a cup of coffee?" he asked.

"You know, Tom, if you're going to be hanging around I think I'm putting you to work. I think you know where the mugs are and you'll spot the coffee."

A sly grin spread across his face as he marched off to retrieve his own coffee.

A few customers strolled in, but one in particular had me wanting to turn the sign to read *Closed* and lock the door. Miss Perky Blonde strolled into the café. I hadn't expected to see her, not without Rory, at least. She'd volunteered to come by for pie with him. Where was he? She plopped down at the counter, setting her Louis Vuitton bag on the counter next to her. Her emerald green blouse matched her long-lashed eyes.

"What can I get you?" I smoothed the apron over my T-shirt and wiped flour off my jeans.

Next to her I was underdressed, but I needed to remember, I was working. No time to play dress-up in Mystic Café. Had she ever worked a day in her life? What had Rory seen in her, anyway? Was it purely looks? Men were superficial that way. Surely someday he'd realize there was more to a relationship than looks and sex. Ugh, sex. I didn't want the image of the two of them going at it like rabbits.

"I'll have a skinny cinnamon dolce latte." Her golden hair curled slightly inward on each side, falling perfectly in place next to her cheeks.

Mary Jane walked behind Kim and made the crazy sign with her index finger. I averted my eyes to keep from snickering.

"Will coffee work?"

"Um, sure. Can I at least get cream and sugar?" Her neatly plucked eyebrows rose into confused arcs.

Mystic Café was the nearest thing we had to a Starbucks in town, but I still didn't offer more than plain old coffee.

"Of course." I placed the mug down in front of her and poured. "It's none of my business, but you seem upset. Is everything okay?" It was none of my concern but nonetheless, I really wanted to know. Why was she here? Maybe if I attempted being nice to her, she'd do the same in return.

"I don't know what's wrong, actually. Heck, I don't even know why I'm in town. I woke up the other morning with this overwhelming need to come here and see Rory. Now we're back together and I don't know what to think."

She might as well have stabbed me in the heart. What would she say if I told that her magic had brought her back? Letting her talk may give me answers, but did I really want to know?

"Oh, really?" I asked.

"He broke up with me last year."

"What?" I almost dumped the pot of coffee.

"Yes." She sipped the coffee, then puckered her lips. "He spread nasty rumors about me, but I forgave him."

This was the opposite of what Mrs. Perkins had said. Could she have had her facts wrong? She was rather old.

"What kind of rumors?" I had to know.

"Basically that I was a nasty person and that I'd cheated on him." Kim pursed her lips together.

"Oh, and you didn't cheat on him?" I tried to hide my emotions.

"Of course not. My mama taught me how to be a lady."

I had to get to the bottom of this. Was Rory really a dirty rat? No, he couldn't be. Kim probably couldn't be trusted. Mrs. Perkins seemed far more trustworthy.

"The fact is I have no idea why I'm here. It's as if I can't control myself, you know?" She poured more cream, and then dumped more sugar into her cup, stirring feverishly.

"That doesn't make much sense." I chuckled.

I knew all too well what she meant. And if she knew it was my fault, she'd probably strangle me with the strap of her ridiculously expensive purse. Maybe she'd jab me in the eye with her stiletto heel. Heck, if she knew my stomach did somersaults every time I saw Rory, she'd really want to clobber me.

"Well, I'm sure you'll figure it out." I waved to a new customer, attempting to appear nonchalant.

She responded with a careless shrug. "I don't know if I will, but maybe this is fate telling me Rory and I need a second chance. I've never really been alone before. When I break up with someone, I always have someone else waiting in the wings. I have to be in a relationship."

There was that fate word again, and hearing Kim confessing to not wanting to be alone made me feel bad for her. Nonetheless, I couldn't allow the spell to continue without trying to stop it. "How do you know Rory really wants you back? If he dumped you once, what makes you think he's interested again?"

She waved a dismissive hand. "Oh, I heard he never got over me. Of course he wants me back. I just don't know what to do."

"I'm sure you'll think of something," I said halfheartedly.

I watched as she took another sip of coffee, then placed her mug down. Kim leapt to her feet, slinging her purse across her shoulder. "Well, thanks for listening to me. I'll sure we'll be back later for that cherry pie he keeps raving about."

My stomach danced. Rory raved about my pie to Kim? "Not a problem."
She placed a couple dollars on the counter and sashayed toward the
door. Why had she come into the café just to take a few sips of coffee
and tell me the opposite of what Mrs. Perkins said had happened
between her and Rory? Maybe she had done it on purpose. But why?
The thought hit me: because she thought I liked Rory. Or because she
knew I liked Rory. Was I that obvious? Did I have an 'I'm smitten with
Rory' sign across my forehead?
Tom sauntered up behind me right after Kim walked out and tapped me
on the shoulder.
I groaned. "Now what?"
"Take it easy, tiger, I just wanted to prepare you for what's about to
happen."
"What's about to happen, Tom?" By the expression on his face, I
guessed he wasn't delivering happy news.

Chapter Eighteen

Before he answered, movement drew my attention to the glass entry door. A man in a wrinkled suit stumbled up the old front steps—the concrete had cracked and crumbled a long time ago.

The bell on the door handle jangled as the man entered. His brown, striped suit looked as if it may have fit him about twenty years ago, which was probably when he'd bought it. His thinning gray hair stuck to his head with perspiration.

"May I help you?" I asked and gave the widest smile my face would allow. The café may be on the verge of closing, but in case this man was a real customer, the least I could do was give him a pleasant dining experience. I'd want the same done for me, although some folks in this town weren't the hospitable type, to say the least.

"This is a legal matter," he said.

My eyebrows rose and I wiped my hands on my pants. "You'll have to speak to my lawyer. I told Ray I wasn't talking to him about this anymore."

I wondered if this wasn't about magic and really had to do with that snake, Ray Russell. No way was he getting the Mustang back. I'd burn it first. Well, maybe not burn it, but still....

Ray had persuaded me to accept his engagement ring with his smooth talk. Thank goodness I hadn't followed through with it. Why had I let him talk me into moving in, anyway? I'd given up my dreams to be with that slimeball. What can I say? I was young and in love—and stupid. I had no way of knowing I was making such a big mistake. My grandma knew, though. And my mother, my best friend, cousins... They tried to warn me when I'd first met him, but when you're twenty-two years old, all the answers seem to be at your fingertips. I knew it all. At twenty-eight, I realized I knew nothing. But deep down, I'd never pictured a future with him. Not a real future, nothing past six months. I'd always lived day by day.

Things had a way of working out for the best sometimes, though. If I'd married Ray, I would never have gotten the café. Grandma Imelda never had liked him. A small price to pay, I guess. After all, I had loved him— I'd been blinded by love. I wondered what Ray would say if he knew I was the owner of this place now. He'd probably want to be involved in some way. Over my dead body.

The man scrunched his brows together and placed his briefcase on the counter. "I'm not sure what you're talking about." He popped the lock on the old leather tote. "I'm with the National Organization of Magic."

So, my original hunch had been correct. Was the situation really that serious? Why was he here?

The man's wide brown eyes gave me the once-over. "I'm lookin' for Elly Blair. Is this her?" He glowered at Tom and pointed at me.

I frowned and waved my hand halfheartedly. "Yes, it's me."

"I'm here to talk about the magic." His lip twitched.

I'd assumed as much.

I swallowed hard. My mouth turned dry. "All right. Please have a seat anywhere you like."

He seemed so formal I wanted to ask if I really needed an attorney. I didn't actually have one, but they didn't know that.

"Mr. Owenton has briefed me on the situation. I understand what has happened to the poor man in question."

Poor man? He had women following him everywhere he went. Did they realize how many men would pay big bucks to be in that exact situation? Sure, it sucked, but it wasn't as if I'd turned him into a toad or a donkey. There were worse fates.

"My name's Bart Wibble." He shifted the ratty leather briefcase clutched in his right hand to his left and stuck out his hand toward me. I reached over the counter and grasped it. His palm was as sweaty as his head.

I eyed him up and down. "You've come to look into *my* magic, I assume?" With Grandma Imelda's perfect track record, I realized how lame of a question that was. Of course it was my magic in question.

"Yes, young lady, I have. This is a serious situation."

He knew my name, why didn't he use it? It was as if my father was scolding me.

Tom avoided my glare. Did he call Mr. Wibble here?

"You called in backup?" I whispered in Tom's direction.

Tom glanced at me, but remained tight-lipped.

Mr. Wibble pulled a stack of papers out of his briefcase. One flew across the floor. Mary Jane reached down and grabbed it. She'd been straining her neck to hear what he was saying from the moment he walked in the door. I should have just told her to come on over before she did permanent nerve damage.

"And? How bad is it?" I asked. Did I really want him to answer?

Mary Jane handed him the paper, but she didn't back away. She lingered nearby.

"I can't answer that just yet, not without a full investigation, but I can tell you it doesn't look good." He stepped closer to the counter, his cheap shoes squeaking as they moved across the hardwood. "Do you want to go somewhere else to talk, or is this good right here?"

"Well, um, we can speak here, if that's all right with you?" No way was I waiting to hear what he had to say. Mary Jane would drill me for the details anyway.

I paused, waiting for him to speak. He didn't say a word as he looked down at his shoes. After a few seconds, he cleared his throat. How long could he keep up the silence? Was he trying to kill me with anticipation? Awkward silence again. Was he praying while looking at his shoes? Was it a moment of silence for my soon-to-be closed café?

"It's fairly straightforward, Ms. Blair. You have to right this wrong." Mr. Wibble cleared his throat and continued, "Or we'll close the café for good."

Tom had said the same thing earlier, but I thought he had been exaggerating. Mr. Wibble appeared to be dead serious. I glanced at Mary Jane and practically saw the little wheels spinning in her head. She lived for gossip and big events such as these. It didn't matter if it was someone getting good news or bad news, as long as there was news.

"Your face looks green." Mary Jane placed a hand on my arm.

"Are you okay? I didn't mean to shock you." He leaned closer to the counter, meeting my gaze.

"I'm fine. I don't need y'all fawning over me." I waved a dismissive hand and grabbed the towel next to me, then wiped my forehead. "Please, do go on." I took the glass of water Mary Jane handed me and gulped half of it. They watched me as if they'd never seen anyone drink before.

Chapter Nineteen

After another few seconds, Mr. Wibble studied one of his papers, then stuffed it back into his briefcase. "Like I said, unless you correct this little snafu, we'll be forced to close the café."

"But I have tried to reverse the spell." I covered my mouth with my hand. "Well, I made a pie. He hasn't eaten it yet."

"Secretly," Tom said and looked at Mr. Wibble. "She didn't know I was aware of what she was up to." He smirked as if proud of himself.

Mr. Wibble frowned and I swallowed hard. "That's the problem," he said. "There's more to it than that. Yes, you must reverse the magic spell, which is more complicated, but first you need to get to the root of the problem."

I quirked a brow. "What does that mean exactly?"

He pulled the paper out again and adjusted his glasses. "This woman...Kim?" He glanced up for confirmation. "She needs to understand why she's here, and Mr. Covington...." He studied the papers again. "He needs to understand his feelings for her."

"So I need to play matchmaker?"

Mary Jane coughed from somewhere behind me.

"If need be, yes." He nodded.

There was no way I could put the two of them together. "I can't do that."

Tom placed a hand on my arm.

"Then shall we put the closed sign in the window now?" He gestured over his shoulder.

"No, no. I'll do it. But I have no idea where to even start." I fidgeted, not quite sure what to do with my hands. How would I even begin this process? A ripple of panic rose in my throat at the thought.

"Obviously, you'll need to talk with the victims." Mr. Wibble pushed his eyeglasses up on the bridge of his nose and stared at me, waiting for a response.

Victims. I loved his choice of words, as if I didn't feel bad enough already.

When I didn't answer, he dropped the next bomb on me. "You have forty-eight hours to correct this problem."

"What?" A pain rippled through my chest. "I have a time limit? There are movie marathons that last longer than that. This isn't some game show. People's lives are at stake."

"Exactly." He frowned. "That's why time is of the essence."

"How can I work under such pressure?" I asked.

"You should have thought of that before you were so careless with your magic."

Yeah, stupid me. "Look, in my defense, I wasn't exactly trained very well."

"This is the way it's done. Most people don't have a problem with it." He waved his hands as if to tell me he'd heard enough.

I continued. "But some do? I'm not the only one who's failed miserably?"

"No." He shook his head. "No, you're not the only one. But it doesn't happen often."

"Well, that's good to know."

He stood, attempting to brush the wrinkles out of his jacket. "I should get going and let you get back to work. I have a case involving mistaken identity waiting for me a few towns over." He glanced over my shoulder in the direction of the dessert case. "I hear you make a delicious pie. No offense, but it'll be hard to beat your grandmother's." He licked his lips and patted his belly.

Had he been here before? Tom had said they'd never had any problems with Mystic Café until now. It probably wasn't unheard of for magical folks to visit other magical folks. Mr. Wibble had probably visited the café for grandma's wonderful food.

"Would you like a slice to take with you?" Was pie a sufficient form of bribery? The answer to that question was probably no.

"Oh, well." He smiled, an expression I didn't think his face was capable of making. "If it isn't too much trouble?"

"No, no trouble at all." Maybe if I gave him the whole pastry display, he'd drop this entire issue. Somehow, I knew not to even ask.

"The blackberry looks good." He pointed at the glass case.

"Excellent choice. It's my favorite." I reached for a container and plastic wrap, then covered up a slice of blackberry and placed the package in a bag.

He clutched the pie in his chubby hands. "I'll be back in forty-eight hours. Remember, I'll close the café if the spell isn't reversed by then."

Yeah, I'd heard him the first time, loud and clear.

"Just like her grandmother," Mr. Wibble muttered as he shuffled toward the door.

Tom frowned. "I'm very sorry. I hope you don't blame me for this. He's my boss, I couldn't keep him away."

"You're just doing your job. I know it's not your fault." I placed the pie dish back into the display case. "What did he mean, I'm just like my grandmother?"

He shook his head. "I have no idea. Mr. Wibble's a bit eccentric."

"I see that."

Tom squeezed my hand, his warm fingers tightened around mine. "Looks like you have some work to do."

I massaged my temples. "I know, but with taking care of the café, when will I have time to talk with Rory and Kim?" If I didn't talk with them, though, it wouldn't matter if I took care of the café or not. I let out a deep breath, but it did nothing to relieve the tension building up inside me.

We watched as Mr. Wibble drudged through the door and around the corner with the pie in one hand and his ratty old briefcase in the other. Who knew they had a whole legal system for magic? Then again, who knew they had magic? Certainly not me.

"All of this is crazy, you know. I didn't know anything like this existed, and now I have to navigate the magical world?"

"You're a smart woman, Elly. If anyone can figure it out, you can." He winked.

Tom offering encouragement? I barely knew him, but this seemed out of character. An aura of cockiness followed him everywhere he went, and this behavior didn't fit that categorization.

Visions of Grandma Imelda's sweet face popped into my mind and I knew I had to make an attempt to straighten this mess out. Giving up wasn't an option.

I began devising a plan. "I guess first thing, I need to talk with Kim, she'll be the hardest. She's positive that fate has brought her back to Rory, and I need to convince her fate doesn't want her here."

Fate or me, maybe it was both. What if Rory had no idea what he really felt? I was almost afraid to find out. What if I got an answer I didn't want to hear? That he loved Kim and always would.

"You have to start somewhere. And I think you're right, Kim will be the hardest. And on that note, since I'm allowed free reign of the café, I think I'll help myself to a slice of pie."

"I never said free reign," I yelled as he walked away. He didn't respond and I watched him saunter toward the dessert case. Keeping these magic people fed was going to cost me a small fortune.

Business had slowed down and I'd just taken a moment to catch a breather when the phone rang.

"Mystic Café, how may I help you?" I propped the phone between my ear and my chin and sorted through receipts.

"Elly, dear, it's your grandmother. How's my favorite café owner doing?" I dropped the receipts as if they were a ton of bricks.

"Grandma, what are you doing?" I glanced around as if she was there, hiding and watching me from a distance. She and my mother had always used that 'I've got eyes in the back of my head' line. Heck, for all I knew she had a baby monitor set up to scrutinize my every move.

"What else would I be doing? Enjoying the sunshine, of course. I played a little golf this morning with a delightful man I just met."

"A man? You want to tell me about this stranger? Is he safe? He's not a serial killer, is he?"

Her snort rang through from the other end of the line, but she quickly fell silent.

"Wait a minute," she said.

"What's wrong?" I swallowed the lump in my throat.

"Don't ask *me* what's wrong. Why don't you tell me what's the matter? There's something going on with the café, isn't there?"

She was good. No wonder I'd never been able to sneak around and skip high school. She'd always known when I was hiding something then, and apparently, she knew now.

"What makes you say that? Everything is going fine. Customers have been steady and I'm following your recipes." Did she sense the doubt in my voice?

She sighed. "How's the magic? I hadn't heard from you, so I assumed there weren't any problems, but now…."

"You're being paranoid, Grandma. Let me repeat, everything is fine."

She ignored my reassurance this time. "It's not just bad, either, I can sense it. Have you met a man?"

I snorted. "What? Ha, no."

"You have. Oh, Lordy, maybe there's hope yet."

"Hope for what?"

"Hope for a great-grandbaby."

"Oh, Grandma." I gave a mirthless chuckle.

While I had her on the phone, I needed to ask about Tom. But how would I pose the question without her knowing something was wrong?

"You still there, Elly?"

To ask or not to ask? There was no time for a heated internal debate. "Grandma, there is one thing..." I let out a deep breath and pushed forward with the question. "Maybe this is what you sensed..." I was for sure going to hell for not being honest with her. "There was a man who stopped by the café. He claimed to be from The National Organization of Magic. His name is Tom Owenton, do you know him?"

"Oh yes, Tom. He's so handsome. He's a little cocky, but in a good way, if you know what I mean? I didn't think he'd pay you a visit. Was there something wrong with the information I provided them about you?"

"I don't think so. He just wanted to confirm things, I guess." Grandma probably sensed a rat. "Maybe he wanted to stop by and welcome me. Kind of like a welcoming committee?"

"Huh...they've never done that in the past unless the person who discovered the magic didn't have anyone to show them, but you have me. Oh no, did I not show you enough? Are they mad at me? It's just you're so smart. I knew you'd figure everything out for yourself."

"No, everything is fine. I promise." Now I'd upset my grandmother. What kind of person was I?

"Are you sure? Did Mr. Owenton say anything about a mistake I might have made?"

Oh, he'd said plenty, but there was no way I could tell her. She'd barely gotten out of sight before I had an investigator at the café. What would she think?

"To the contrary. He said everything looked to be in order. I just wanted to make sure he was who he claimed to be. I wanted to make sure this organization was real. There are a lot of crazies out there. You can never be too sure, you said that yourself. Remember your warning about me moving to New York?"

"I remember, and I'm glad you're actually listening to me. Sometimes I feel like an old woman just talking to myself."

"Grandma, don't say such things. You're not an old woman."

"Well, Mr. Evans certainly didn't think I was old when we were playing golf this morning. But that's neither here nor there." She snickered.

"I'm not sure if I want to hear why...."

"To answer your questions, yes, the organization is real and Tom is exactly who he says he is. Well, that's if he told you he's an investigator."

I cringed at her words. What if the little lightbulb went off in her head? Surely she'd know they wouldn't send an investigator unless something needed investigating. As much as I might not want to hear about her new golf buddy, a subject change was in order.

"Tell me about your golf friend, Grandma."

"Enough about me," she said. "I want to know about this man you met."

"Oh, look at that, here comes a customer. I'll call you soon. Enjoy the golf."

"But—"

I hung up before she uttered one more *but*. Not since I was eight-years-old and lied to my grandmother about climbing the big oak tree in her front yard had I felt this rotten. I plopped down at the counter, resting my head in my hands. Did I really think I could get by with withholding information from Grandma Imelda? She sniffed that stuff out better than any bloodhound.

****

With my head buried in the dessert display case, cleaning out the dried remnants of whipped cream, the clearing of someone's throat caught my attention. I spun around and almost let out a gasp when I saw Kim standing in front of me. What was she doing in the café again? Not that I was complaining. I'd had no idea how I was going to talk with her and find out her true feelings for Rory, as Mr. Wibble had instructed me. Had fate brought her to me, or was it a little magical help from Tom? For someone who didn't seem to like Mystic Café, she'd been in a lot.

"You got a minute?" she asked.

This time she wore low-rise jeans that hugged her body in all the right places. Even if some of those places could stand to be filled out a little. Her white T-shirt made her abs almost visible through the fabric. She would have looked casual if not for the extremely high wedge heels and abundance of jewelry. Why had she changed her clothing in the middle of the day? This wasn't a fashion show.

"Sure." I placed the soiled towel on the counter behind me and gestured toward the table in front of us. "Have a seat."

"Thanks for taking the time to talk with me," she mumbled.

"No problem. Can I get you some coffee?" To think I thought it would be hard to talk with her. It seemed as if Kim was an open book—all I needed was to find the correct page. And she was thanking me!

Mary Jane placed two glasses of water in front of us. I knew she wanted to hang around and overhear the conversation, but I gave her the look. The look that said: you'll lose your cool and blow my chances. Kim probably wouldn't talk if anyone else was around.

"Let's be honest, woman to woman." She sat, crossing her long legs.

"Okay," I said. This probably wasn't going to end well. A vision of her pinning me to the ground and pulling on my hair flashed through my head.

"Do you have a thing for Rory?" She placed her hands on the table and stared me right in the eyes. She was dead serious.

I almost choked on my water. Why hadn't she asked me this earlier? Kim was playing games and I hadn't been handed a set of rules.

"At the grocery, there seemed to be something between you, a connection of sorts. The way you two stared at each other, as if you were communicating telepathically."

"I don't know what you mean. We just happened to run into each other." I twisted a napkin in my hands.

"Please. When he thought you knocked on the window, he ran out from that store as if someone had yelled fire. Are you trying to take him away from me? If so, I warn you things will get ugly." She glared at me. Her emerald eyes grew darker.

The thought of finding a spell to turn her into a toad crossed my mind. Lucky for her, it wasn't an option. She could use a little time-out. Basking in the sun, eating a few flies for a couple hours might make her tone down the sassiness. A tinge of guilt immediately washed over me. I should be ashamed. Magic was for good only. But I still chuckled to myself when the vision of Kim as a toad ran through my mind.

"I'm not trying to take him away from you, if that's what you think," I said, grinding my teeth ever so slightly.

She stared for a beat, then continued. "Well, good. I'm glad we have that settled."

"Is that it? That's all you had to say?" I met her gaze. Backing down and allowing her to think she could intimidate me wasn't an option.

"Pretty much. I've spoken my piece, don't you think? I won't let anything stand in my way with Rory." She knitted her eyebrows together. "Or anyone."

"Oh, really? That sounds pretty harsh." I folded my arms across my chest.

"Sometimes I have to be that way. It's my character. But I get things done and I get what I want. Always." She smirked. Her lip-gloss sparkled under the overhead light.

"Let me ask you a question, since we are being honest and talking woman to woman. Where do you see yourself five years from now? With Rory, and married? Do you have children? A home with a white picket fence? Is that what you want? No offense, but you seem like a party girl and not exactly the soccer mom type. You seem like someone who wouldn't want to be tied down with a husband and children."

She picked at the napkin in front of her. "Well, I guess I hadn't thought of that part."

Her wheels were turning, I knew by the sickened expression on her face. I continued with my strategy. "I don't think it would be fair to Rory if that's what he wants and you want something entirely different. He doesn't seem like the partying type. Not that I know him, mind you." I was treading dangerous waters here. "He's probably rather dull, actually."

She sat up straighter. "He is not. Why, he likes to do all kinds of things. He's very adventurous."

"Really? Name one thing he wanted to do that you wanted to do that seemed adventurous."

"Well, we, well." She paused. "I guess I can't think of anything. Still, Rory isn't dull."

Okay. I sensed Rory wasn't dull, but anyone that wasn't wild would seem tame to her, so I needed to plant that seed in her mind. With any luck, it would grow into a giant tree and she'd abandon her mission. "He likes this town, so I hope you enjoy living here. I doubt you'll get him to move. Where did you say you're living now?"

Mary Jane watched as she wiped off a table next to us. She was like a pit bull waiting for her attack command.

"I didn't. But I moved to New York City." She waved off my question as if swatting at a fly.

I tut-tutted and shook my head. "No way."

"No way, what?" Her brows furrowed and her eyes narrowed to slits.

"No way will he move to a big city. He's a small-town boy. I think you should really think this over before you give up all your hopes and dreams. You do have hopes and dreams, right? I mean, a girl as smart as you must have."

She nodded. "I do have dreams. I plan on being a fashion designer."

"See, you can't really do that while living in Mystic Hollow. I guess you'll have to give it all up to live here. Hey, I know." I straightened in my chair and leaned forward. "I could really use some help here at the café, you could wait tables. Mary Jane would show you the ropes. Tips are good with the morning crowd and, as pretty as you are, I bet you'd make a ton."

She jumped up. "You think you're so smart. I know what you're trying to do. You don't want me to be with Rory. You want him for yourself. Well, I won't let you have him. He'll move to the city with me, you wait and see. And keep away from my man, or else." She pointed a French-manicured nail in my face.

Mary Jane inched closer to our table like a cat waiting to pounce. Kim turned in a whirl and stormed out the door.

I turned to Mary Jane and she shook her head. "That wasn't so good, huh? I wasn't very convincing."

"No, not really. But the part about working here was great. Tips from the morning crowd are good." She nodded.

"Everything I said was the truth. There's no way he'll leave Mystic Hollow for her." I studied her face for a reaction. "Is there?"

She managed a shrug. "I don't know, honey. I stopped trying to figure out men a long time ago. And if you're wise, you'll stop, too."

That was probably the best advice Mary Jane had ever given me. But it was easier said than done with someone like Rory. His dimples set my stomach on fire and I lost all reasonable thought. The spicy scent his body exuded set off tiny tickles in the pit of my stomach and his gorgeous eyes made me weak at the knees. I was doomed.

"I hope she doesn't convince him to leave before I can reverse the spell. I *will* be able to reverse it, right?" I was full of questions. If I didn't have the answers, I wasn't sure why I expected Mary Jane to have them. But I needed reassurance, even if it was a lie.

"Sure, of course. It'll happen soon enough. It's certainly not for your lack of trying, that's for sure."

Had I really tried? Maybe this just proved magic wasn't in the cards for me.

"Thanks for helping out extra around here today. I needed the time to talk with Kim. I'm just surprised she came here. I thought I'd have to chase her down." I replaced the coffee pot and stood next to Mary Jane at the register.

"Sometimes trouble has a way of tracking you down, I guess." Mary Jane wrapped her arm around me squeezed my shoulders.

Yes, sometimes trouble did have a way of finding me.

I poured a cup of coffee for the man who'd just sat down. With his slumped shoulders and the dark circles under his eyes, he seemed as if he could use a little perking up. I'd make sure to give him a little magic in whatever food he ordered. Simple magic spells was the only thing for me. Nothing complex like fixing screw-ups.

Chapter Twenty

I crossed my arms in front of my chest. I didn't know what else to do with myself. If only I'd had a chance to comb my hair before he showed up looking gorgeous. Rory's jeans and T-shirt hugged every muscle. It was a nice look for him. He looked darn good in a tight pair of Levi's, but he probably looked delicious in everything he put on...and didn't put on, too. Oh my, the question popped into my head: boxers or briefs? No, I had to clear my mind.

Silence hung in the air. What else was there to say? I studied the cute little scar above Rory's right eyebrow and wondered how he'd gotten it. What I wanted to know most though, was who Rory was. What he liked and disliked. What he did for fun and how his lips tasted.

"Can I get you a slice of pie?" Small talk was not one of my better skills. But I was almost giddy with the knowledge that soon the spell might be reversed. All Rory needed to do was enjoy one little slice of pie.

Then I remembered what Mr. Wibble said. Rory eating the pie wasn't enough. Was there a chance Mr. Wibble could be wrong? What if the pie was enough? Though if it were that simple, wouldn't Tom have told me to do that in the first place? In spite of not wanting to know Rory's feelings for Kim, I had to follow my orders. Find out if he wanted Kim. Truly wanted her.

"I hate to say this...but no." Rory moved closer.

"Oh, not in the mood for flaky-crusted cherry goodness?" Butterflies frolicked in my stomach.

He shook his head. "No, no pie for me."

I studied the imperfections in the hardwood floor and shuffled my foot. "So, if you're not here for pie, what other reason is there?"

To tell me he was leaving with Kim and that I'd never see him again? No, he barely knew me. He wouldn't bother telling me something as personal as that.

Rory's cheeks turned red and heat rushed to mine. "I think you know why I'm here."

He knew about the magic? My heart thumped until I thought it would pop out of my chest. "Not for the pie? Maybe a flying cheeseburger?" My voice faltered and I chuckled, trying to cover my nervousness. He didn't return the sentiment.

Rory stared straight at me. "I don't really know how to say this, so I guess I'll just come right out and say it. Elly, will you come on a date with me tonight?"

"Yes!" Mary Jane yelled from a table a few feet away.

I shook my head and Rory frowned. "No, you won't go out with me?"

"What!" Mary Jane stomped toward us.

"No. I was shaking my head at my crazy best friend." I gestured her way.

"Never mind me, I'm invisible." Mary Jane walked backwards away from the counter.

His smile made my heart rate spike every time he flashed his pearly whites. I needed Mary Jane to come back over to make sure I didn't say anything stupid. A poke in the side from her every time nonsense slipped out of my mouth might work, but there was no time for that now. She needed to help me before I did something I might regret. Like plaster a big kiss on Rory. I wasn't sure, but the way he was looking at me, I thought he wouldn't mind if I did, though.

His gaze remained focused on my face. I licked my lips; there was no stopping my involuntary reaction to his stare. Had someone turned off the air conditioner? Heat gathered in my cheeks and my legs shook. I glanced down, but lost my balance. When I looked up, it was too late to avoid the chair in front of me.

I stumbled forward and Rory grabbed my arm. "Whoa. Easy does it."

"Thanks." My cheeks tingled again, but that wasn't all that tingled. His touch made my whole body quiver like Grandma Imelda's Jell-O.

He leaned against the counter, waiting for my answer. If I didn't answer him soon, Mary Jane would probably have a heart attack. I fiddled with my apron, buying myself time to allow the redness to disappear from my cheeks.

"Mary Jane told me she'd cover for you tonight. You know, do all of the cleanup here at the café." He studied me for a reaction.

A big piece of duct tape had Mary Jane's name written all over it. That would shut her up.

"Did she now?" I shot an evil glare her way. She didn't look up, but I knew she felt it.

"What can I do to get you to say yes? I'll do anything. I'll let you spray me with whipped cream again. You can knock another burger out of my hands." One side of his mouth hitched up, then the other as his taunting grin burst into a wide smile. "Come on, we'll have fun."

I bit my lip to stop from laughing. I wanted to say yes. But should I? There were many reasons to say no, but many to say yes. No woman in her right mind could say no to that smile.

Rory gave me a long, appreciative look. Blood rushed to my cheeks. His masculine voice drifted across the room, knocking thoughts of my magical ineptness out of my head. "What do you say? Tonight's the first night of the county fair. Or we could go for a walk? Maybe get some ice cream?"

If I didn't answer him soon, he'd think I was brain-dead and retract his invitation.

From behind Rory's back, Mary Jane scolded me silently by waving her index finger so hard I figured she'd need a trip to Urgent Care.

When I thought she'd almost burst from frustration, I said, "I'd love to."

Chapter Twenty-One

Darkness had settled over Mystic Hollow. The sounds from the Ferris wheel, Tilt-A-Whirl and other rides echoed across the night air. My arms ached from pushing the mop over the dirty café floor and my feet hurt from standing for so long. That mop grew heavier every night—and it had only been a couple. In spite of that, I was anxiously awaiting Rory's arrival.

Traffic had slowed to only a few passing cars. Fireflies flickered in the nearby tree and a cricket sounded from somewhere beside me. While I waited for Rory, I contemplated walking to the fairgrounds and meeting him there. It was a short walk, but my dogs were barking so loud, and anyway the thought of strolling to the fairgrounds with Rory by my side was more appealing than going alone.

My cell phone rang, startling me from my reverie.

"Hello?" Mary Jane yelled. Her voice was barely audible over the roar of the crowd and the rides. Well...what constituted a crowd in Mystic Hollow.

"You're already at the fair? I didn't know you were going." I shouted into the phone.

"I decided why not go, what have I got to lose? Are you with him?" I might as well have asked Mary Jane to come along on the date. Was it a date? Either way, she'd want a play-by-play.

"Not yet. You're not at the fair to spy on us, are you? I don't think we need a chaperone." I sat on the bench in front of the café to rest my feet.

"If you're lucky, you will." She giggled.

"Well, in that case, I guess I'll see you there." I laughed. "I'm assuming you're applying for the job?"

"I have no intentions of being the third wheel. You probably won't even see me."

"Now that I think of it, I might need you. How much of a third wheel can you be in a couple of hours? Come on, what will I talk about?" I gulped.

"And they have the candy apples you love," I said, suddenly desperate to persuade her to be there. "Just think of the gooey, nut-covered yumminess."

"Darn you, you know I can't resist caramel and nuts. But why do you need me?"

"So I don't say anything completely brainless and embarrass myself."

"Honey, you snatched food out of his hand and drenched him with whipped cream. There's nothing left to be embarrassed about."

"You make a valid point. Nonetheless, I'll see you there," I chimed.

I hung up and stuffed the phone back into my pocket. Before Rory arrived, I dabbed on a little lip-gloss, not bothering to use the compact mirror in my purse to apply it. Staring at my reflection and realizing what a mess I looked wouldn't help my nerves. It was almost pointless to wear makeup with this kind of heat, anyway. The sticky air made breathing difficult. Fighting the humid temperature for a little cotton candy and gooey apples wasn't worth the effort, but seeing Rory sure was.

Something didn't seem right, though. Being happy didn't seem appropriate.

For all I knew, I only liked Rory because of a stupid magic spell—along with every other woman in town. Not to mention, he practically had a wife following every move he made. Okay, she wasn't his wife, but in her mind, she'd probably already sent out the invitations.

"Am I late?" The voice startled me and I spun around. My heart thumped wildly, as if I'd run several sprints.

"No. The café was slow tonight, so I closed a few minutes early. Mary Jane didn't need to cover for me, after all. I was just sitting here enjoying the night sky." I shifted on the bench.

Rory took a seat next to me on the old bench, stretching his long legs out in front of him. His thighs bulged under the restraint of his jeans. His blue shirt was buttoned up except for the first two buttons; the sleeves were rolled up exposing his tanned muscular forearms.

"It is beautiful. So, are you ready to go to the fair?" He ran his fingers through his hair, making it even more mussed. Just the way I liked it.

"I wouldn't miss it for the world."

The light from the café sign lit his gorgeous face, showcasing the strong cheekbones, blond hair, and dreamy eyes. Rory looked out of place in Mystic Hollow, unless he was modeling for a magazine. But I was positive a photo shoot would never be held in Mystic Hollow, much less right outside my front door.

The lip-gloss didn't seem like such a stupid idea now. I peered down at my clothing. Remnants of flour and chocolate remained on my jeans. I hadn't had time to change. Rory took me by the elbow and helped me up from the bench. His masculine scent circled me again, making the butterflies return, not that they'd completely disappeared since he'd showed up in the café that first day.

I surreptitiously wiped at the flour on my jeans, hoping he wouldn't notice. Was he thinking about what it would be like to ride the Ferris wheel with me? Not that I'd go. Heights and me don't mix. Maybe Rory was daydreaming about sharing a cotton candy? Or about winning me a stuffed animal? Or was he thinking of something even better, like a kiss? Twinkling lights filled the night sky with not a cloud in sight. The fairgrounds sat a few blocks away from the café in an open field. We set out down the sidewalk through town, our bodies so close that we almost touched. I tried not to look back and check out his butt. He'd had enough ogling for the day.

As we strolled along, I said, "I'm sorry about the way I look tonight. I didn't have time to go home. If I'd known we were going out, I would have brought a change of clothes."

"Don't apologize. I should have given you more notice." He brushed at my nose with his finger. "You had a bit of flour on your nose."

His unexpected touch made my knees wobble, and my stomach tingled against my will. "Oh, sorry." I let out a nervous chuckle. Why hadn't I checked my face? The magic and running the café had me befuddled, not to mention the thoughts of spending time with Rory that had filled my brain since he'd asked me out.

"I didn't think. I just really wanted to spend some time with you. And I think you look sexy, flour residue and all."

When I realized my mouth hung open, I snapped it shut and let out a chuckle. Thirteen-year-old girls were less giddy than me. But in my defense, this gorgeous man had called me sexy, and I was now in need of a cold shower, or possibly a ventilator.

To the left of the field was a wooded area, full of tall, thick pines. Too spooky to walk past by myself. I was glad I had waited. We turned down the isolated road toward the sound of the screams from the rides and the rickety roller coaster making its ascent echoing through the night air. It reminded me of my childhood when my parents took me to the fair every year. My dad always won me the biggest stuffed animal in the place—one of his hidden talents. I missed him; we had lost my father several years before.

Remembering the taste of corn dogs with an overload of mustard made my mouth water. But this was far different from my childhood memories. So far, the night was nothing short of romantic...magical.

The first person I spotted when we entered the gate was Mary Jane. Had she been waiting for us? I told her I'd see her there, but I didn't think she'd patrol the entrance waiting for us.

The smile on her face reached from ear to ear.

"I didn't expect to see you here," I said. Rory probably saw past our charade and knew the meeting was planned.

Mary Jane winked. "Yeah, I finally got my boss to let me get away from the café for a night. I came for the candy apples," she offered, looking at Rory as if he'd asked.

"Candy apples sound good to me. If you'd like, I can get us some." He gestured over his shoulder.

"Um, no, I have to meet friends." Mary Jane started to walk away. "Nice seeing you again."

At least she hadn't taken him up on the offer, although I was sure she wanted to. But my chaperone was now gone. It was up to me to make intelligent conversation with Rory for the rest of the evening.

"The candy apples are really good. Mary Jane will miss out." He smiled. I couldn't help but grin. The tingly feeling had returned.

"Come on. What are we standing here for? Let's get a candy apple." He motioned for me to move forward with him as he took a few steps.

My stomach danced as I realized this was like a real date. Not that it *was* a date, but it was *like* one. I couldn't call it a date unless I fixed all that was wrong first, then it could be called a date.

The laughter and screams from the thrill seekers on the roller coaster, and children playing games around us, was intoxicating, only adding to the excitement.

We walked up to the concession stand. The smell of cotton candy and funnel cakes lingered in the air.

Rory turned to me. "Would you like caramel or candy?"

"I'd like caramel with nuts, please." Why not go for the messiest, right? I'd already embarrassed myself around him where food was concerned.

"Two caramel apples, please." He held up two fingers to the young girl behind the counter.

Rory smiled as he handed me my apple. The way his dimples appeared on each cheek made my insides light up. "I'm giving you the one with the most nuts."

There was something to say about that comment, but I wouldn't go there.

"That's sweet. Thank you. Here, let me pay for mine."

I dug around in my pocket, pulled out a couple crumpled dollars, and pushed them toward him. He brushed them away.

"It's on me. You want to take a walk around and check out the sights? That's if you don't mind eating and walking at the same time?"

"I think I can handle it." I chuckled.

We strolled along with the crowd, men and women yelling at us to try to win a prize as we passed the booths.

"This brings back memories. My dad and I went straight for the caramel apples first thing when we came to the fair. My mom always got the cotton candy, but my dad ate most of it because she'd never finish it." I took a bite of my apple.

"I always hit the biggest, meanest-looking roller coaster when I came." He laughed.

I hoped he didn't want to hit the meanest-looking one next. My face probably blanched at the mere mention of it.

"So, you hesitated earlier when I asked you out. Did you not want to come with me?" Rory asked.

He really got to the point; I liked that. Maybe he didn't hide his feelings like my ex. Rory was probably the type of guy who liked to get things out in the open. Too bad I was doing the exact opposite. I should tell him about the magic right here in the middle of the county fair next to the House of Mirrors.

"No. I mean, yes, I mean no." I attempted to wipe caramel from my chin.

He scowled.

I took a deep breath and tried again. "I mean, I didn't really hesitate. And I wanted to come here with you tonight. If I didn't, I wouldn't be here."

"I thought maybe Mary Jane was here to give you an out in case I turned out to be a creep." One corner of his mouth lifted in a sexy grin. "I'll try my best to be a perfect gentleman."

"No, Mary Jane was coming anyway. She was worried about running into us and being a third wheel. That's why she took off when you offered the apple. If you were a creep, I'd just take off and leave you here." I took a bite of my apple, dropping little pieces of nuts on my shirt.

He laughed a hearty laugh again. "Sounds like you got a great emergency exit plan."

I brushed off the bits of peanut. "It may not be foolproof, but it's a plan."

We continued our leisurely walk around the midway, eating our candy apples and making chitchat between bites—mostly talking about the sights of the county fair.

"You mentioned your father. He brought you to the fair a lot?"

"Yes." I nodded. "He brought me every year. Sometimes we'd go to the surrounding county fairs, too. My dad had this crazy knack for winning prizes. His favorite was tossing pennies into the little dishes. He was fantastic. Unfortunately, word spread quickly and they hated to see him coming."

Rory chuckled. "I bet. I'm sure he wanted to impress his little girl."

"Maybe so." I grinned.

We walked in silence for a few seconds. With memories of my father in my mind, I felt the need to share some of those thoughts with Rory. He seemed to care. Ray had never been all that sympathetic with the mourning process.

"I lost my dad several years ago," I said.

"I'm sorry." Rory looked down as he said, "My father recently passed, too."

"I'm sorry," I said softly.

"Do you mind if I ask what happened to your father?" Rory asked.

I shook my head. "He had a heart attack. My mama was always on him to eat better, but he liked his fried food *extra* fried. What about your dad?"

"Actually, it was the same thing."

"Really? I hate to hear that. I plan on making the food at the café as healthy as I can make it. Southern food doesn't have to be bad for you. There are a lot of alternatives to frying and fat."

Well, I'd wanted to make the food healthy, but now I wasn't sure I'd get a chance to do anything if the café was closed.

He smiled softly. "I think that sounds like a wonderful idea."

"Thank you. The only problem is convincing people that it *is* a good idea. Some people think it couldn't possibly taste good unless it's the full fat version. But enough talk about the café."

"Where is your mother now?" Rory asked.

"Um, she's still in Mystic Hollow, although she's not here now. I haven't seen her since I came back to town. She's in Ireland. She's been planning this trip for six months. My parents used to travel a lot, so a year after my dad died, mom decided to keep doing it. I think it makes her happy, as if he's still with her. She feels closer to him, sharing something they loved, you know?"

My parents had shared something special. Something I thought possibly unobtainable for the average person. But maybe I hadn't met the right person. I'd felt I settled on Ray just because I hated dating. The whole routine of it put me off.

"What about your mother? Is she in Kentucky?"

"No, she lives in Texas. That's where I'm originally from. She's in the Austin area. My father wanted to buy a farm here, so I agreed to come with him. Not long after we got here is when I lost him. My brother's been here a few times to help and I have people who work for me now, so it's going well, so far."

"What did you do in Texas?"

"I worked with him there. He sold the farm because he wanted to work with thoroughbreds in Kentucky."

"Do you like it here? Sometimes moving to a small town and being the outsider can be tough."

"I do."

"Are people being nice to you?"

"They've been very kind. Some more than others." Rory glanced over his shoulder. I knew he meant the women who followed him around the fair. "I like it even better now." He smiled at me.

"What made you decide on Mystic Hollow?" I asked.

"I'm not sure. It was my father's idea. He found the farm and within a few days he'd bought it."

"You don't work all the time, do you? What do you do in your spare time?"

"Well, let's see, I like to read. Stephen King is my favorite. I love old horror films like Bride of Frankenstein and Dracula."

We neared more booths. The blinking lights and music lured us closer.

"Hey, let's play. What do you say?" Rory pointed at a booth.

I tossed the apple core in the trash and nodded. "Okay, but I must warn you, I'm not very good."

He placed his hand on the small of my back, steering me toward the booth. "You aren't trying to trick me, are you? I bet you're an expert marksman."

Rory handed the attendant the money and we picked out our water guns. I selected the red one and Rory picked blue. The bell chimed, indicating the game had started. Rory and I pushed the triggers at the same time. We laughed as we both raced to get the little figure to the other side.

"Yes!" I exclaimed. "I won."

Was it all right to brag about beating the guy I secretly had the hots for when he was standing right next to me?"

"You're good. See, I knew you were trying to fake me out. You are your father's daughter."

"I did no such thing." I crossed my heart. "I got lucky."

"Don't forget to pick out your prize." Rory smiled and gestured toward the stuffed animals.

"Anything from down here." The attendant gestured to the bottom section of toys.

"All that effort for a tiny toy?" I picked a little yellow bear and we headed on our way.

"That's a great bear." Rory inspected my new stuffed friend.

"Yeah, he's kind of small, though." What could I expect for a few dollars?

"Do you want a big one?" His words slipped out with a sexy southern drawl.

I coughed, almost choking.

Chapter Twenty-Two

"What? Oh, you mean a stuffed toy." Heat rose in my cheeks.

"Come on, I'll win you a bigger one than that." He grabbed my hand and pulled me along. My toes tingled from his touch.

Considering I'd just beaten him, I wasn't sure another game was a good idea. Embarrassing my non-date when he didn't win me the biggest stuffed animal at the fair was probably bad dating decorum.

He pointed at a game with a huge hammer. "There's one."

"That looks really hard."

"I work on a farm. I'm used to lifting heavy things."

Judging by his muscular arms, I was sure Rory was strong, and I hoped he didn't think I was insulting his manliness. But these places have been known to rig the games.

"Okay, let's see what you got." I followed him toward the game.

While Rory paid the man for the chance to cause permanent injury to his shoulder, the sensation of being watched swept over me. When I glanced over my shoulder, I noticed several women standing behind us, staring at Rory's backside. Talk about uncomfortable. They stared, barely blinking an eye, definitely unconcerned with my presence.

Rory flexed his muscles and flashed his perfect smile. The somewhat predictable macho insecurity was making a tiny appearance, but I expected as much from any man. Rory paid the attendant and lifted the huge hammer. He glanced over his shoulder at me and winked. I think my knees wobbled slightly.

He swung the hammer and I thought the little bell at the top might rocket on into the night sky. A few people standing around clapped. Rory had proved his manliness. But I hadn't needed a stuffed animal to know he was all man.

"Congratulations," the man said, "which one do you want?"

I must admit I almost swooned at the whole scene. Knowing Rory wanted to win me a stupid stuffed animal bad enough to almost pull his shoulder out of its socket was invigorating. I picked out the biggest brown teddy bear on the wall. It was almost as big as I was.

As I clutched it in my arms, I smiled at Rory. "Thanks, but you didn't have to do that."

"I wanted to." His gaze met with mine, then traveled down to my lips.

I didn't know for sure, but I sensed he wanted to kiss me. The desire to press my lips all over his pulled at me, calling me like a Carnie lures fairgoers to play their overpriced games for cheap prizes. I wanted Rory to kiss me. There was no denying it.

But with the crowd standing around, I didn't think it would happen. Not to mention the gang of women of all ages who'd been following us all night. I worried I'd need a stick to beat them off. If need be, I'd use the giant stuffed bear.

The feeling of being watched swept over me even stronger this time. Probably the buffet line of women following us, but perhaps it was nothing more than the fact that there were a ton of people standing around. Rory didn't linger, maybe he felt the stare, too.

"It's such a beautiful summer night. I love the smell of food from the fair carrying across the air, although it looks like there are some storm clouds moving in." Why was I blathering on about the weather? I needed an on-off switch for my mouth.

"How about we go on a ride?" Rory beamed as if this was his first trip to the fair. His eyes sparkled under the blinking lights.

A slight whimper stuck in my throat and my stomach flipped. Why hadn't I anticipated that question? We were at the fair surrounded by the death traps. Of course he'd want to get on one. My worst fear had now come to pass. "Oh, I don't know..." My eyes widened as I peered up at the massive monster of nothing more than wood and bolts in front of us. "I'm afraid of heights."

He grabbed my arm. "Come on, you'll be fine. I'll protect you."

I did like the idea of his strong, muscular arms holding me tight so I didn't collapse, but would he still want to protect me when I lost my candy apple all over him?

"Maybe we should try something a little tame, like the Ferris wheel?"

That was his idea of tame? Did he realize how high in the air that thing went? I was more of a Tea Cups kind of gal. At least we'd be snuggled together in a little metal box, so it wasn't an entirely bad thing.

After buying tickets, Rory led me toward the ride. My stomach roiled at the thought of soon being strapped into that torture device. A combination of panic and fear was not a good look for me. The attendant latched us in and I felt as if I was a caged animal. There was no way out now. But feeling Rory's thigh touch mine as we squeezed into the little seat next to each other almost made the agony worth it.

"I take it you don't ride these things often?" He quirked his lips as he studied my face.

"No, not really." I shook my head while twisting my hands in my lap. "I gave them up years ago, really. My dad took me on the kiddie rides. I tried to convince them I was a kid when I was fifteen, but they didn't buy it."

The music tinkled to life and the ride lurched forward. I gripped the bar in front of us, my knuckles turning white. Rory draped his arm around me and I thought I might melt into the seat. Okay, I hated how high we were, but with his arm around me, I'd stay on this thing for hours.

So much for staying on this death trap all night. I loved the feel of being wrapped safe in Rory's arms, but my stomach wasn't too keen on it. My insides churned and whirled. Creaks and groans from the metal, as it strained to spin the big wheel around, sent a shiver up my spine.

"Okay, I'm ready to throw up, er, I mean get off now."

Rory squeezed my shoulders. "It's almost done now." He chuckled.

One more loop and I'd lose the apple for sure. True to his word, he had taken care of me, though. The feel of Rory's hand stroking the back of my head made my heart dance. The ride lurched to a stop, swaying back and forth until the attendant steadied it to a stop. Luckily, we were the first ones off. I'm not sure what I would have done if I'd been stuck waiting at the top.

"You made it. You only whimpered at the top. I'm impressed." He gave a flash of gleaming white teeth.

I took a bow. "What can I say, I'm a whimpering coward."

Rory laughed and I steered us away from the Ferris wheel before he suggested we go for another spin. The smell of funnel cakes lingered through the air as we neared the Tilt-A-Whirl.

"Are you up for another ride? How about this one?" He pointed to the machine that looked as if it had morphed from an innocent carnival ride into a mutant evil Easter egg basket. The pastel purple and yellow with pink did nothing to soothe my churning stomach.

The tilt of his lips made my heart go pit-a-pat, but no way was I getting on that thing. Did he think because I hadn't barfed on him that I could handle the next phase in this so-called fun? "I'd prefer to live a while longer, so I think I'll pass on this one."

As we moved away from the ride, a shrill voice shouted out Rory's name.

"Look at me, Rory."

We whipped around to find the source of the voice. I recognized her as the woman who made her living by writing the equivalent of a gossip column for the local paper. Much to my chagrin, picking out Geneva Beale's screech in a crowd was never a problem. Her voice sounded like a braying donkey with an upper respiratory infection.

Geneva desperately tried to capture Rory's attention. Mission accomplished. Not only did she have his attention, but all the other fairgoers, too. Her brown hair was piled high on her head and her face was flush as if she'd run a marathon. She waved her arms at Rory while everyone around us gawked, shifting their attention from us to the crazy woman on the Tilt-A-Whirl as if they were at a tennis match.

Geneva was old enough to be Rory's mother, but that didn't stop her. Never had I imagined the magic spell would have been this powerful. Each whirl of the basket made Geneva's face turn greener. But in spite of her pea-colored hue, she still wanted Rory to notice her.

"Rory, over here!" She waved her arms, then quickly grabbed the safety bar in front of her.

Rory's face turned as dark as ketchup. "I have no idea why she is trying to get my attention."

"Maybe she wants to tell you something." I tried to smooth it over.

"I really don't know the lady. She must have me confused with someone else."

"She did call your name." Okay, I wasn't helping matters. Did I really need to point that little tidbit out?

People still watched and she still tried to wave, but the ride zoomed around at such a rate she finally couldn't flail her arms about anymore. The velocity of the whirling had momentarily stolen her voice. Thank heavens for small favors.

Maybe it was best if I got Rory out of there, even if I did want to spend more time with him. Although, we couldn't avoid these women forever, something had to change soon.

Rory must have read my mind. With a tilt of his head, he gestured toward town. "I thought maybe we'd have a nice summer treat. It's not too late. Would you like to go for that ice cream now?"

This night was doing nothing for my waistline. "Sure, I'd like that."

"We can drop off your teddy bear, if you'd like?"

"That's probably a good idea. He'd end up covered in chocolate."

In fact, the evening had been so fantastic that I'd all but forgotten about my mission of discovering Rory's true feelings for Kim. How easily I'd put that little forty-eight hours clause out of my mind.

Rory placed his hand on my back and steered me in the direction of the exit. Yes, this was the best night I'd had in a long time...since I couldn't remember when. Rory didn't seem affected by the craziness of what had happened at the café. Of course, he didn't know the whole story, either. At least I hadn't sprayed him with whipped cream this time. But ice cream was in our future...maybe the teddy bear wouldn't be the one to end up wearing chocolate. So why, if the evening was going so well, did I feel the need to mess it up?

I took a few steadying breaths. For a moment, no words formed, but finally I said, "There's something I need to tell you about the burger."

"I'm listening."

My heart thumped. Was I really going to tell him the truth? What would Tom say? What would he do to me when he found out what I'd done?

A brief moment of reasonable thinking ticked through my brain, and told me it wouldn't be a good idea yet. Yes, he deserved to know, but if I could fix things without him knowing of the magic, it would be better for him. He didn't need the extra burden of dealing with this magic business. How long would I have this internal debate?

"I didn't knock the burger out of your hands because I thought it wasn't your order."

"No?" He raised a brow.

"No..." I cleared my throat. "I was worried I gave you expired meat. So you were right to be concerned about getting food poisoning."

He stared for a beat. "Well, it's a good thing everything turned out okay, huh? I'd have probably been unhappy with you if you'd killed me with a burger." He flashed a wicked grin.

I chuckled. "I wouldn't blame you for hating me if I did that."

Great. Now he thought my café was unhealthy. But did he really buy my excuse? Maybe he thought I was completely insane. I wanted the conversation to die a quick, painless death, so I changed the subject. We walked across the parking lot and through the small crowd.

"Thanks again for the bear." I clutched it to my chest, wishing it was Rory.

"I couldn't let you see me lose and not even attempt to win anything," he said, flashing me a small smile.

"So it was a macho thing and not just you wanting me to have Mr. Bear." I patted the bear on its belly.

He shrugged. "Hey, what can I say, I'm a guy. We're all like that to some extent."

"Yeah, it's to what extent that matters."

He chuckled. "I guess you're right."

We made our way down the gravel path back toward the road and I silently cursed at having the stuffed animals in my arms. Maybe Rory would have held my hand. Maybe not, but I'd never know. Only a little gesture, but any contact would have set me ablaze at that point.

"Did you have fun tonight?" He reached out and touched the bear's ear.

"I had a great time. I'm glad you asked me." My heart thumped faster.

"I was hoping you'd say yes. If you'd turned me down, I might never have had any of that cherry pie again. Though I'll probably hold the whipped cream in the future."

Oh no. I hoped this wasn't the point in the evening when he told me he thought I was a complete idiot.

"You were glad I said yes?" Add another mark to my 'stupid things I've said' list.

He nodded. "I wanted a chance to get to know you better."

"It seems like you've been real busy lately." Why did I say that? Did I want to draw attention to the fact that so many women wanted him?

"You could say that, yes."

He didn't mention the women, so I let it drop. If I'd had a shovel, I'd have buried my words right there. Forever forgotten.

The moonlight shone against his face, revealing a smile that showcased his white teeth and highlighted his strong jaw. Long, thick lashes outlined his gorgeous green eyes. The black ceiling of sky glittered with stars, a symphony of crickets chirped, and a slight breeze whisked across my arms. Along the path, tree leaves rustled as the wind picked up. The moonlight trickled through the branches, breaking some of the darkness. The moon cast a shadow across the road. The trees hovered above, their dark gesticulating branches reaching out as if a canopy stretched over us.

Temptation got the better of me. I gave in and scoped out his rear when he wasn't paying attention. He did look good in those jeans and his sexy southern drawl made him even more irresistible. Thoughts of what his lips would feel like next to mine continued to flood my brain. And, oh heavens, what his chest would feel like pressed against me. I needed to lasso my hormones. My knees felt like rubber around him. Instead of thinking of mending magic, my thoughts went to his lips, chest, and cute dimples. So much for lassoing my hormones, I was out of control.

Chapter Twenty-Three

After dropping off the bear in my car, we headed toward the ice cream. He ordered a vanilla cone, and I had chocolate. He insisted on paying again. That added fuel to my internal debate about this being a real date. If it looks like date and sounds like date, then it must be a date, right? But I couldn't consider it a date with the magical accident lingering over my head. With sugar cones in hand, we left the Dairy Queen parking lot, making our way back onto the sidewalk.

"So, this Tom guy helps you?" Rory asked as we strolled past the shops, side by side, licking our ice cream cones. I avoided looking at his tongue as much as possible. That was the last visual I needed in my head right now.

"Um, yeah." How did I explain what Tom did? "He's helping with the accounting."

I hated lying and I had to stop this charade before I ended up with an antacid addiction. I needed to tell Rory the truth, but would he still speak to me?

"What did you do before the café? I heard your grandmother retired." The more we walked, the nearer Rory got to me. His arm accidentally brushed against mine.

"I was an administrative assistant for the most evil boss on the face of this planet at a marketing company in Manhattan." I licked the melting ice cream from the side of my cone.

Wow, saying it aloud brought back bad memories I'd being trying desperately to repress since I'd gotten back in town.

"Really? A southern girl like you? What made you go all that way from home for work?"

"The thrill of big city life, as if there was something I was missing by being in little Mystic Hollow. But to be honest? The main reason I left was a man. And not a very good one, I might add."

He laughed. "So it didn't work out so well for you?"

"You could say that." I took another lick, trying to keep up with the quickly melting ice cream.

"But things seem good now?"

I swallowed hard, looking away. Could he read my face and know I was lying? Not telling him the truth was almost unbearable. "Yeah, things are good. I love the café. And baking."

"I don't think I've ever tasted a pie that good. The burger, well, it's good if you can get it," he teased.

At least he could laugh about what happened. I didn't think I'd ever find it humorous at first.

I felt Rory's stare on me as I licked the cone.

"How's the ice cream?" he asked.

"Delicious." I avoided his gaze. "So, what about you? I still don't know anything about you." I picked a honeysuckle off a bush as we walked by and sniffed.

"I have a small farm on the outskirts of town. That's why you always see me dressed like a bum."

"I don't think you look like a bum. I think you look great," I said softly. The little line crinkled between his eyebrows and he smiled. "Thank you."

"What do you have on your farm?" My hand accidentally brushed against his as we strolled along, sending a tingly feeling from my toes to the top of my head.

"Some corn, some soybeans. I rescue retired racehorses, too."

"You do? I love horses. Well, actually, I love all animals. Dogs are my favorite."

"I have a Golden Retriever. You should come see him sometime."

"I'd love to." My stomach did a flip at the thought of being alone in Rory's house—just the three of us, me, Rory, and the dog. No Kim within hundreds of miles.

"Do you enjoy running a farm?"

"I do. It's what I love." His eyes lit up when he answered.

"Did you live in Austin?"

"I lived in Cedar Creek, just outside of Austin. It's a small town like this one. But I like it here better. I don't really have a desire to live anywhere else. Travel, sure, but I always want to come back home."

I nodded. "Yeah, I'm glad I'm back. I missed the rolling hills and everything is so green here. You don't get that in New York City."

Rory slowed his pace. My heart rate spiked and it wasn't from the cardio of our walk.

When he came to a stop, Kelly Smith, the local beautician guilty of creating those little football helmets attached to the senior women of Mystic Hollow, smacked right into the back of him. Amy Strong, the bank teller who used to eat crayons in elementary school, narrowly missed crashing into me. Had they been following us all this time? Rory was now like the pied piper of women. They giggled and blushed. For a brief time, I'd been able to pretend the spell didn't exist. Unfortunately, it wasn't meant to last.

"Hello, ladies."

"Hi, Rory." Kelly twisted a lock of her brown hair between her fingers. "Fancy seeing you out and about tonight."

Yeah, imagine that. They'd probably been stalking his house and followed him. How could the magic work so well for a love spell, but reversing it was so complicated?

"Nice seeing you, ladies." Rory placed his hand on the small of my back, guiding me toward the park, away from his adoring fans.

"Bye, Rory. Come see me at the bank sometime." Amy blew a kiss in his direction.

"Not much privacy around here, huh? Do you want to sit on that bench over there? Maybe they'll take the hint and realize this is a private conversation." Rory led me by the elbow toward the little white wooden gazebo with white twinkling lights draped around its ceiling. It called to us, whispering of romantic times to be had while sitting under the stars. A girl could get used to evenings like this.

"I'd like that." I walked with him down the stone path, enjoying the view of the perennials along the way.

"Bye, ladies." Rory tilted his head and waved over his shoulder. They still stood and watched us.

"I don't understand this. It's all so weird. Women never followed me before. Sure, the occasional woman might have flirted, once an older woman propositioned me, but this is bizarre. Some men may like the attention, but I find it unnerving."

I had to ask about the older woman propositioning him story—it could be entertaining.

"Do you care to share this fascinating story of the older woman with me?"

He laughed. "There's not much to it, honest."

"Then you won't mind sharing with me then?"

"You're going to force it out of me, huh?" He grinned.

"Oh, yes." I smiled.

"Like I said, it was nothing really. I worked at a pet store when I was in college. This woman came in every day to buy her cat food. She never bought enough to last the whole week, or even a few days, just one can a day." He held up his index finger. "Soon the other guys I worked with started giving me slack about what she was doing. They said she wanted me. I thought they were crazy because she was old enough to be my grandmother. Obviously, they read her signals better than I did, because I was clueless. The first day I noticed anything, it was just a little squeeze on the hand and a wink." He gave a brief glimpse of his gleaming white teeth. "The next thing I knew she was behind the counter, trying to kiss me. I had bright red lipstick all over my face. For an older woman, she really was fast. Her hands moved like lightning."

I snickered, barely able to contain my laughter.

A hint of a smile quirked his lips, giving a peek of his dimples. "The guys never let me live that down.

"How did you...how do I put this? Let her down gently?"

"I told her I had a girlfriend, which I didn't at the time, but she didn't seem to care. Finally, I quit the job."

"Oh my gosh. You had to quit to get away from her?"

"She was persistent. I was graduating anyway and didn't need the job. I'd taken on a higher-paying position at a farm and ranch supply store at night and worked on the farm during the day. I had student loans to pay for."

"It's expensive." I nodded. "That's quite an interesting story. So you've had your share of female admirers?"

"Not really. Or if I have, like I said, I didn't read the signals."

It was hard for him to miss the signals from the Mystic Hollow women, though. From over Rory's shoulder, the women glared at me until finally giving up and turning in the other direction. It felt as if they'd stabbed a knife in my chest before walking away. I was positive the thought had crossed their minds.

As we stood in front of the bench, Rory smiled and I melted worse than the chocolate ice cream cone in my hand. Just like Kim had noticed, ever since I had set my eyes on him, I felt the connection. But whether or not I'd ever know if the feelings were real or magic, I had no idea. Sure, I'd been attracted to him when I first saw him, but would my feelings have gone this far if not for magic?

Rory reached for my hand, his touch warm against my skin. His long fingers and wide palm engulfed my small hand. My heart thumped, hammering in my ears. His gaze focused on my lips and I wanted him to kiss me more than anything. He looked up at me again and I met his gaze, neither one of us knowing what to say. Since we'd set out for ice cream at the Dairy Queen, I'd had a smile spread across my face from ear to ear. How could I not with someone as sweet as Rory by my side? He stepped closer, reaching out and touching my cheek with his hand. He brushed a strand of my hair back and tucked it behind my ear. The silence lingered, but we didn't need words. His gaze focused on my lips again and I began to stare at his as he leaned in closer. Rory's breath was sweet like the vanilla ice cream. He tilted his head and pressed his lips on mine.

The cold from the ice cream tickled against my lips. The taste of his mouth against mine was divine. His soft touch made my body tingle in places that hadn't felt that alive in ages. I opened my mouth and our tongues began a tango right there in the park. Before I knew it, my hands were entangled in his hair, my chest pressed flat against his. I pulled away slightly, remembering we were in a public place. Granted, it was nighttime, but still. Another kiss like that, and I'd surrender without an ounce of struggle. He made my insides melt faster than ice cream.

He leaned back and grinned, brushing hair away from my face. "I hope that wasn't too forward."

Before I had a chance to answer, an annoying voice rang out like a metaphorical slap to the face. Kim approached. I hated this magic right now.

"What's going on here?" She glared at me, stopping in front of us and placing her hands on her nonexistent hips.

"We're having a conversation," Rory said.

Her bottom lip trembled. "I swear, Rory Covington if you don't come help me with my car, I don't know what I'll do. I think I might cry." She swiped at a fake tear in her eye.

"What's wrong?" He crossed his arms in front of his muscular chest.

"It won't start and I'm scared out here all alone at night." She jutted out her lower lip.

Rory turned to me. "Do you mind if we take a look at her car?"

In my sweetest voice, I said, "Sure, no problem."

How convenient that her car had problems at that exact moment. I followed them like an unwanted outsider. Kim sashayed across the street to her sports car, her arm looping around Rory's. When she glanced back and realized I was coming, a deep frown spread across her face. If she thought I was staying by myself in the park, she had another think coming. It was too scary for her to be alone, but not me?

Rory lifted the hood of her car while she glared at me from over his shoulder. I definitely felt like a third wheel which, if the scowl on her face was any indication, was exactly what she wanted. It didn't appear as if she'd give up on her pursuit of Rory anytime soon, either.

"I'd better get going," I said.

"What?" Rory looked up from the engine. "No," he said. "I'm sure it's nothing major. I'll have it fixed in a jiffy."

"I have to get up early in the morning, anyway. I'll see you." I waved, never looking at Kim. I didn't need to see the sly grin on her face. She'd won this battle.

He frowned. "Okay, can I walk you over to your car?"

"It's right there. You can see me from here." I gestured with my thumb over my shoulder. "It's not necessary, really."

I turned and hurried away before he had a chance to stop me.

Something I hadn't expected happened, though. I still felt the imprint of Rory's touch on my back and the way his hand caressed mine. I still tasted him on my tongue. He'd heated up parts of me that hadn't been warm for a long time.

When I glanced back, Kim had monopolized his attention again. I'd get her for messing up my evening with Rory Covington. But maybe getting even wouldn't be so difficult, after all. As I approached my Mustang, a group of women gathered around Kim's car, all offering to help Rory with the problem. Any other time I wouldn't have liked it, but right now, it was just fine.

Chapter Twenty-Four

I slipped into my car and headed in the opposite direction, not looking back at the mess I'd caused by not using magic responsibly. It was too painful to watch. One thing was for sure: I was going to fix it and fix it now. I needed Tom to stop playing games and help me. What if I had messed up the magic? There was no reason Rory had to suffer because of it. Kim too, for that matter. She didn't want to be with Rory. At least, that's what I told myself to feel better. She said she had no idea why she'd come back. This forty-eight hours business was completely unnecessary.

I pointed my car in the direction of Tom's hotel in search of answers, once and for all. I'd dodged a bullet, though. What had I been thinking, going out with Rory? Perhaps the heat was getting the better of me. The last thing I needed was the complication of another man in my life, anyway. I'd gotten rid of a rat when I moved back to Mystic Hollow. Rory in my life would not be a good thing. So why was I fantasizing about sitting close to him on my front porch and gazing up at the stars with him? I could almost smell his spicy scent—like sandalwood and soap. I almost felt his hand caressing mine. The fantasy stayed with me the rest of the way down Main Street.

Within a couple of minutes, I pulled up in front of the small motel. The building looked like it hadn't changed since the 1950s. All that was missing was poodle skirts and an Edsel parked in front. Tom had said he was staying in room four. I wedged my car into a parking spot between a minivan and a beat-up truck. The sight of the Mustang between the two vehicles would have made Ray weep like a little baby. Too bad he didn't have any control over where the car was parked anymore. I knocked on the door, tapping my foot while waiting for an answer.

The door opened. "Hey, gorgeous, fancy seeing you here." He stretched his muscular arms over his head and yawned.

I suddenly had second thoughts about this plan. Perhaps going to a sexy man's hotel room wasn't one of my better ideas.

"I need to talk with you," I said, as I scanned the room.

"Come on in." He gestured with a wave of his hand.

"Okay, but only if you leave the door open." I held my purse in front of me as a shield.

He held his hands up in surrender. "Whatever you want."

A basketball game played on the TV in the background. He wore a T-shirt that revealed his tanned arms and well-worn jeans. The casual attire suited him. The smell of pepperoni hit my nostrils and I noticed a box with a half-eaten pizza on the table next to the bed.

"Have a seat." He pointed. "What's on your mind?"

I blew out a deep breath and tucked a stray strand of hair behind my ear. After studying his face for a second, I said, "I think you know what's on my mind, Tom. I need answers. Shouldn't the organization be helping me a little more instead of just leaving me to figure this mess out on my own?" My words became more hurried. "And don't look at me with that little grin."

"Sorry, it's just that you're cute when you're panicked."

"Tom, quit kidding around," I said, willing my lips not to curve upward.

"Who says I'm kidding?" A hint of a smile materialized on his lips.

"I want to know what's going on."

"I'm working on it. When I say I'm helping you, you need to trust me."
I blew a shallow breath through my teeth, then said, "I can hear the clock ticking. With every second that passes, it's as if a little voice chimes in my head, 'the café will be closed forever.' Can I at least talk to Mr. Wibble? Isn't there a way we can convince him to give me more time?"

"I'll see what I can do to get Mr. Wibble to speak with you, but I can't make any promises."

"Fine, fine, whatever. It's a start. I need something, anything right now." The weight in my chest grew heavier.

"Elly, the organization has been around for many years. So many years I think they've lost track as to when it was actually formed. Anyway, they have their reasons for doing things the way they do. It may not make sense, and maybe they don't always make the best decisions, but it keeps some form of order to magic. Without them, who knows what would happen?"

"Life isn't always fair, huh? How many times do I have to learn that lesson?"

"It's easy to forget," Tom said in a low tone.

"So you can't tell me everything that's going on, huh?"
He shook his head. "As soon as I know anything different, I'll let you know."

I nodded. "I'm just freaking out a little."

"It's understandable. Look, I'm going to tell you one more thing to freak you out even more." He leaned forward, trying to narrow the distance between us.

"I'm not sure I can handle any more." I gripped the side of the chair, bracing myself for the blow.

"It's just that, you can't do any magic for now. Put a hold on it, at least until I talk to you again."

"Why?"

"Just stop with the spells, okay?"
I watched the TV in an attempt to ignore his request.

"Are you listening to me, Elly? There are consequences if you do the magic."

"Oh yeah, like what? They'll close the café? I heard that already."

"There's more to it than that. Things like having your magical rights taken permanently away. Any descendents wouldn't be allowed to do magic, no matter what level of talent they possessed."

"I doubt I'll have descendents. And I hadn't anticipated being allowed to ever do magic after the café," I groused.

"You have natural magical talent, Elly. You don't want to ruin your chances of ever doing magic again."

I had no idea why all of a sudden my magic was being restricted, but I didn't intend on listening for any further reasoning. Tom was talking in circles as far as I was concerned. I'd heard enough rules from the magic bureaucrats and this was one I wouldn't be following.

"I shouldn't have come here and bothered you."

"You're not bothering me, Elly."

"I've got to go. I'll see you later."

Before Tom had a chance to react, I jumped up and hurried out the door.

"Elly, don't go, please. I don't want you to leave here upset," he called as I climbed in my car.

When I pulled away, Tom stood in front of his room, barefoot and holding his hands up in frustration. Maybe he did want to help. But like Grandma Imelda always said: if you want something done right, you've got to do it yourself. That's what I intended on doing: fixing this magic debacle myself.

Chapter Twenty-Five

Before going home and passing out for the night, I decided to head back to the café and prep a few things in the kitchen. I wanted to release my frustration and anxiety before attempting sleep. As wired as I felt now, there was no way I'd get any rest. Maybe work would tire me out.

I slipped into the café and flipped on the light. The space was eerily silent; there were no clanking dishes, no chatter, or demands for refills. I ambled across the room, touching a chair, then moving on to brush my finger across a picture of Mystic Hollow from 1952 that grandma had hung on the wall.

As I studied the photo, I realized the town looked strangely the same back then as it did today. Grandma Imelda may be in Florida enjoying the sand and surf, but her presence still lingered in the café. What would she have done in my situation? What a silly question. She would never have made a mistake as I had.

Grandma had placed a calendar on the wall behind the register. I looked over at the date. Hours ticked away toward my forty-eight hour deadline. It felt as if I was watching the sand pour through an hourglass, and I had done nothing to stop it from falling completely to the other side. With running the café, there was hardly time to think of anything other than pancakes, eggs, and bacon. I needed to stop messing around. The answer to my problems wouldn't fall at my feet. How would I find the time to reverse a magic spell? I had to make the time. Somehow, some way.

As I moved toward the kitchen to begin work and attempt to relieve my melancholy mood, the bell jangled on the door.

I spun around and clutched my chest. "What are you doing here?"

"The better question is what are you doing here?" Mary Jane propped her hand on her jutted-out hip.

I sighed. "I knew I couldn't sleep, so I came here to work off my troubles."

"I'm sorry to say it probably won't help, but you can give it a try. Do you want to talk about it?"

"Not really, but..."

"But you know you will." She grinned. "I expected you'd still be with Rory. Last time I saw you guys, you were by the Tilt-A-Whirl." She covered her mouth. "I didn't spy. Honest."

I smiled and shook my head.

"What happened? It looked as if you were hitting it off," she said.

"I thought we were, until Kim popped up."

Mary Jane flushed red and dropped her purse on the floor. "What!" Her voice boomed across the café.

I filled her in on every detail, even up to the point where I sat in Tom's hotel room.

"So that's what happened. And now I'm trying to figure out why I feel like this." I sighed and leaned against a table.

"You love him." Mary Jane wiggled her eyebrows. "Not to mention you have a lot of crap hanging over your head right now."

"I do not love him," I huffed.

"You do. I can see it in your eyes." She pointed.

"You can't." I looked away. "I think I'm still at the in lust phase."

"Good point. But it could definitely turn to love."

"I don't know him, and besides, if the end of the night was any indication, I think he's spoken for again. Kim has her eyes and heart set on getting back together with him. I don't think she'll stop until she's succeeded." I pulled out a chair.

"In a span of twenty-four hours, I learned Rory's favorite doughnuts...chocolate glazed, and sports team...Cincinnati Bengals, for heaven's sake. All things I discovered during our chitchat at the county fair. These are things I doubt Kim would care to learn."

"Wow, you did learn a lot. I'm impressed by your skill."

"I bet she knows nothing about him after dating him for two years." I shook my head in disgust.

But it didn't matter how little she knew about him, she had the history with him and I didn't. But that didn't mean she loved him or that they belonged together because of it. My stomach acid churned and I rubbed my chest. Between the caramel apple, ice cream and the stress, I'd need a vat of acid reducer soon.

Mary Jane walked up and put her arm across my shoulders. She'd been absentmindedly rearranging the sugar packets on the table. "It'll work out. Just you wait and see. The café will stay open and you'll sort out this thing with Rory. Kim doesn't want him. She messed with his heart and mind once, she'll do it again. He deserves better than that. He's a fine man and not just on the outside."

"The good ones are always taken. Come on, let's go back to the kitchen," I said, jumping up from the table.

She nodded. "Sometimes the bad ones are taken, too. As in Kim."

"You think she's a bad one?"

"What do you think? The way she treated him?"

"She claims the opposite," I said.

"If she really believes that, then she's crazy. She's only lying to herself. She knows the truth. And there are plenty of people who can back up the story. Rory didn't realize it at the time but, in my opinion, it's the best thing that could have happened to him."

The bell on the café door jingled and I walked over to the kitchen door. I thought everyone in town knew we didn't stay open this late.

"Sorry, we're closed," I said as I opened the swinging door from the kitchen.

It was Kim.

Making a sound somewhere between a grunt and a dying cat, I stopped in my tracks.

"Oh, look now, it's back. Er, well, she's back," Mary Jane said when she peeped out the little window.

"I'll go talk to her." As if I thought for a second Mary Jane would stay behind and not listen to this conversation. Maybe I'd need her for backup, though. Kim probably wanted to clobber me.

I hadn't expected to see her in the café again so soon. She hated that I didn't have any fancy coffee drinks. I had a suspicion as to why she was there and it had nothing to do with coffee and everything to do with Rory. Why wasn't she still with Rory? What happened to her 'broken' car?

The usual scowl was displayed on her face.

"I need to talk with you, Elly, if you have a minute?" she asked in a clipped tone.

I didn't like the sound of this. She had to have seen us kissing. No doubt, she'd been stalking us all evening, way before she popped up in the park.

"Sure. You want to have a seat at one of the booths?"

She stared at me for a moment while tapping her foot. "I'd rather not. This won't take long."

"Okay." My lips twisted into a wry expression. I couldn't believe she was staring me down.

Her back stiffened as the blood rushed to her face. "I'm tired of playing games with you. Stay in your stupid little café and leave my Rory alone."

"I'm not playing games with you," I said through a smile.

She held up her hand. "I'm not finished. He doesn't want you. I tried to be nice to you, but I see that doesn't work." Pinning me with her green eyes, she continued, "Now, I'm warning you. Stay away."

Kim spun around and stormed out the door. The bell moved so violently that it wasn't able to make a sound. The door rattled when it slammed shut.

"Go dye your roots!" Mary Jane yelled in her wake.

"That's telling her, Mary Jane."

Mary Jane's face was fire-engine red and her eyes narrowed. She'd always had a temper. "How dare she come in here and tell you that," she ground out.

"Come on." I wrapped my arm around her shoulders and led her to a table. "Forget about her for right now. Let me get you a piece of pie." A little dose of pastry with a general spell for a calming effect would be good right about now.

"Can't you do a magic spell on Kim to make her not want Rory?" Mary Jane asked.

"That would be a negative spell. And it specifically states in the book on page one that there are to be no negative spells."

"I bet someone has done a negative spell."

"Yeah, lots of people probably have, but it doesn't turn out well for them in the end. Well, at least that's what Grandma Imelda told me, anyway. Even if none of this magic was in play, I still believe in karma. It's like grandma always said: what goes around comes around."

"You really believe that?" Mary Jane asked.

"I do, always have. Then again, I've been hearing it from my grandmother since I can remember. My mom, too. But regardless, I do believe it."

"So if a negative spell is out of the question, what do you do now?"

I handed Mary Jane a plate with a slice of peach pie and a heaping pile of whipped cream on top. "Wait, I guess. Find out what Tom says I can do next."

"There has to be something you can do on your own instead of waiting around. Rory needs to tell Kim that he's not interested in a relationship with her." She speared a hunk of peach with her fork.

"Ideally that would be nice, but I don't know how the magic works. Maybe it stops him from saying what he really wants to say."

She shrugged. "I guess. What about Tom? Do you really trust that guy?"

"I guess so, I haven't checked up on him, though."

"Maybe you need to. Sometimes people aren't always who they claim to be. Perhaps a little background check is in order. What can it hurt?" Mary Jane asked before stuffing a forkful in her mouth.

I chewed my bottom lip, considering the question. "I wouldn't even know where to start. Who would I ask?"

"I don't know, Elly, but we have to think of something. Mystic Café is where you need to be. This is what you need to do. You're good with people. And I must admit, I didn't think you'd do so well with the cooking, but you've managed to keep the burnt items to a minimum."

"Gee, thanks for noticing." She ducked when I threw a towel at her. "What do you know about this National Organization of Magic place?" She licked her fork.

"Well, I asked my grandmother and she backed up everything Tom claimed about them. And I trust her. She says they keep law and order within the magic world. So I have to do what they tell me to, if I want to keep the café."

"What happens to you if they close the café?" Mary Jane asked, then frowned.

I knew she didn't want to hear the answer. The last thing I wanted was for Mary Jane to be out a job. "I guess I'd move. Maybe go back to the city and look for a job and pray I found one."

"I'd miss you. Things wouldn't be the same around here without Mystic Café."

"I'd miss you, too." I reached across the table and hugged her. The smell of peach pie tickled my nose.

"Hey, it's not goodbye yet, we don't know anything. Everything will work out. We have to keep a positive attitude." Her words were garbled by a mouthful of pie.

"Think positive." I nodded. "You're right."

"Besides, maybe you wouldn't have to move, maybe there's something else in this town you could do."

I raised a brow. "Seriously? I don't think so. Even you know that."

At the sight of my lifted brow she said, "Well, I'm not going to stand around and let that snake, Kim, ruin everything." She placed her hands on her hips. "Besides not wanting you to lose the café and my need to keep this job at least until I finish night classes, I want you to be with Rory. You two would make a perfect couple."

Just her mentioning us making a perfect couple made me blush and I was sure Mary Jane noticed my flushed cheeks.

"You do like him. Admit it."

I shrugged. "He's okay."

She dipped her finger in the whipped cream and licked it off. "And he likes you, even if you did spray whipped cream in his face."

"Thanks for reminding me, I was trying to forget."

"I'll never let you forget that. He probably got a good laugh out of it, too."

"Oh, he laughed all right, but I think he was laughing at how much of a fool I am."

"Nonsense, he likes you, too. I think he doesn't know what to do now that Kim is back in the picture. I don't see how any man could be with that woman. I mean, sure at first, the pretty package on the outside is tempting, but once they open it up, they have to want to return it immediately."

I laughed. "I know I'd want to return her as soon as possible."

Chapter Twenty-Six

Twenty-four hours until the café was closed for good and I intended to make the most of the day. I'd make the best food Mystic Hollow residents had tasted. Well, the best food they'd tasted since Grandma Imelda left. And unless I figured out something in a hurry, the café would be history and so would any romance with Rory.

"So, Mary Jane, you got any wild plans tonight?" I asked, as I handed her a customer's order.

"Me? Wild plans in Mystic Hollow? You know better than that. Wait. Maybe I'll head over to the Dairy Queen and check out the new blizzard flavor. Or cruise around the town square a few hundred times."

I rolled my eyes. "You've made your point."

She delivered the food, then returned to where I stood. "No, no plans. Not tonight or any other night as far as I can tell. There's slim pickings around these parts."

"Oh, come on, there has to be somebody you're interested in."

She stared at me for a beat. "I know that look in your eye. Your grandmother tried her magic on me before and it doesn't work."

"It doesn't work? Then why does Rory have women following him around like little lost puppies? Why is his ex-girlfriend back in town? Is it just a coincidence that after I did magic for those specific things that now they're happening?"

"No, no coincidence." She sighed. "The magic works, but let me clarify something. It doesn't work for me. Okay? So get that little glimmer out of your eyes." She pointed, giving a dire warning.

"Do you think the magic doesn't work for some people?"

She shrugged. "I think some spells don't work for some people. Like when Imelda did the spell for my hangover, it worked. But I know for a fact she's tried love spells on me before and, needless to say, they didn't work. So, to answer your question: I don't know."

"I think maybe I'm only attracted to Rory because of the love spell. Somehow the magic may have gotten to me, too."

"Oh, Elly, I don't think so. In my opinion, there has to be something about the individual people and magic, because I haven't been affected by the spell. Don't get me wrong, Rory is gorgeous, but when I see him, I think of my slightly older brother. So don't be so sure that your feelings for him are based on magic."

She had a point. I hadn't noticed her being googly-eyed around Rory like the other ladies. If I only knew how the magic worked. Were some people more susceptible to it? Maybe there had to be underlying feelings for a spell to affect one person and not another. Or some kind of connection? I liked to think of the magic as a little booster of fate. It was only pushing forward what would inevitably happen anyway.

There should be some kind of magical orientation for this stuff. Classes or, at the very least, a pamphlet explaining this stuff. The magical folks were so secretive...even grandma. It was as if they wanted me to learn as I went, and how could they not expect me to make mistakes like that?

I nodded. "You're probably right. I've got so many thoughts in my head at this craziness I don't remember which way is up. Anyway, let's talk about Mystic Hollow's handsome Sheriff Jasper..." An innocent little smile curved my lips. "I saw the way you looked at him the other day when he came in. I think you have the hots for him. You'd really like to butter his biscuit." I wiggled my eyebrows.

She threw a towel at me. "Stop. He's not interested in me."

"How do you know?" I placed a hand on my hip.

"I just do. He doesn't pay any attention to me when he comes in. I saw him just the other day at the Piggly Wiggly and he didn't even notice me."

"Did you speak to him?" I crossed my arms in front of my chest.

She looked down, picking at the edge of her shirt. "Well, no."

"Did you do anything to let the man know you were in the store?"

"Not exactly." She picked at a loose thread on her shirt.

"Uh-huh. Just as I thought." I clucked my tongue.

"What was I supposed to do? Go streaking through the store?"

"Sure. If need be, why not?" I smiled.

"'Cause I'd get arrested, that's why," she chided.

"Well, he'd be the one arresting you, so is that such a bad idea?"

"I'd prefer if the first time he saw me naked wasn't under the harsh lights of the produce section. It's bad enough with the lights off."

I chuckled. "Seriously, I think I'll get him in here for a little lunch. Or maybe breakfast? You know how he loves those pastries. If the café has to be closed and I can't practice magic, at least I'll have done one last kind act before I'm locked out. And admit it, he does have nice biscuits." In spite of her nonchalant demeanor, as I stared into her bright eyes, a small spark of hope flickered.

"Whatever you say, but I don't want someone to like me only because of some magic spell."

I shook my head. "Mary Jane, Mary Jane. You know that's not how it works."

She tossed a sugar packet in my direction. "Shut up. You don't even know how it works."

"I do know how it works. I've been reading *Mystic Magic*."

She quirked a brow. "You've been reading the book, huh?"

"Okay, I don't know exactly how it works, but practice makes perfect. I'll just do a spell to make him notice you. Sometimes men can be clueless. What am I saying? A lot of times men can be clueless."

"I can't argue with you on that one."

"He just needs his eyes opened, that's all. He's too busy looking down to notice. He needs to lift his head up and see the world around him. I'll find a recipe for something wonderful. I've wanted to try something new anyway. He won't be able to resist. Plus, it'll help me get a little closer to the truth behind this magic stuff. Why certain spells work for some people and not others. Now, make sure to put your lipstick on." I pointed at her face.

She rolled her eyes. "What for? He isn't coming in here right now. You're too much, do you know that?"

"You love it. Don't tell me you aren't a little excited at the prospect. You two would be perfect for each other. Movies and late night walks under the stars holding hands. A little smooching and..." I wiggled my brows.

"Stop it. Your eyebrows are going to fall off if you keep doing that." Her cheeks blushed.

"Okay, I'm getting busy finding a new recipe." I moved toward the kitchen.

"I heard he likes cherries."

I turned around. Her face was still flush. "Is that right? And where did you hear that?"

"Through the grapevine." She traced an invisible line on the table with her index finger.

"You've been checking up on him and haven't told me? What's wrong with you?"

"I haven't been checking up on him, per se. Just asked a few people some questions, that's all." She studied her fingernails.

"But you don't come to your best friend for a little help? I'm hurt." I held my chest as if I'd been stabbed through the heart.

"You're busy with other stuff. You don't have time to worry about my love life." She waved off my feigned hurt.

"I don't have time? Mary Jane, you're my best friend. I always have time for you. Don't say such things. Now why don't you help me find a recipe? Grab a few of those cookbooks." I pointed toward the shelf across the room. "I've got some more in the back. I'll go get them."

I headed to the back room and collected a few of the dessert and breakfast cookbooks. I'd help Mary Jane find her happily-ever-after man. If I couldn't help myself, I'd help her. Rallying around others was much more fun, anyway. Seeing a smile on Mary Jane's face would make me happy.

When I returned, she'd sat at one of the tables. The sun shone through the window, casting a yellow glow over the area. Mary Jane whistled and swung her leg as she flipped through the pages, never looking up to notice me watching her. She was happy already just thinking about Sheriff Jasper. Wait until something really happened, she'd be over the moon. Mary Jane hadn't been this excited since Ruby Hawk opened a nail and tanning salon across the street from her house.

"Here's a few," she said as I approached. "Cherries with lots of icing." She pointed to the page.

"Sounds delicious. The more cherries, the better off we'll be." I set my books down and grabbed hers.

We settled on the cherry pie recipe. But not just any cherry pie, it was a new recipe—bigger and better. I decided to call it cherry crumble pie since I modified the ingredients from the original.

Earlier, I'd mixed together silky smooth flour with salt, butter, and water so I'd have dough waiting in the refrigerator for me when I needed it. As I placed my hands into the soft dough, I filled my mind with good thoughts. Having negative thoughts while preparing the crust wouldn't help when I cast the spell. Grandma Imelda always said a loving heart made for heavenly cuisine. With one glide of the rolling pin, Rory's smile popped into my head. Another slide across the dough, and Grandma Imelda's sweet voice echoed through my mind. I rolled the pin again and the smell of my mother's gardenia perfume filled my senses.

Once I finished with the rolling pin, I patted the crust down with my open palms. When I was sure my crust was smooth, I placed it into the pie dish, covering the glass as if I were covering a baby with a blanket. In the center of the pie, I'd added a little heart, made from extra crust and cut with a heart-shaped cookie cutter. This would be the ultimate love pie—the magic spell would come later. Proud of my work, I poured the filling into the crust. The smell of cherries filled the air around me as I dotted butter across them, then placed the top crust on. With a knife, I trimmed the top crust, then folded it under the bottom pastry.

I crimped the edges against the rim of the pie dish, making sure to leave a glimpse of the plate visible. I ran a clean cloth around the outer edge to wipe away any excess filling. With the finishing touch of egg brushed over the top, I popped my matchmaking creation in the oven.

I thought about the pie's edges. When I baked a pie, I'd always been so careful with the sides; trying to make sure the filling never oozed over the boundaries of the pastry, making a mess. Without proper care, the contents would trickle down the sides and burn, but I was always confident that when I pulled the pastry out of the oven, it would be perfect. Why wasn't I as careful with my life?

I ignored the edges of my life, taking for granted that everything would stay within the boundaries of my own pie crust. Did I believe my pie plate would expand, allowing the contents to go on forever? Never did I dream of the mess it would make once my life baked to a boil. I was now at that boiling point. The fillings of my life were seeping over the edges, and if I didn't stop it soon, the mess would be so bad, it would be almost impossible to clean.

****

When I pulled the yummy goodness from the oven, Mary Jane wasted little time pinching off a forkful, testing it out for accuracy.

"He'll love it." I inhaled the scent of golden crust and warm cherries. The scent of cinnamon tickled my nose.

"I think he will." Mary Jane smiled. "Now, how do we get him in here?"

"You leave that part to me. I have a plan." I didn't really, but I didn't want her to be discouraged, she seemed so happy.

"Should I be afraid of this plan?" She sliced off a sliver of pie and dug her fork in for another bite. "You know I've gained ten pounds since working here?"

I scoffed. "I'll have you know I'm a fantastic planner."

"This is so good." She gestured toward the pie with the fork.

"I'll be back in time for the breakfast crowd. Put on your lipstick because I'm bringing one hunk of a sheriff back with me."

"Oh." She jumped up in her seat a little. "I'll be ready."

A few fluffy clouds dotted the sky and the sun shone, blanketing the area in brightness. I stepped out onto the sidewalk and headed toward the police station. I'd seen Sheriff Jasper's cruiser parked in front of the building when I drove by this morning. My fingers were crossed he was still there. Now I had to come up with a way to get him back to Mystic Café without him catching on. He'd probably think I was flirting with him.

I made my way down the sidewalk, cutting across the church parking lot to avoid the hotel where I thought Kim might be staying. Only a few cars dotted the lot but luckily, I didn't see her lime green VW Bug. I crossed back over to the corner of Summer Drive. I avoided the cracks in the pavement and enjoyed the flowers the Mystic Hollow Women's Club had placed in various planters at the beginning of summer. Geraniums were my favorite.

The police station was housed in the courthouse, an imposing gothic style structure that loomed tall over town with its ornate stained glass windows, intricate archways, and bell tower. The puffy clouds hung so low that they almost appeared to touch the roof. Sheriff Jasper's car was still there, parked out front in the same spot. As I neared the courthouse, I noticed a man leaning against the building.

When he spotted me looking his way, he approached. "What are you doing?" he asked.

"Um, walking." I glanced over my shoulder to make sure he was talking to me.

He wore dirty pants that may have been a light shade of khaki at one point. His wrinkled blue and white plaid short-sleeved shirt was buttoned all the way to the top.

"I know you." He wiggled his finger as he fell into step beside me.

"You're Imelda's granddaughter, Elly. She told me about you. You came back to tend the café." The smell of whiskey hung around him like the little dirt cloud hung around Pig-Pen. "Your grandmother's a fine woman."

"Well, thank you, I'm sure she appreciates that."

"I may be a drunk, but I hear and see more in this town than anyone." His lips twitched into an all-knowing smile.

I thought it an odd announcement and I wasn't sure what his statement meant, but for someone drunk he seemed awfully sharp.

The man inched closer. "Your grandmother had that book. It must have been something special."

I stopped in my tracks. "What do you mean?"

He reached out and touched my arm with his rough, leather-like hand, then hiccupped. If there was any question whether or not he'd been drinking, he just answered it.

"She had that big ol' book in the café. I asked every now and then, but she never would tell me what it was." He smiled, displaying the gap where his front teeth used to be.

So maybe he didn't know the true meaning of the book. "She keeps her recipes secret." I chuckled, avoiding his gaze.

"I think there was more in there than recipes, but I don't know what."

"Nope. Just recipes." I moved forward and he followed.

"Well, have a nice day, Elly. I think I'll take a little nap. No rest for the wicked." He chuckled.

"Do you live in the hotel?" I stopped and pointed toward the inconspicuous building.

"Sure do. It's nice."

I smiled. "It seems nice."

He held out the bottle of whiskey. "Do you want a drink?" He wiped the top with the bottom of his shirt.

"Thanks, but I'm good." I waved my hand.

He shrugged. "If you say so. No hair off my back."

"My name's Henry, by the way." Henry leaned close and stuck out his hand.

I almost passed out from the whiskey on his breath.

I shook his hand. It scratched like sandpaper. "It was nice to meet you, Henry. Come in the café any time. Breakfast with hot coffee is on me."

Maybe there was a magic spell for sobriety? If there were though, I'd bet grandma had already tried it.

"That's sweet of you, darlin'."

He glanced over his shoulder, then stood a little taller. "Beware of that woman in the green car, she's trouble." His eyes widened, seeming to sober up a tad.

Chapter Twenty-Seven

Henry had to be talking about Kim. He closed his eyes for a brief moment, and I thought maybe he'd drifted off to sleep. I reached out to touch him, but before my hand reached his arm, he snapped open his lids. "There are bad people in this town." He lowered his voice, as if calming down and continued, "Of course, a lot of nice ones, too. Like you, beautiful lady." His eyes remained half-shut.

"Thank you, Henry, but what do you mean by 'bad' people?" Grandma Imelda hadn't mentioned anyone I should avoid. Sure, some people were nosy, but bad?

"The new ones. Strangers coming to this town and causing a ruckus." He gestured with a tilt of his head toward the hotel.

Did he mean Kim? I'd thought she had lived here for a little while with Rory. But with small towns like Mystic Hollow, if you hadn't lived here all your life, then you were considered a stranger indefinitely.

Henry turned around and shuffled back toward the hotel. I stared for a second, then continued on my way, contemplating as I walked up the steps of the building how Henry had arrived at this dark place in life. Maybe if I could get enough coffee in him, he'd sober up. I'd certainly give it a shot.

My stomach jumped with anticipation. What made me think I could play cupid? If I messed this up, Mary Jane may never forgive me. I pushed open the big door and walked into the station, a blast of cold air hitting me in the face. About five or six desks sat around the room. File cabinets were flush against the left wall. The smell of new plywood lingered in the air as if they'd recently remodeled. The walls were painted a soothing beige color, probably to ease the anxiety of anyone who entered.

Sheriff Jasper sat behind the desk right up front. "Hi, Elly, what can I do for you? Is anything wrong?" His brown uniform was crisp, the shirt starched to attention with shiny collar pins, and cuff links. His nametag and badge rested over his breast. He smiled, showcasing his white teeth. He had thick dark hair, and long, full lashes outlined his gorgeous brown eyes. No wonder Mary Jane had her eye on him.

Stacks of papers covered the top of his desk, exposing only small glimpses of wood. I picked out a piece of peppermint candy from the jar on the edge of his desk, attempting to appear casual.

"Oh no, nothing wrong. I was just walking by and thought maybe you'd like to stop in for some breakfast? I got coffee cake, doughnuts, pastry, omelets, oh, and cherry pie. I made a special recipe just this morning. I'm trying to drum up some business. I can use all the business I can get, you know how it is." I popped the candy into my mouth and grinned.

Continuing my nonchalant act, I studied a few wanted posters covering the wall next to his desk. It made visions of a magical wanted poster with my face plastered on it pop into my head. Thank goodness there was no such thing, or I hoped there was no such thing. Was there?

"I hear that. We're sure going to miss your grandmother around town. You say you got cherry? It's my favorite. How did you know?" He slapped a few papers down on the desk and snapped me out of my trance. Shifting in his leather chair, he smiled, folded his hands together, and placed them in his lap.

"It is? I had no idea. Well, isn't this your lucky day?"

"As much as I'd love to, I'm afraid I can't come by, I've got too much work here." He picked up a pen and flipped it between his fingers.

"Well, maybe next time." I smiled and turned to head toward the door. I wouldn't give up that easily, though. As I reached the door, I turned and said, "You know, I could have Mary Jane deliver you a piece. If you'd like? She has a few errands, anyway."

His eyes lit up. "You'd do that?"

"Sure thing. Cherry pie, right?"

Now he'd want cherry pie delivered all the time. This plan could backfire on me if I wasn't careful. Mary Jane would be making deliveries here all the time. I'd lose a waitress. Maybe I should have thought this through more. Oh well, too late now.

"I'd love cherry pie. Do you think I could get a cup of your coffee? We have some here." He pointed to the tiny coffeemaker set up in the corner. "But it's nothing like yours."

"Sure, no problem. Coffee and cherry pie coming up. Mary Jane'll be here with them soon."

I hurried out the door like a kid with a secret to tell. I couldn't wait to see the look on Mary Jane's face. Sure, she'd be nervous, but she'd have to go. I hoped I didn't have to push her all the way there. I hurried my steps and made it back to the café. Mary Jane was looking out the front door like a kid on Christmas Eve, waiting for Santa.

She opened the door and let me in. "Well, did you talk to him?"

"I did." I nodded.

"So, is he coming?"

I smiled. "He wants cherry pie."

"Oh." She looked toward the door. "Will he be here soon?"

"Not exactly."

She scrunched her face. "What does that mean?"

Chapter Twenty-Eight

"I kind of told him you'd deliver it." I stepped back in case she wanted to punch me.

"Oh no." The color drained out of her face.

"It'll be okay. Breathe." I patted her on the back.

Her expression was somewhere between a grin and a grimace. She sputtered, "I don't think I can do it."

"You can do it. What's the big deal? It's not like you haven't talked to him before."

"But he probably knows what we're up to. Not the magic part, but the fixing up part."

"He doesn't know. How could he? I told him I happened to pass by and was trying to get more business. His eyes lit up when I told him you'd bring it back."

"They did?" She stood a little straighter.

"Uh-huh." I wiggled my eyebrows, proud of my matchmaking abilities.

"Don't toot your own horn just yet," she said.

I held my hands up. "I'm not, but...it does sound promising. Now get back there and let's get this pie ready. The lipstick looks nice, by the way."

She rubbed her lips together. "You think? This shade's not too dark?"

"No, it's perfect. It looks really good on you and I'm sure Sheriff Jasper will be dying to kiss it right off."

She blushed. "Oh, stop it."

I sliced a piece of the pie, then took down the spell book and the spices. Casting the spell on the whole pie would have been easier, but I didn't want to be overly ambitious. Heck, Mary Jane might decide she doesn't like the guy, then I'd have wasted a whole pie. Besides, one slice should do the trick.

Pinching out a dash from each one of the spice jars, I sprinkled them on top and waited for the sparkle. I was getting the hang of this magic thing even if Tom and his magical associates didn't think so. The familiar feeling radiated through my body, whizzing and swirling. The zing of energy ran through my whole body like tiny zaps of static electricity. The wind whipped above the pie, blowing my hair away from my face and propelling items around the pie onto the floor. The light show eased until it vanished just as suddenly as it had appeared. The wind departed leaving nothing but tranquil air, and the power inside my body faded, leaving that somewhat drained feeling that came after doing a spell. Finishing the spell, I placed the slice of pie in a bag. I poured coffee into a cup, put on the lid, and rushed Mary Jane out the door.

"Go on, he's waiting for you."

A look of horror spread across her face.

"Everything's fine. He's not going to bite." I placed my hands on my hips.

"That's what I'm afraid of. I want some nibbling on my ear," she deadpanned.

I laughed. "Well, with any luck, that's what you'll get."

"How do I look?" She adjusted her clothes and repositioned her black Fedora.

I picked a piece off lint of her shoulder. "Fantastic. Remember, men can't resist food. You know, the way to a man's heart is through his stomach or some such theory."

She wiggled her hips. "Sure there's food, but adding a little sway to my walk wouldn't hurt, either."

"He'll never be the same again."

"If this works out, you'll be like my fairy godmother," Mary Jane said.

I snickered. "I'm missing my magic wand, though."

She let out a deep breath. "Yeah, here I go."

I waved her on. "Let me know how he likes the pie."

She smiled and I watched her walk away as if she was my first child going off to kindergarten. I sure hoped it worked. Not just to prove my magic abilities, but for Mary Jane to get herself a hunky man.

While Mary Jane was gone, the breakfast rush hit, which meant I was cooking and serving all by myself. Just what I'd been afraid would happen.

"Where's my pancakes?" a bald man yelled out.

"Coming right up," I yelled back. A bead of sweat trickled on my forehead. That whole 'if you can't stand the heat, then get out of the kitchen' saying was so true.

Thirty minutes since I'd opened and almost an hour since Mary Jane took Sheriff Jasper the pie, I hadn't meant for her to go on a date with him right there and then, only to line up a little rendezvous for another night. After all, he was supposed to be working, too. Maybe I should go check on her after the breakfast customers leave.

I'd just finished the thought when the bell on the door jangled. Mary Jane bounced through the door toward me with a sheepish grin on her face. Her carefully applied lipstick was missing.

"What took you so long? I thought I was going to have to come look for you."

"Sorry, I guess time slipped away."

I raised an eyebrow. "I guess so. And that's not all that slipped away. Where's your lipstick? Oh, wait. I know where it is, it's on Sheriff Jasper's face."

She giggled. "He kissed me."

"I see that."

"Elly, he smells so good and his dark eyes shimmer like moonlight casting off the ocean. His muscles are like—"

I held up my hand. "Not to stop you from waxing poetic about him, but... Let me stop you right there before you get carried away."

She blushed.

"So the spell must have worked. He noticed you. It was easier than I thought," I said.

"Maybe I didn't need the magic, after all." Her face glowed with excitement.

"Probably not, you just needed the confidence."

"Where are my pancakes?" the man yelled from across the room.

"I need more coffee," another angry voice rang out.

"I've got it." Mary Jane picked up the coffee pot.

"Thank you," I mouthed as she brushed past.

"Again, I'm sorry I left you alone with the breakfast rush."

"Don't be sorry. I'm the one who wanted you to go in the first place, remember? Are you happy?"

She nodded with a grin.

"Then I'm happy and there's no need to be sorry. Now let's get these people fed before they form a revolt against us. It could get ugly."

She laughed and grabbed the plate of pancakes and hurried over to the starving man. I looked up when the bell dangling on the door handle echoed across the café, hoping that it was Rory. Instead, it was Sheriff Jasper. He sure hadn't waited long to see Mary Jane again. Could I have messed up the spell? What if he became obsessed and started stalking her? That would be the end of me.

Magic was a big no-no for me right now, anyway. I wasn't supposed to do any magic per Tom's orders until he gave the all clear. If they found out I'd cast a spell and messed it up, I'd be in magic jail for the rest of my life. Wherever magic jail was. Would I really practice magic if it weren't for Mystic Café? Cooking up spells was the whole purpose of my magic—the entire reason all of this was happening.

"Mary Jane, Sheriff Jasper is here. Should he be here so soon? You just left him."

"He said he'd come right over for more coffee." She brushed back her hair and adjusted her chest.

That was not a good enough reason. He'd never made a special trip just for coffee, not when he had a coffeemaker just a few steps from his desk. Although by the appearance of the pot I saw this morning, it looked more like mud than coffee so maybe he was in need of a top off. But a refill probably wasn't all that was on his agenda. I think he just wanted to see Mary Jane again. That made me nervous. I had to wait and see what happened, I guess. These spells were apparently full of some powerful mojo.

Maybe it was just the first hours of new love. Love at first sight? Did I believe in love at first sight? Visions of Rory popped into my head. I guess I did believe it was possible for some, and if for some, then why not me?

I wished Rory didn't have the evil-ex following him around town. I'd never get a chance to find out if love was written in the stars for us. If I attempted to give him the magic reversal again, I'd for sure be busted. A little spell for Mary Jane was all I could endeavor for fear of being caught by Tom. I'd been warned for the last time. The thought of losing grandma's café brought tears to my eyes. She'd never forgive me for that. I watched as Mary Jane and Sheriff Jasper made eyes at each other, and a tinge of jealousy settled in my stomach. Don't get me wrong, I was happy for her, but it was only natural to want that feeling for myself.

"More coffee, please." The customer's request brought me out of my reverie.

When Tom rushed through the door, as if he were on fire, the coffee poured across the table, missing the customer's mug. He headed straight toward me with determination in his eyes.

When he was close enough for me to hear him, he whispered through gritted teeth, "Why are you still doing magic? What part of 'don't do magic' do you not understand?"

Chapter Twenty-Nine

"Let's talk back here." I motioned over my shoulder.

Mary Jane grabbed a towel and wiped up the confused customer's table. Tom hurried behind me. Without asking, I sensed his frustration and tensed muscles.

"What's wrong? Why are you so upset?" I crossed my arms in front of my chest.

He looked like a tightly coiled spring with his shoulders slumped, eyes narrowed and lips pressed into a thin line. "I told you no magic right now. Can't you control yourself? I know you have natural talent, but that's no excuse."

"I have natural talent?" I perked up. "Really? Grandma Imelda said I did, but I figured she had to say that. Like when I was nine and my mom said she loved that Chia Pet I bought her."

"Never mind that right now. Answer my question," he demanded.

"I just did a little spell for Mary Jane." I pinched my thumb and index finger together, indicating a small amount.

"There's no such thing as a little spell. Now knock it off before you get me in trouble."

"Fine." I crossed my arms in front of my chest again. "Don't get your boxers in a bunch."

"Cute." He smirked.

"Maybe he's wearing tightie-whities, or bikinis. You know, he's awfully handsome when he's angry." Mary Jane snickered.

"Too bad he's so annoying," I said.

"That's his job, to be annoying, right? He probably gets paid extra to be annoying."

"He must be very wealthy." I stuck my tongue out at Tom.

"It's not nice to talk about people like they're not there," Tom retorted.

"It may not be polite, but it's a heck of a lot of fun," Mary Jane quipped.

Tom sat on one of the stools in front of the counter, then rubbed his forehead with one hand.

"I think a customer needs you, Mary Jane," Tom said.

"It's nice to see you again too, Tom." Mary Jane marched away, shaking her head.

"So, what's happening? Any news?" I leaned forward, placing my elbows on the counter and propping my chin on my hands.

He frowned. His only response was to reach for a napkin.

"Don't keep me in suspense, tell me what happened."

"I'm afraid it's not good news." He let out a deep breath.

"Tom, do you ever have good news? I really didn't expect you to come in and say you had good news." I leaned back, standing up straight. "It's like there's a black cloud hanging over you and it's full of nothing but bad news raining down on whoever you stand next to. Maybe I should lock the door and not let you in, that way I wouldn't get the bad news."

"Oh you'd get it." He turned the mug over that was set in front of him.

I poured it full of coffee and placed flatware in front of him.

"I'd just wait until you came outside to catch you." He picked up a spoon, dipped it into the sugar, then dumped the heaping spoonful into his mug.

"You play dirty like that, don't you?"

"I'm one of the dirtiest." He wiggled his eyebrows. "I do what I have to do. It's my job." He dipped the spoon into the mug, stirring his coffee.

"So I'm ready. Tell me the bad news."

"They're not happy with the progress." He took a sip from his mug.

"I'm not happy either, but what can I do about it?" My voice raised a few decibels, garnering attention from around the café.

Tom leaned across the counter, lowered his chin, and looked into my eyes. "They're considering going ahead with the closing of Mystic Café, effective tomorrow."

"They can't do that." I grabbed his arm. The urge to shake some sense into him rushed through me. But apparently, no amount of pleading and begging would stop this. "This is completely not fair. What kind of organization is this, anyway? This is my café!"

"Elly, you knew this was going to happen. Are you making any progress? Other than kissing Rory?"

My blood boiled. Did he think I didn't care about the café? "How did you know about that?"

"I have my ways." He took another sip.

I let out a deep breath, attempting to calm my irritation. "As a matter of fact, I talked to Kim." I stood straighter, locking my gaze with his.

"Well, you'd better step up your efforts or this place will be a used bookstore, or maybe a consignment shop." He gestured around the café.

My stomach clenched. I narrowed my eyes. "This place isn't closing."

Chapter Thirty

My bed had never felt so good. I settled under the covers, hoping to pass out quickly and forget about the whirlwind of a day I'd experienced. Plus, I needed to forget about the fact that tomorrow the café would be closed for good.

Apparently, exhaustion had won the battle over me, because I woke the next morning to my phone ringing, still lying in the same position as I'd started in the night before.

"I think you need to get over here right away," Mary Jane yelled into the other end of the line.

I rubbed my eyes and stared at the clock, bleary-eyed. "Where are you?"

I was almost afraid to find out what had sent Mary Jane into this tizzy. She had a tendency to be overdramatic at times. Like the occasion when she cut her foot and swore it would need amputating. The nurse ended up spraying it with Bactine and slapped a bandage on it. With any luck, this was one of those instances.

"The café." Her words came out in a gasp. "Someone broke in and the police are over here right now."

"I'll be right there." Jumping from bed, I stumbled over the woven rug next to my bed and bumped into the dresser.

I grabbed the first pair of jeans within my reach and yanked a T-shirt from the drawer. My hands trembled as I slipped into the denim and pulled the shirt over my head. The top was too tight around the chest, but this was no occasion for a fashion show.

There was no time to tie my sneakers. I snatched up my purse and jumped into the Mustang, speeding off as fast as the law allowed without issuing a ticket.

The drive through the winding country roads seemed endless until I finally reached town. Maybe Mary Jane was wrong. There could be another explanation for the damage. How did they know someone had broken in? Who would break into the café? The crime rate in Mystic Hollow was almost nonexistent. The worst that happened around here was old man Phelps driving his lawnmower through town after he'd knocked back a beer or ten.

When I pulled up to the café, police cars surrounded the area with their lights flashing. I parked the Mustang as close as I could and hurried out from behind the wheel.

"What's going on?" I asked the first policeman I approached.

"Who are you?" He held his arms straight out, stopping me from moving closer.

"I own the café. My name's Elly Blair." I glanced over his shoulder, trying to catch a glimpse of the scene.

"I'm sorry." He lowered his arms back to his sides. "Someone apparently knocked out your front window and did some damage to the place. You want to go in and tell us if anything is missing?" He gestured with a tilt of his head.

I nodded. My stomach churned. Thank goodness I hadn't left any money in the register. What else could the intruder have taken? Plates and glasses? I didn't really have anything valuable except to another café owner. Other than...the magic. My stomach turned again. Was the book safe? What about the spices? This would not help my case for keeping the café open, if I couldn't even keep those items safe. Not only did I screw up magic, but I lost it, too?

No need to panic yet. I hadn't even looked in the café; I shouldn't jump to conclusions. The police officer motioned for me to follow him. The sun had begun its ascent, covering the area in a warm glow, birds chirped in the nearby trees and a warm breeze slipped past, so why did my insides tremble with unease?

When we neared the entrance, the extent of the damage to the window became evident. Someone had smashed it, all right. Shards of glass littered the ground. It looked as if I'd be busy cleaning up that mess for quite some time. How much would it cost to replace the window? Regardless of the price tag, it was money I couldn't afford to part with.

Another officer joined us. "I'm Officer Westman."

"Nice to meet you." I shook his hand.

Under different circumstances meeting him would be nice, but in this situation...not so much. Nonetheless, I'd remain polite. It wasn't his fault someone had decided to smash the café up.

"Where's Sheriff Jasper?" I asked.

"He's busy at the moment, but we'll make sure he knows all about the situation."

I guess the sheriff didn't bother showing up for little things like vandalism.

"Can you tell us if anything is missing? Otherwise, we'll assume it was just some stupid kids out playing pranks."

"Were any other stores or shops affected?" I eased around the glass to peep inside the café. "I can't imagine why someone would pick my place."

He frowned. "No, not that we know of, but that doesn't mean it couldn't happen to another business later. We'll patrol the area and be on the lookout." He gestured toward the door. "Why don't you have a look around?"

I stepped around the broken glass. "Yeah, okay."

Nothing stood out as unusual as I made my way from the front of the room. Tables and chairs were just as I'd left them. I reached the register and scanned the area. Nothing had been touched. There was a small safe in the back of the café. That was the main thing a burglar would have targeted other than the register. But since I hadn't left the money at the café last night, any would-be thief would have been out of luck. For the first time since taking over, I'd dropped off the cash at the bank on my way home. That was a good move and an even better lesson.

When I reached the kitchen and I stepped inside, I saw that the safe had been untouched. The kitchen, on the other hand, was a mess. Pots and pans were strewn about and flour and sugar dumped on top of my workstation. My gaze traveled to the shelf and my heart sank.

As I'd dreaded, the book was gone. The spices were missing as well. Grandma Imelda's voice rang in my head, whispering a warning I'd disregarded. "Don't let anything happen to the book or the spices." Ugh. What had I done now? Who would want an old book and spices, and why? From what I'd been told, hardly anyone knew about the magic. Even worse, I couldn't tell the police about the missing items. Had Tom taken the book and not told me? But that wouldn't explain the broken window.

The police officer adjusted his hat. "Well, someone has been in here." Good work, Barney Fife.

"Unless this is the way you leave your kitchen?" He regarded me with a raised brow.

I frowned. "No, I clean up all the time. It's one of my pet peeves. I like everything to be in order."

"This isn't in order. I've seen neater pigsties. Anything missing?"

I shook my head. "No, there doesn't appear to be."

Someone cleared their throat behind us and I whirled around. Tom stood with a look of astonishment on his face.

"Hey, buddy, you can't be in here right now." The officer motioned for Tom to clear the area.

"It's okay. I'm a business associate." Tom scowled.

I nodded. "Yes, he's with me."

Tom Owenton was an associate, all right—a pain in the butt associate. This was not going to go well.

Tom ran his hand through his thick hair. "You want to explain what is going on here?"

By the look on his face, I was guessing Tom didn't have the book.

"I'll be outside if you need me." The officer walked toward the kitchen door, but stopped just short and turned toward us again.

"Thanks." I'd almost rather he arrested me than have to face the interrogation from Tom.

"You're sure nothing's missing?" the officer asked again before leaving.

"No, everything seems to be here," I told him again with a forced smile spread across my face.

He nodded. "We'll write up a report and you can sign it. I'll be outside." I walked across the kitchen to retrieve my broom. "I need to sweep up that mess outside before anyone gets hurt."

"Are you going to answer my question?" Tom crossed his arms in front of his chest.

Did I have a choice? He might as well put the *Out of Business* sign on the front door now; I knew it was coming today, anyway. And to think I was just beginning to get used to small-town life again. I wondered if I could get my old job back. Probably not since my resignation consisted of a voice mail message of me singing "Take this Job and Shove It."

With broom and dustpan in hand, I moved my way across the floor and out the front door. "Exactly what it looks like: someone broke into the café."

"I see that part. What's missing?" His brow furrowed in concern.

"How do you know these things? And don't you dare say magic." I frowned. "You know what's missing without me telling you, so why are you asking? Just to torture me? To make me say the words out loud?" I continued sweeping the shards of glass.

He remained straight-faced. "This is a very serious situation, Elly."

Chapter Thirty-One

"I realize that." The clinking of the glass when it hit the metal dustpan made me cringe.

"I'm not sure if you do. You're not acting all that worried." He studied me.

I threw my arms up and the broom fell to the ground. "What am I supposed to do? Can't you sniff it out with your bloodhound nose?" I made air quotes with my fingers. "Can't you sense it with your magic?"

"It doesn't work that way."

"How does it work?" I whispered as an officer walked by. "Why don't you tell me because I'm a little confused. My grandmother leaves me this place and she, along with all you magic people, expect me to just know what to do. Well, I don't know what to do. So why don't you quit blaming me and help me?" I poked at his chest. Just as I'd suspected, it was hard as a rock.

"I plan on helping you, Elly. The only reason I'm here is to help you." His eyes held a sadness that I hadn't seen before.

I inhaled and slowly exhaled. "You could have fooled me. I thought the reason you were here was to close the café."

"Well, you're wrong. I can't lie and say that won't happen, but I want to help you so that it doesn't happen."

I steadied myself with a deep breath, then picked up the broom and stared at him. "That was actually very sweet of you to say. Thank you." I swept more glass into a pile. "So what do I do now? The book is gone and so are the spices."

"We'll have to close until we find them. If we find them soon enough, then the boss doesn't even need to know about this. But even if we find the book, that still doesn't leave us much time to remedy the other situation."

He didn't need to remind me. The pain of my reality sat on my chest like an elephant.

"Can't you get in a lot of trouble for not telling your boss about the missing items?"

He shrugged. "A little."

"A little?" I raised a brow.

"Okay, a lot. But what's one more thing, right? I think you're worth it." He moved closer and my stomach tingled.

What was he doing? His tone had changed. He no longer sounded like my magical warden.

He placed his hand on my arm. "I want to help you, Elly. Now quit being stubborn and let me, okay?"

I took in a deep breath and his spicy scent hit my nostrils. "Okay. I'll do whatever you say from this point forward."

"Like I said, we need to close until we locate the magic."

"I thought you'd close the café for good this morning, anyway. Aren't my forty-eight hours up?"

He stared at me. "You have until this afternoon."

I nodded, not sure of what to say. Tears threatened to fall from my eyes. My throat ached from holding them back and I bit my lip to keep it from trembling.

"You need to replace the glass, anyway." Tom reached for the dustpan. His tanned arm flexed as he reached down. "That should give us time to find the book and spices."

"You think a couple hours will really help? It sounds as if we'll be looking for a needle in a haystack."

"You'd be surprised. Mystic Hollow is a small town, remember?" He shook his head gently.

"Whatever you say, but I've never been a sleuth, so I don't know how we'll locate them."

"All we can do is try, right?" He touched my arm again.

"Right."

Footsteps caught my attention and I spun around. Rory approached us. He frowned when he saw Tom's hand on my arm. Tom noticed Rory's glare and a sly smile appeared on his face. I wriggled out from under Tom's hand and walked toward Rory.

"Are you okay?" he asked with a frown aimed at Tom.

"I'm all right, but someone smashed the café window out." I tilted my head toward the broken glass.

"Did they steal anything?" He shoved his hands in his pockets.

"No, not that I know of." What a liar. If only I could tell him the truth. It would feel so much better to confide in him. I'd never been a good liar, anyway.

"Do you need help cleaning up the mess?" He gestured for me to hand him the broom.

"I think I have it under control, although I'm not sure of what to do with the gaping hole in the front of the café."

"I'll get a few boards to nail over the broken part until you can have it replaced." Rory moved closer, inspecting the window frame.

"That would be wonderful. Thank you, Rory."

"Think nothing of it." He smiled as if to say ha to Tom.

Why did they dislike each other so? The only common denominator was me.

"I'll be back soon." Rory frowned while he gave Tom a departing glance, as if he didn't want to leave me alone with him. But leaving the café wasn't an option, and it didn't appear Tom was going anywhere, either. Didn't he need to start searching for the book? On a good note though, while Rory went for wood, Tom and I could discuss how we'd find the book...if we'd find the book. I hoped he had a good plan.

Rory drove off and I turned to Tom again. "So, where do we start?" I asked.

"First things first. We need to find out who knew about the magic."

Chapter Thirty-Two

"You want to explain to me how you know who is aware of magic and who isn't?" I asked.

"We have a list."

I stared for a beat. Was he pulling my leg? "So when I became aware of magic, was I added to the list?"

"Absolutely. The person telling you about the magic has to call in with your details."

"This is weird."

"I never said it wasn't. It's just the way it is."

"I know, I know, like the sky is blue and birds fly, blah, blah, blah."

He laughed. "Exactly. Now you're catching on."

"That's debatable." One thing was for sure, I wanted to get him out of there before Rory returned to repair the window. The last thing I needed was more heated looks and sneers back and forth from them.

"Why don't you go ahead and start while I clean up here?" I leaned against the brick building, suddenly aware of my too tight T-shirt when I noticed Tom's eyes fixated on the area. I held the broom in front of my chest for some semblance of coverage. "I won't be long and then I can help you in the search. Call me if you find out anything."

He shoved his hands in his pockets. "Okay, you'll be all right here?"

"I have been before. I'll be fine now."

He nodded. "I'll call you soon. We need to be on top of this and move as quickly as possible. No waiting around for the answer to find us."

Too bad he didn't feel that way about reversing the spell.

"Gotcha." I saluted.

Tom walked toward his car and I finished sweeping outside. While I waited for Rory to return, I'd clean up the mess in the kitchen. Standing in the middle of my once-clean kitchen, I ran my hands through my hair and let out a huge sigh. I couldn't believe the mess. It made no sense. Who would want to do something like this? As I set the dustpan on the kitchen floor and started sweeping, Mary Jane entered.

"Where've you been?" I asked.

"I had to run home real quick and check my house. I was worried someone might have broken into my place, too."

"I don't think you have anything to worry about. This person isn't targeting you. They want the magic."

"What?" She looked at me wide-eyed.

"The magic book is gone and so are the spices." I pointed to where the book and spices had rested for years until I'd been left in charge.

"Are you kidding?" She glanced at the shelf.

"Nope. I wouldn't kid about something like this."

"Does your grandmother know?" Mary Jane moved her finger across the spot where the book had been.

"No, she doesn't, but Tom does. He showed up not long after I got here. I didn't want to tell him, but he knew. Somehow he knew...."

"He's kind of creepy like that. It is strange having them sense the magic, huh? Tom should be able to find the book and spices easily, though." Mary Jane grabbed the dustpan.

"You'd think so, but he said it wasn't that easy. He can trace it somewhat, but not completely. The person will use the magic to hide. They have a list of people who know about the magic, so he's going to start there. He said we'll have to close the café until we find who did this. But we have to hurry, or this afternoon it'll be permanent."

"Let me help you," she said and grabbed the broom from my hands.

"Oh, and Rory is on his way to repair the window."

"That's sweet of him. I'm surprised the evil woman hasn't showed up looking for him already." Mary Jane dumped the contents of the dustpan in the trash.

"She probably will before he's done. The sooner we get this over with, maybe the sooner I can get her out of town. She doesn't want to be here anyway."

Mary Jane frowned. "I think she'd suffer through anything right now. She has a plan to get Rory back and nothing will stop her from doing that."

I wiped off the counters and looked at the clock. Rory should be back soon. I just wanted to get that window closed before anything else happened. Although how anything worse could happen, I didn't know. After another five minutes, Rory returned through the kitchen door.

"I've got the boards." He smiled. "They're on the back of my truck."

"Oh, thank you." I followed him outside the café.

"Can you give me a hand while I nail them in place?" He slid a board from the back of his truck. His muscles flexed as he carried the wood over to the broken window.

"Sure." I tried not to stare. "And again, I can't thank you enough for helping me."

"It's what I do. No thank you necessary." He pulled the hammer from his back pocket.

It wasn't exactly the answer I'd been looking for. I'd hoped he'd say something like: anything for you. His words made me think he'd help everyone and I was nothing special to him. But that was the thing with Rory. He would help anyone, even if they didn't deserve his help. Or his attention, like Kim and her stupid car. I held one side of the boards while he hammered in the nails one after the other, all the while admiring his biceps with each swing of the hammer. The bright sunshine lit up the area giving me a fantastic view of his body.

Forcing myself to look away from Rory's first-rate physique, I studied the street in front of Mystic Café. Why hadn't anyone seen the person who'd done this? If it had been during the night, the streetlight right in front would certainly not have allowed them to use the cover of darkness. The whole area was awash with light in the evenings.

"That should do it until you get the window replaced. The hardware store can get you a replacement fairly quickly. I can stop by there sometime this morning, if you'd like?"

He snapped me from my musings. "No, you have too much to do." I shook my head.

"I'll be going by there anyway, it's no big deal." He placed his hammer back in the cab of his truck.

I stood beside his truck, leaning against the bed. "If you're sure it's no trouble."

He flashed his dazzling smile. "Anything for you, Elly."

Had he read my mind? They were exactly the words I'd wanted to hear. So much for listening to Kim's warning about leaving Rory alone.

My breath caught as he ran his finger across my cheek. "I need to get going, but I'll be back later. You'll call me if you need anything?"

With a smile spread from ear to ear, I said, "I will." I felt like a giddy teenager.

Chapter Thirty-Three

"I have the list," Tom said. "I'll interview everyone and see what I can find out." He waved a couple sheets of white paper through the air.

"What can I do in the meantime?" I'd been staring at the old picture on the wall and wishing grandma was here when he walked in.

"Would you like to help me interview people?"

"I'm not sure I'm cut out for the sleuthing game. I never thought I'd make a good private investigator."

"There's nothing to it. You just ask questions. With the magic, they'll be more truthful. But they can still try to hide things from us, so we'll have to be thorough."

"They can break your magic and lie?"

"Some might be able to, but I pride myself on my magical investigation abilities. How do you think I got this job?" He wiggled his eyebrows.

"No comment." I flashed a big smile. "But seriously, I hadn't thought about how you became an investigator. Bad luck? You drew the shortest straw?"

"Very funny. I like your wit." Tom waved his index finger at me. "You've got spunk." He smiled.

"When do we start?"

"Right now. I'll take this half of the list." He separated one sheet from the other. "And you take this half."

"What about the magic? Where does that come in?" I looked over my shoulder to see if anyone was listening.

"I'll find a way with each of them, leave it to me. Sometimes it's as easy as saying an incantation, with others it can be a little harder."

"How will I know if they're being truthful?"

"You'll know. Trust me."

Again with the 'you'll know' business.

"It's worked so far, hasn't it?" He pushed the sheet of paper toward me.

"I suppose."

I studied the list of names. "Six? Only six? I thought there would be at least fifty."

He shook his head and a lock of dark hair fell across his forehead. "Oh no. Six for you and six for me." He combed his hair back with his fingers.

At the top of the list was Mr. Hanley from the barbershop, the one with the magic scissors. If Tom thought I was getting a haircut just to talk with Mr. Hanley, he had another think coming. Mr. Hanley had been in yesterday and had eaten a slice of peach pie so I figured I'd take him a piece in an attempt to get the information I needed out of him. After talking to him, I'd swing by the little boutique around the corner.

"Mimi Adams knows about the magic?" I raised a brow.

"She sure does. Her grandmother had the magic skills, but they weren't passed on to her. She found out by accident."

"And you expect me to believe that a lot more people around Mystic Hollow aren't finding out by accident?" I asked.

"It's very rare."

"I really find that hard to believe."

Tom's raised eyebrows let me know he thought my skepticism was a little unnecessary. "Well you'll have to trust me on that one, because it's the truth."

I grabbed my purse and scooted out from the booth. The thought of closing the café made my stomach twist into a knot, and a lump formed in my throat. With each passing minute, it looked more and more as if Mystic Café was in its final hours, so I'd better get used to it. Soon, I'd be seeking employment elsewhere. Grandma Imelda still wasn't aware of the latest incident. But that call was at the top of my to-do list, honest. She wouldn't be happy. I'd probably interrupt her receiving a massage from some guy named Sven while she enjoyed a Piña Colada.

"We'll meet back here in a few hours, if that's okay with you?"

"I hope I have enough time to talk with everyone." I studied the list again.

"Don't worry if you don't, we'll get around to all of them. Let's just get started." He motioned for me to move with him.

Don't worry? Had he forgotten about the time restraint? Had the urgency of the situation temporarily slipped his mind?

"Where are you headed?" Mary Jane stepped out from the kitchen, wiping her hands on a dish towel.

"Apparently, I'm going to talk to people who know about the magic to see what I can find out." I adjusted my purse strap and pasted on a smile.

"Do you need my help?" she asked.

Tom cleared his throat, drawing our attention to him. He raised a brow. "As a matter of fact, Mary Jane, I need to talk with you."

"Mary Jane? She doesn't know who did this. If she did, she would have told me."

"I understand that, but she's on the list and if you're on the list, then I have to talk with you."

She waved off my objection. "It's okay. I'll talk with Tom. If you need me when we finish just call me, I'll come help you."

Mary Jane didn't know anything and it was a waste of time to ask, but apparently these magical law enforcers had their policies and weren't about to break them.

I hugged her. "I think I'll be okay, but I'll call you if I need anything. Don't let him try any funny business." I waggled my finger in Tom's direction.

He didn't appear threatened by my words of warning.

I left the two of them at the table and made my way to the Mustang, still parked next to the curb. It seemed as if Tom had kept the easy list and I'd gotten the more colorful characters. Mr. Hanley never liked to talk with women, and he only chatted with the men if they were getting a haircut. I pictured myself with a shaved head. No way.

I slipped behind the wheel and pulled away from the curb. Through the rearview mirror, I glanced back at the Mystic Café sign dangling above the door. My stomach turned. I'd miss that place. I'd only been back for a short time, but it hadn't taken long for me to get used to the place again, and the people. I'd just started to get the hang of things. A chill ran up my spine when I realized the sign would soon no longer be a fixture in town. It had been there for so many years. Within hours of my arrival back in town, things had changed forever.

It was a short drive to my first stop. The quaint historic section of town captivated everyone with its old buildings lining the cobblestone streets. It made me envision what the town may have looked like years ago when the horses and carriages clomped through. Brick sidewalks spanned the length of Main Street, lined with ornate black lampposts and matching planters filled with red geraniums standing proud, showing off their vibrant color.

Southern charm was undeniable down every street, along the alleys and in every enticing shop that lined the main thoroughfare. Businesses ran the gamut from old-time barbershop—the one I was about to visit, which gives the shortest haircuts I'd ever seen—to antiques. Two antique shops, to be exact, one of which had the most beautiful credenza I'd ever seen displayed in its window. The buildings were all restored and in great shape.

The small pizza joint on the corner had a prime spot next to the bookstore, two of my favorite places. There was nothing like buying a new book, then strolling over for a big slice of pepperoni. A small hardware store sat on the corner, but how it stayed in business, I wasn't sure—the new Home Depot on the outskirts of town was a force to be reckoned with. There was even an old-fashioned soda fountain with the best chocolate milkshakes I'd ever had.

I made my way through town, pulled up in front of the barbershop, and parked the car. With the heavy traffic, it would have been faster if I'd walked. By heavy traffic, I meant the huge tractor inching its way through town with a line of cars stuck behind it.

I hopped out from behind the wheel and made my way to the door. The barbershop pole beckoned me and the *Open* sign blinked in the window. I swallowed the lump in my throat and moved forward. A few men sat around, chatting, but all talk ceased when I walked through the door. You'd think they'd never seen a woman before.

Chapter Thirty-Four

"Can I help you? You didn't come for a cut, did you?" The bald guy with the scissors in his hand didn't glance up. He looked about as out of place there as I did. He reminded me of a cleaned-up version of a mountain man, except hairless on the top of his head. His dark beard was sprinkled with grey and neatly trimmed. He wore a plaid long sleeve button-down shirt with brown pants.

"No, I didn't." I stayed close to the door. My hand hovered near the knob in case I needed a quick exit.

"What can I do for you, young lady?" He placed his scissors down and grabbed the little brush, knocking the hair off the guy in the seat who'd just had most of his head shaved.

Talking in front of the other men wasn't an option. But it felt strange to ask to speak to him in private. The other men would think it out of the ordinary, for sure. Heck, it was out of the ordinary in their world for a woman to set foot in the barbershop.

"I'm Elly Blair. I took over my grandmother's café." I gestured over my shoulder with my thumb, then handed him the little bag of peach pie. A look of recognition lit up his face when he opened the sack. Thank goodness, because now this awkward situation would be a whole lot easier.

"I need to speak with you about my grandmother." I motioned toward the sidewalk.

He nodded. "I'll be right back, fellas."

When we stepped outside he asked, "This is about the magic, right?"

"Yes." I looked over my shoulder to make sure no one was within earshot. Inside the barbershop, all eyes focused on us. I wasn't sure what Mr. Hanley would tell them about our conversation, but that was for him to decide; I had enough problems.

"I heard someone busted out the window on the café and stole your grandmother's book, well…your book now."

"That's why the organization sent me."

"They don't think I had anything to do with it? 'Cause I'll tell them a thing or two." His face and ears grew red. Mr. Hanley had always had a permanent red hue, though, always sweating and appearing as if he'd pop a vein at any moment.

"No, no." I waved my hands. "They just wanted to know if you saw anything, or heard anything."

"I'm afraid I can't help you there. But if I hear anything, I'll let you know. I can't imagine anyone who'd do such a thing."

"Me, either." I sighed and peered back into the barbershop window. The men remained transfixed. "Yeah okay, thanks anyway. Let me know if you hear anything."

Mystic Hollow was a small town but obviously, we weren't immune to lawbreaking. But someone wanted *Mystic Magic*. I guess if they took the book that was one way to get me to stop the magic.

Well, so much for contestant number one. Now on to my next stop and with any luck, it would provide more information than the first. At least I didn't have to get a haircut.

The hot sun beat down on me as I rushed back to my Mustang. The temperature had spiked already. The asphalt held in the heat, making the area like a giant frying pan. The next location on my list sat between the only dry cleaner in town and a ceramics shop, the kind of place where you get to paint your own hideous creation.

I slipped into the Mustang, shifting as the hot leather burned my skin. The torn piece on the driver's seat poked my legs as I positioned myself behind the wheel. The air in the vehicle hadn't spit out cold in ages, but at least the radio still worked.

I parked the car right in front, not a lot of shoppers out at that time of the morning. The Plaid Peacock sign dangled high above the sidewalk—a plaid background and a colorful peacock in shades of lime green, red and blue. A young woman pushing a stroller with one hand and holding onto a toddler crying for ice cream with the other hurried past. I pushed the old door and stepped inside, relishing the blast of cold air that hit my face. A bell chimed, announcing my entrance. An aroma hit me—a mixture of old building and scented candles—I detected cinnamon, apple and maybe pumpkin. I liked the place instantaneously. It made me feel comfy and hopeful.

"Welcome to The Plaid Peacock," a sweet southern voice drifted from behind the counter. The short brown-haired woman shuffled papers, her round face popping up to attention. "Can I help you?"

"I'm just looking, thanks. I thought I'd check your place out." I glanced around, pretending interest in a floral arrangement. I wanted to get a sense of how she felt before springing the questions on her.

Homemade folk art signs with lively sayings such as *Home Is Where Your Story Begins* and *It Is What It Is* dotted the walls. Knickknacks lined the many shelves.

"Aren't you Elly Blair?" Her rosy cheeks spread to reveal a huge smile.

I furrowed my brow. "Yes, I'm Elly."

Was there a wanted poster of me already? The magical screw-ups most wanted.

"I'm Mimi Adams. I heard about you taking over your grandmother's café. Let me tell you, lately I've had one, okay, ten too many pieces of pie and ice cream from her place, not to mention the chocolate. My waist just keeps expanding."

"I know how that goes, the pastry is hard to resist."

Mimi moved right along with her chatter. "I read in one of those celebrity magazines about all those movie stars wearing those fancy girdle underwear things." She paused for a quick breath, then continued, "I heard even Oprah wears them. Now, I don't know where all the extra fat is squished to, but I digress."

I bit my lip to suppress my laughter.

She looked at me with a dead-serious expression. "I ask you; where the heck does it go to? I mean, for heaven's sake, where does the fat go when wearing that torture device?"

I shrugged, but she didn't slow down.

She waved her hands in the air. "Anyhoo, I decided to try and find some of that fancy underwear and give it a test run. But of course, there's none to be found in Mystic Hollow. I couldn't find even one store that sells it. So I drove all the way to Louisville for a pair and, I swear, I think the darn thing is made from discarded car tires."

Biting my tongue no longer worked. My snicker escaped, but Mimi didn't slow down.

"Of course, I'm a tad bit vain, and I opted to get the extra-small size."

My eyes widened as I looked at her round waist.

"Honey, I swear this pair would have been tight on a flea. Why didn't I get the hippopotamus size that was more fitting to my girth?"

I giggled.

"If I could have flipped my belly fat around to the back, I'd have a great J. Lo booty thing going on. Well, let me tell you, if there'd been a camera in that dressing room, I'd be on my way to Disney World or somewhere as winner of *America's Funniest Home Videos*. I pushed and pulled. I rammed and crammed until every bit of extra me was tucked in. I had to have the check-out lady cut the tags off right there in line, 'cause there was no escaping."

I leaned against the counter, waiting for the outcome of this little yarn. Sure, I was wasting time when I should have been questioning others, but I had a feeling Mimi wasn't letting me out of the store without finishing her story first.

"I'm downright stupid, because I failed to think ahead of the time when I actually would have to take the vise off my body to pee. Wouldn't you know, right after the store I had to go pee? So what did I do? I stopped to eat at Taco Bell and rolled myself off to the ladies' room. Lord have mercy on my soul, extricating myself from that thing was like stripping off about ten layers of human skin from my body. I believe I actually exposed raw bones in the peeling process. I'm not lying, would I make this up?"

I shook my head.

"It was a wonder I didn't go flipping and flopping and flying through the air like a balloon that's been blown up and suddenly let go of."

"That's quite a dilemma."

"I think I should redesign these suckers. I could make a million dollars by just making them crotchless, or by making a detachable flap. But let me tell you, if you need any patches to repair your car tires or hot air balloon, I can cut up that sucker and send some your way."

Listening to her story was exhausting. I needed a glass of water and a place to sit down.

"Mimi, I've never heard a story quite like that."

She snickered. "Well, I'm full of them. Let me know when you want to hear more." Her expression turned serious. "I heard about what happened to you regarding the magic, and let me just say it's terrible. I can only imagine how you must feel." She paused to catch her breath again. "How are you holding up?"

Word sure spread quickly with the magical folks. It was like being on the cover of some sleazy tabloid.

"Thank you, Mimi. I'm doing okay. Things are working out okay." I diverted my eyes, looking around the store.

"Does your grandmother know?"

"No, not exactly." Grandma probably knew, but she always had wanted me to deal with problems myself. She said it made for a strong character.

"Tell me what you're looking for, darlin'."

Mimi had cool grandmother written all over her. The one everyone always wondered what it would be like to have. The kind of grandmother who'd hop on a motorcycle, then go home and bake a batch of chocolate chip cookies. Her black mini-skirt and tights combination revealed legs like a twenty-year-old's. The dark blouse she wore matched perfectly.

"I'm not sure. I suppose I'll know it when I see it. I really love everything in your store. It's so charming." I was stalling; coming right out with the question was my best option, so why was I looking at knickknacks?

"Thank you. Aren't you precious?"

I picked up a candle. "These are great."

"Those candles are locally made, you know." She pushed buttons on her calculator.

"Really?" I picked up another one, taking a long sniff.

"You're not here for candles though, are you?"

I stared at her for a beat, then shook my head. "No. No, I'm not."

"Well, spit it out, dear. What's the matter?"

"The National Organization of Magic sent me."

"Okay. Is this about Imelda?"

"Not exactly. The café was broken into. The *Mystic Magic* book is missing. I'm just trying to figure out who did it. Someone who knew about the magic had to take it."

"I'm so sorry to hear that. Your grandmother will be devastated."

I didn't need to be reminded of that right now. "I'm afraid I can't be of much help. I came here really early to work on stock. I drove past the café, but I didn't look over. Sorry to say I was messing with the radio."

"Oh well, I was given a list of people to ask. I'm very sorry if I bothered you."

"You're no bother. I just wish I could help. There is one thing," she said while tousling her hair. "Henry, the town drunk, has been known to slip into stores with unlocked windows. But I doubt he'd ever do something like break a window or steal. He'd never hurt a fly."

"You're right, I don't think he'd hurt a fly. I met him already." But he had mentioned the book. He'd seen Grandma Imelda with it and it had made an obvious impression on him, but enough to steal it? And what would his motive have been?

"He's a smart man and very charming, even more so when he's sober," Mimi said.

"What happened to him? How'd he come to live in the hotel?"

"His wife died several years ago and he's never been the same. He sold their home and moved into the hotel. He lives off his retirement money. Money for his room and money to drink on, that's all he needs."

"That's a tragic story." We stood in silence for a few seconds, then I said, "Thanks again for helping."

"Wish I could do more."

After contemplating Mimi's words for a few seconds, I snapped out of my reverie and selected a few candles for myself—cinnamon, lavender vanilla, and blackberry, then handed Mimi the candles.

"Would you happen to have another one of those iron candleholders over there in the display window?" I asked.

"Isn't it lovely? As a matter of fact, you're in luck. I did order a few more. The shipment should be here any day now."

"Well, I want one, so I'll check back. You'll be seeing more of me, Mimi. These candles smell wonderful. I'll take these three." I took another whiff before handing her cash for my purchase.

"I'd like that. You come by anytime you want." She handed me the white bag containing my purchase. It had lime green tissue paper peeking from the top and a lime green ribbon secured to the handles. "Just come by to chat if you'd like." Her big brown eyes twinkled in the light.

"I will." I waved over my shoulder as I bounced out the door.

That trip had been unproductive other than me spending money I didn't have. The other visits yielded nothing, either. Someone had to have seen something. With any luck, Tom had turned up a clue. Or even better, he might have already solved the mystery of the missing spell book.

The Mustang sputtered through the narrow streets, passing an old, weather-beaten gas station and a produce stand along the way. As I neared the café, a red light caught me. I tapped my fingers against the steering wheel and looked around. That's when I spotted them.

Unless my eyes were playing tricks on me, I saw Kim standing next to the building across from Mystic Café. I didn't need eyeglasses. Nope. It was her in a tête-à-tête with Tom. As I sat at the red light, waiting for it to change, I watched them. Why would he be talking to Kim? Was it about the magic? She hadn't been on the list.

Kim touched his arm and laughed, tilting her head back as if he'd said the funniest thing she'd heard in ages. I'd only seen Kim a few times, but it didn't take long to discover the touchy-feely thing was part of her attempt to charm everyone she came in contact with. But in spite of her efforts at charisma, there was an aura of intimidation about her. As if she'd better get what she wanted, or there'd be hell to pay.

The stoplight was taking an insane amount of time to change. Of course, I was a wee bit curious and wanted to know what they were talking about, so that may have had something to do with the drawn-out time. I tapped my fingers against the steering wheel harder, taking my gaze off them and glancing at the light every few seconds. Okay, a lot curious.

Mostly it seemed as if Kim was doing all the talking, though. Tom nodded a half a dozen times, then he finally stepped away. Kim watched him for a moment, then sashayed down the sidewalk. At least she hadn't followed Tom to the café. I didn't want to deal with her at that moment. Actually, I didn't want to deal with her ever, but I digress.

When the light turned, I punched the gas and steered over to the curb in front of Mystic Café. Time ticked away for me to find the book and reverse the spell. I sensed it. Soon, it would be too late.

Chapter Thirty-Five

When I pulled up to the café, Tom was waiting for me. He was leaning up against the side of the building. "It's about time you made it back."

"Some people are chatty." I left my purchase from The Plaid Peacock in the car. No need for him to know I'd shopped while interrogating Mimi. I figured she'd be more likely to talk if I bought something. Men wouldn't understand that line of thinking.

"What did you find out?" he asked.

"Other than where to buy local candles and how to escape a buzz cut? Nothing. Nothing at all. No one saw anything and they certainly weren't telling me if they took anything. I didn't sense any lying from them either, if that's what you were getting ready to ask."

He held his hands up in surrender. "Don't be so sensitive."

"It's hard not to be, I'm under a little pressure here. What did you find out? It didn't take you long."

"I've been doing this for a long time, I know what to ask, and I get right to the point."

I did spend too much time sniffing the candles at Mimi's place, but I didn't need to share that with Tom. I opened the door to the café. Tom held the door open for me while I walked through, then he followed.

"Where's Mary Jane?" I asked.

"She went home."

"What did you do to her?" I set my purse on the counter.

"What makes you think I did something to her?"

I looked him up and down, then frowned. "Oh, lucky guess."

"I didn't do anything. Guess you'll have to ask her."

"Fine. I want to wish her good luck on her test in the morning, anyway. I'll call her and if you did anything, she'll tell me." I stuck out my tongue. "What did you find out from her?" I poured myself a glass of water.

Tom frowned. "Nothing."

"See, I told you." I took a gulp.

"I have to talk with everyone, those are the rules."

"Rules, rules. I'm kind of sick of hearing about the rules." I ran my finger along the rim of the glass.

"Well, if we don't find the book, you won't be hearing about the rules for much longer. There's no need for rules if you're not doing the magic and the café is closed."

"Thanks for reminding me. I'd almost forgotten." I plopped down at the nearest booth and Tom sat across from me. "What did you find out from the others?" I looked at him, searching his face.

He folded his hands together and placed them on the table. "Nothing."

"I thought you were an expert at this investigating stuff?" A wry smile pulled at my lips.

Tom didn't respond to my sarcasm. "Mrs. Perkins said she heard the glass break. She lives all the way across town and never goes out at night."

"How did she hear anything?" I asked. "As a matter of fact, I thought her hearing was bad."

He took my glass of water. "She has an ear for magic. She may not hear anything else, but she can hear magic from miles away, especially when it's bad. Her words, not mine."

I placed my head in my hands. "This is not going to work and nothing will help."

"You're not being very optimistic." He held the glass to his lips for a moment, then took a long drink.

I looked up. "By the way, I thought I saw you talking to Kim." A casual way to mention it, I thought. Smoothly slid into the conversation.

"Oh yeah, she stopped me. Not sure what she wanted. She asked if we were dating." He set the empty glass down.

"What? I can't believe her." I shook my head in disbelief. "What business is that of hers? You did tell her no, though, right?"

He frowned. "You mean you wouldn't date me?"

My stomach flipped. I hated being put on the spot like that. Tom was handsome and he was growing on me, I had to admit. But he was there for business and not good business, either. It was never good to mix business with pleasure. Did he expect me to become his magical investigative assistant when they closed the café? Plus, I couldn't get Rory out of my head.

Tom grabbed my hand and squeezed. "What about when my business here is done?"

Before I could answer, Rory opened the door and I was like a deer caught in the headlights. Like a robber who'd just been caught with one leg out the window and a bag full of loot.

"I'm sorry, I didn't mean to interrupt. I saw the light on." He froze on the spot.

I jumped up and hurried over. "You're not interrupting anything." I pointed toward Tom. "We were just discussing business." Yeah, while holding hands was what it looked like to him. Some business meeting. Of all the rotten lousy timing.

"It's none of my business." He held his hands up. "Y'all continue and I can talk with you later." Rory frowned and moved toward the door, grabbing the handle.

"No need. I was just leaving," Tom said as he jumped to his feet.

Rory backed away from the door, and Tom rushed out without saying another word. He seemed upset and I didn't know what to think. I hoped I hadn't hurt his feelings. What if he closed the café without helping me anymore? Was he really interested in dating me?

"I didn't mean to interrupt," Rory said again once Tom had disappeared out of sight.

"Really, it's not how it looks. We were only discussing business." It never ceased to amaze me how easily I put my foot in my mouth.

He held his hands up once more. "Like I said, it's none of my business. You can do whatever you want."

Maybe a subject change was in order.

I gave an awkward smile, then said, "Kim asked if Tom and I were dating. Isn't that an odd question?"

Okay, that stupid statement wasn't much of a subject change. The fact that he wasn't the only one who thought we were dating only reinforced the idea.

"She's nosy like that. She always wants to know what's going on. I'd ignore her if I were you." He dragged his hand through his hair and let out a deep breath.

Believe me, I tried. I wished he would follow his own advice. Did Rory know what he wanted?

"Do you want to have a seat?" I gestured toward a chair. "Can I get you something to drink or something to eat?"

He moved closer, invading my personal space. "Something to drink isn't what I want."

When he looked at me, it sent a tremor of longing through my body.

I swallowed hard, then held my breath, wondering what was next. "What do you want?"

"This." He pressed his lips against mine. They were cool and my lips tingled as his brushed across mine. Rory wrapped his arms around my waist and pulled me closer. Being in Rory's arms felt natural, as if I'd come home.

A knock rattled the window. Rory released me from his embrace. We spun around to find at least ten women huddled around the front door, peering through the glass. Talk about a mood killer.

"It looks as if we're wanted," I said, gesturing with a tilt of my head. Though I knew it wasn't both of us, but Rory they wanted.

The pack of ladies waved feverishly. They were a mixture of ages—a couple of grandmothers, mothers and daughters. Fortunately, there were no teenagers. That was the last thing he needed.

I stepped out onto the sidewalk. With any luck, I'd disperse the crowd before they had a chance to pack Rory off like a piece of meat. Rory followed me, although in hindsight, he probably should have run out the backdoor.

The women didn't seem to notice me. They never looked in my direction as they reached out their hands toward Rory. It was like a scene from *Night of the Living Dead*.

"What do you think they want?" Rory looked at me wide-eyed.

I winced at the thought of answering his question truthfully. A couple women ran their fingers through his hair, while others rubbed his chest. He pushed at their hands as politely as he could.

"Please, ladies. What is wrong with you?" He brushed a grandma's hands away from his hair. "I have to get out of here." He twisted, stepping to his left. By his expression, he must have been too stunned by their behavior to run.

"Don't leave, Rory," a blonde woman said.

"Let's go for a walk." The redhead looped her arm through his.

Why? So they could capture him and chain him up in a basement as their love slave? No way. I felt so bad for him, but what could I do? Beating them off with my rolling pin wasn't an option. Or was it? No. No violence. I'd have to think of something else.

Rory stared at me with a look that was a cross between apologetic and desperate, as if pleading for my help. There was no way I'd not put up a fight for him if they tried to drag him away. They were like zombies looking for their next victim to drag off into the night. I'd seen clips of Elvis being attacked like this. But I was no Colonel Parker. How would I save him?

I sucked in a deep breath and pushed forward as if plowing through a blockade.

"Hey, back off, honey," Amy Strong protested. I hadn't seen her sidle up. Were there more women coming? This would turn into a mob soon. "He doesn't want you." Was that my mom's friend yelling at me while poking me in the ribs with an elbow?

I grabbed Rory's arm and pushed him back, away from the women. "Ladies, back off." I nudged Rory's arm and he took off in a run. "Rory, hurry."

We ran toward his truck, which was only parked a few feet away. I yanked open the passenger door, jumped in and locked the door.

Rory glanced my way and I motioned for him to jump behind the wheel. "Hurry. Save yourself."

Once he rounded the front of the trunk and hopped in, the women converged around the truck like a pack of wolves circling their prey. He let out a few deep breaths and cranked the engine. He gestured for the women to get out of the way. After a brief pause, they slumped their shoulders and stepped away from the truck. But not without some protesting that I'd taken him away. A few pumped their fists at me.

What did I say to him? He had to be extremely embarrassed. Maybe if I acted as if it was no big deal? If Rory knew the truth, he wouldn't be embarrassed. No, if he knew the magical facts, he'd never speak with me again. I opened my mouth, but the words didn't form. Why was I such a coward? Of course, Rory would be mad at me. But I needed to suck it up and deal with the consequences. Thoughts whirled in my head and I clutched the leather seat with a death grip. Maybe if I braced myself, I could push forward with telling him the truth. But no. I sat there and continued to allow Rory to think there was something wrong with him...something wrong with the world.

Finally, I came up with a lame plan for escape. "Drive around the block and maybe they'll leave. You can drop me off at the café and get out of this mess," I said.

"Honestly, Elly, I have no idea what's going on, but I want to apologize. I don't know these women." He clutched the steering wheel with both hands.

"I know. They're probably fascinated with you because you're new in town," I said.

"I've been here for quite some time now. I don't think that's it." He shook his head. "I just need some time to think. I'm so confused that I don't know up from down."

We glanced in the truck mirrors every few seconds, looking for any sign of the crazed women as Rory drove around the block. So far, the coast was clear. Would he have to cope with this for the rest of his life? There was no way I'd let him deal with this. I'd demand something be done to reverse the spell. What kind of crazy magic was this, anyway?

As we pulled back in front of the café, all signs of the women were gone. It was as if it was a nightmare and had never happened. By the way the adrenaline flowed through me, I knew it wasn't a dream.

"Stop here quick and I'll jump out. I don't want you hanging around so they can find you again." I hopped down from the truck.

"I'd love to stay and start back where we left off, but I need to get back to work, anyway."

I nodded. "I understand. I'll see you later." I closed the door and waved as he drove off.

His sad puppy dog expression made tears form in my eyes. Later that afternoon, the café would be closed permanently and my chances with Rory gone for good.

****

Tom had said he'd meet me at the café by seven. In reality, he'd showed up at nine. Not that I was in a hurry for what was about to happen, though. Mary Jane had wanted to stay until the very end, but I insisted she go to her night class. Her tear-stained cheeks and red eyes had almost been more than I could handle.

"I'm sorry," Tom mumbled. His expression was apologetic.

Did he actually say he was sorry? Did he really utter those words? A lot of good it did me. I appreciated the sentiment, but my world had crumbled around me and no words would ease my pain. Time had run out for Mystic Café and me. I removed Grandma Imelda's key chain that read *Magic Happens* and handed him the keys. Hot tears threatened to spill down my cheeks.

"I can call your grandmother." He turned off the lights and shut the café door.

"No, I'll call her."

"I'll need to talk with her anyway." He stuffed the keys into his front pocket.

"Please, let me call her first. It's the least I can do. I don't want to be a coward. Facing life's problems is the only way to truly overcome them."

He nodded. "All right, sure." He cleared his throat. "Um, we'll go over the details of the closing tomorrow. Someone will be by in a few days to allow you inside to retrieve your belongings. Since your grandmother left you the place, you'll have to sell it. I'm not sure of the time frame they'll give you for that."

"I don't believe this has happened." I blew out a deep breath and wiped a tear from my cheek. Exasperation filled my chest. What kind of organization closes a business over one spell? "You only gave me forty-eight hours. What could I possibly have done in that amount of time?"

He shifted his feet. "I don't make the rules, Elly. If I could stop this, I would. I'd give anything to make it not happen."

I studied my shoes. "You've been kind to me and I appreciate that. I didn't mean to accuse you."

He lifted my chin with his index finger and wiped the tear from my cheek. "I can't stand to see a woman cry. You're killing me here, please stop."

"It's not like I turned on the waterworks purely for your benefit."

"Can I give you a ride home? Maybe you shouldn't be alone at a time like this. Sometimes it helps to have someone around."

"I wouldn't make for very good company right now." The past few days had been the happiest of my life and, ironically the most stressful. There was nowhere I'd rather be than in the little kitchen of Mystic Café. The smell of the magical spices, mixed with the pancakes, bacon, and biscuits would remain a part of my memories I couldn't erase. Oh, and the home fries...the spicy potatoes.

I'd discovered too late that Mystic Café was where I belonged. It was the shot of love my heart had needed. Grandma Imelda may not be there in body, but her presence would always be there. The café walls were like her arms, wrapping me in a tight embrace. But it was history now. Somehow, I'd make it through this. I had to, for Grandma Imelda's sake. Life was never easy and I didn't want to let this stop me. But what would happen to the people of Mystic Hollow? Grandma said this town would fall apart without the magic.

He stared for a beat. "If you're sure?"

I nodded. "I'll be fine. I just need some time."

Tom reluctantly placed a huge *Closed* sign on Mystic Café's door. Without looking back, I hurried to my car and jumped in. My heart ached, my throat was tight, and my eyes stung. I'd never look at pancakes or pies the same again. And just like that, the café was closed. No magic wand needed.

Chapter Thirty-Six

A bad sensation started in my throat and moved downward, churning as if circling a drain, before finally settling in my stomach like a block of cement. It was that feeling you got when, as a teenager, you're waiting for your parents to return home after they'd left you alone all weekend because you promised you were old enough to conduct yourself as an adult, but the moment their car was out of sight you invited fifty friends over for a party where said friends proceeded to wreck the house and you have no idea how you'll explain the broken sofa or the ketchup on the ceiling. Yeah, I had that feeling. The phone call to Grandma Imelda had to be made. I'd have to tell her that in spite of being twenty-eight, apparently I wasn't old enough to conduct myself as an adult...at least not where magic was involved.

Halfway home, I pulled the Mustang over on the side of the road and stared at my phone. I dialed half of Grandma Imelda's phone number three times before finally getting the nerve to punch in all of the digits and hit send.

Just when I thought she wouldn't pick up, she answered with her usual sweet voice. "I wondered if I was ever going to hear from you. The café hasn't been too overwhelming, has it?"

I sucked in a deep breath. "There's something I need to tell you."

Grandma hadn't even had time to reply before my tears started.

"Don't cry. Tell your grandmother what's bothering you. You know you can tell me anything."

She thought I could tell her anything, but I wasn't sure she was prepared for this news.

Letting out a shaky breath, I said, "There was a problem at the café."

"What kind of problem? Was there a fire? Did someone get food poisoning? Did Mr. Atwood claim he fell on the steps again? Don't believe a word he says. He's been trying those scams since 1969."

I swallowed hard. There was no easy way to put this, so I'd have to come out with it. "I gave someone the wrong spell."

She let out an audible gasp, and a slight sucking in of breath whispered across the line. Fantastic. I'd caused her to have a heart attack.

"Grandma Imelda, talk to me. Are you all right?"

"I'm fine. I'm fine. You just caught me off guard. Who got the spell?"

"A man. His name is Rory Covington."

"Oh." She paused. "I've met him. He's a handsome fellow, don't you think?"

"I suppose he is. But listen, Grandma, Mary Jane accidently set the wrong order in front of him and he ate it. I tried to stop it, but I was too late. The spell was meant for Oscar Harrisburg."

"Exactly what type of spell was this?" she asked.

Although cowardly, I was glad I was talking to her on the phone. There was no way I could have looked her in the eye with this kind of news. "It was a love spell...Rory's ex-girlfriend came back and women in town are going gaga over him."

"Oh, no..." Not the words I wanted to hear from my sweet grandmother. "Elly, someone will be by soon to tell you what to do." Her voice remained calm and steady.

"Um, that's the thing, they've already been here."

"I see." She knew what was coming next without me having to tell her.

"They closed the café." My sobbing started again when the words left my lips.

"There now, don't cry. You're going to make me cry and my mascara will run. I'll look like a raccoon. If it was meant to be, darlin', then it will be. I left you in charge and I believe you handled everything appropriately. If it was the café's time, then there was nothing you could do to stop it." Her voice held a steely determination.

It was in her character to take this news without as much as a whimper. If only I could learn such a quality.

"I didn't tell you when it happened because I thought I could fix it, but I can't. An investigator came and I had forty-eight hours to reverse the spell, but it wasn't enough time. I ruined all your hard work. I ruined the magic for Mystic Hollow." Tears flooded my eyes and I sobbed. With each blubber that escaped my lips, my chest heaved.

"Now listen to me, Elly, you have to get a hold of yourself. Nothing is worth being this upset over. Life goes on and you make things work. You have many blessings to be thankful for, so when something bad like this happens, remember the good things you're blessed with, pick your chin up, and carry on."

I nodded as if she could see me. If only I could talk to her all night. I didn't want to hang up because then grandma would be left to think about Mystic Café. She needed relaxation. The last thing she needed was to worry about me. Her only focus should have been feeling sand between her toes and watching the sunset.

"Elly, did Mr. Wibble come to see you?"

Her voice snapped me back to reality. "Um, yes, he was there, too."

"Mr. Wibble has been kind to me over the years." Her tone sweetened.

"What do you mean? You made mistakes?" I asked.

"I made a few, but nothing ever serious."

What she meant was nothing ever as stupid as my mistake.

"So Mr. Wibble looked the other way? He ignored your mistakes?"

"Oh, he always came out to investigate. But he covered my fanny. Well, not literally...you know what I mean." She snorted.

I snickered. "I believe you, Grandma. So that's why Tom said there was nothing in your file."

"I always suspected Mr. Wibble fancied me. But I was married to your grandpa, so he never made a move."

Why hadn't Tom done the same for me? Covered for me, I mean, not made a move.

Grandma continued, "Mr. Wibble came to me with the intention of closing the café during the first mishap, but by the time he left, we were friends."

How many mistakes had she made? Maybe someday she'd share her stories.

"He seems cranky."

She chuckled. "He's a sourpuss, but a softy deep down."

So she'd made a few mistakes, but they were nothing compared to mine. She didn't even know the whole story yet. What would happen when I told her the book and spices were missing?

"There's one more thing, Grandma."

She paused, then said, "I'm listening, dear."

"Someone broke into the café and took the book and the spices. The organization knows and we're looking for them. I'm sure they'll contact you soon."

"That doesn't change what I said. Mystic Café had a good run. The organization has always been fair to me and I know they'll do what's best. Everything will work out. Have faith, okay?"

It was hard to have faith but, with her positive thinking, how could I not trust her words? Confidence oozed from her and wrapped around me, forcing me to believe that I had no choice but to make things work.

"You call me tomorrow, okay?" she said. "If I hear from the organization I'll call you."

I sniffled. "Okay. I love you, Grandma."

"I love you too, Elly, now you go get some sleep. And tell Rory hello for me."

She hung up before I could answer. I'd probably never see Rory again. There'd be no chance for me to relay the message. Grandma Imelda had been supportive when I'd made the phone call. But I hadn't really expected anything less from her. She had always handled negative situations with grace and aplomb. Her help for Mystic Hollow residents had always been unwavering and unrelenting. Of course, she couldn't say much in between my sobs and sniffling. I'd been mostly incoherent. The memory of Tom locking the door on Mystic Café would haunt me for the rest of my life.

Somehow, I'd managed to drive the rest of the way from where I'd pulled over on the side of the road, but I didn't remember any of it. I was too wrapped up in my emotions. I parked the Mustang in front of the tiny cottage grandma had left me and wiped the tears from my face. After the long day, I wanted nothing more than to collapse into bed, burying myself under my down comforter.

After forcing myself to move, I swung out from behind the wheel and brushed past the rosebushes, hurrying down the gravel drive to the side door. A rustling noise sounded in the nearby bush. I prayed it was a cat. My legs moved a little quicker when I contemplated all the creatures it could have been. My nerves were working overtime because of the day's events.

The entrance led into the tiny kitchen. When I opened the door, the emptiness hit me. The quiet, dark space did nothing to alleviate my unease. I tossed my purse and keys on the table and flipped on the light above the sink. The artificial glow flooded the buttercream colored walls; Grandma Imelda believed in painting with colors named after foods.

I locked the deadbolt on the door, then marched straight to the bathroom and slipped into the hot shower, allowing the warm water to relieve my stress. I reflected on the events from the last few days. Rory's face was etched into my brain and images of Kim, magic books, and food haunted my thoughts.

The tingle from Rory's kiss remained, as a phantom pain would. Only this was far from painful. No, it was amazing and breathtaking rolled into one. But in spite of the feelings Rory gave me, the unease and uncertainty had a tight grip around me and it didn't want to let go.

When the water had turned cold and my tension hadn't circled the drain along with the soap suds, I climbed out and wrapped myself in my old pink bathrobe. I ambled into the living room and pushed the blinking light on the answering machine. I expected the message to be from my mother.

The gravelly voice that now irritated me worse than an air horn being blown in my ear screeched from the machine. I'd been ignoring Ray's calls for days. When he left voice mails on my cell phone, I deleted them without listening.

"Elly, please talk to me. You haven't answered your cell and I'm worried about you. I know I should have told you about..." He coughed. "Um, my relationship with Elana, but I was confused. I'd never hurt you on purpose. It just happened between us. There was nothing I could do. I want us to be friends. Call me back, okay?"

I hadn't told him I was coming back to Mystic Hollow, so I had no idea how he'd found me. He'd probably assumed I'd come running home the minute things got tough. Regardless, there was nothing left to say. I'd moved on. Our relationship was over a long time before I'd caught him in his little fling. There was no connection between us. Every day for the past year, life with Ray was just going through the motions.

I plopped down in the overstuffed chair and zoned out in front of the TV with a bag of Hershey's Kisses on my lap. What a pathetic sight I was, drowning my sorrows with chocolate. I may have lost the one thing my grandmother worked hard for years to make a success, but hey, a girl hasn't lived until she's made a complete failure of her life and everyone else's around her, too.

On one tiny bright side, at least I'd gotten away from Ray. Even knowing that I could shut him out of my life so easily gave me delight. I'd set his belongings on the curb a week before Grandma Imelda had called. Hey, at least I had packed them all neat and orderly before I did it.

Ray worked as an accountant at a not-so-prestigious firm. I had no idea he had been cheating on me the entire time we'd lived together. For as long as I lived, I'd never understand why he'd insisted I move to New York to be with him. Wouldn't it have been easier to woo other women with me not around?

No, he enjoyed the thrill of cheating, being with someone who he wasn't supposed to be with. Ray, or Rat as I liked to refer to him in my mind, craved an amount of attention that one woman alone could never possibly lavish on him. Frankly, I was glad I didn't have to try any longer. Yes, he was nothing short of a rat.

I'd caught him with his pants down around his ankles. Literally. One day I went out shopping and came home to find him with his co-worker. Elana, or something like that, was her name. They were halfway to my bed, when I innocently walked into my bedroom and caught them ripping each other's clothing off. Silly me. What was I thinking walking into my own bedroom like that and spoiling their fun?

I'd met her once, at his office Christmas party. She stood out in my mind back then because of her beautiful black dress. I'd envied it from the moment I saw her. The silk had hit just above her knees and the front had gorgeous beading that came down in a low v-shape. I'd asked her where she bought it, but she claimed she didn't remember.

They'd probably been cheating back then, too. Sure, the signs had been there all along, but hindsight was the only way I'd acknowledged them. Rat had worked late on special projects on occasions too numerous to count. He had important business trips that I couldn't attend and took private client phone calls just out of my earshot. But that was the past, and I was home in Mystic Hollow now. But for how long?

This mess with the café had caused me to dig deep and really think about what I wanted. And in the course of figuring out what I wanted, I discovered something about myself that I'd never acknowledged. Sure, my motto was what you see is what you get. But on the inside, I didn't really feel that way. In an epiphany, I realized there was a recurring thought that ran through my head: that the world would end if someone didn't like me or if they were mad at me. Whether it was grandma, my mother, some magic representative I didn't know, Rory or Ray, for that matter, I hated thinking I'd upset someone. Heck, I'd actually worried that I'd upset Ray when I tossed him out on the street. As if he hadn't humiliated me and treated me like dirt by cheating. What was this weird longing I had to be liked and accepted? To be needed. What I had failed to recognize was I couldn't please everyone all the time. I didn't have to please everyone.

When I finally peered up at the clock, I realized it was after midnight and time had slipped away from me. It was a shame I hadn't gotten to enjoy one last day running the café before it was closed forever.

Knowing I didn't have to wake up at the crack of dawn didn't make me happy. That was something I never thought I'd say. I'd never been one to give up, but I hardly saw any other way out of this situation.

I pushed to my feet, yawned, and made my way toward my bedroom. When I reached the hallway, a loud crash rang out, making the back door shake. My Hershey's Kisses went one way and the remote control flew the other. I froze in my spot. The noise sounded as if it had come from the back porch. I swallowed hard, cursing myself for forgetting to pull the kitchen shade down. Was someone outside my window peeping in? Visions of various slasher films ran through my mind. I didn't want to be the woman hacked to death. I'd prefer to be the heroine who saves the day.

Chills prickled along my arms and down my back. I hurried over and pulled down the shade on the back door. I didn't think I had the nerve to go outside and investigate. So instead, I went around to all the windows, checked each lock and pulled down the shades.

After thirty minutes of fidgeting in the corner chair, and no further disturbances, I slipped into a pair of pink sweatpants and a well-worn Kentucky Wildcats T-shirt and crawled into bed. The noise must have been a stray cat or a rabid raccoon. I stretched out in the middle of the mattress. A big lump poked me in the back, so I slid to the left side. A spring gouged my calf making it impossible to sleep, so I shifted again. The right side wasn't much better, but at least no sharp coils jabbed me. It would have to do until I could buy a new mattress. One good thing: my sheets smelled like lavender. I pulled the covers up tight under my chin and listened for more mysterious sounds. Nothing like being all alone to bring out the odd sounds and visions of the boogieman.

My tears flowed freely down my cheeks, dropping onto my pillow and soaking the cotton. I was alone with my thoughts and, after what had happened to the café, my thoughts were the worst place to be. I'd remained tough when I'd discovered Ray boinking his coworker. I'd held in my emotions when I broke off our engagement. Sure, there had been tears, but I kept it together. Right now, being resilient wasn't an option. There were only so many things I could handle, and letting Grandma Imelda down wasn't one of them.

A storm had moved in, and rain pounded against the window as thunder crashed overhead. The noise had drowned out my sniffling, but I jumped with each flash of lightning. Tree branches scratched against the windows making an eerie scraping sound. I slipped out of bed and padded over to the window. When I pulled back the shade, a lightning bolt split across the sky and landed nearby. I scurried back to bed, pulling the covers over my head.

I wasn't sure how long I listened, but Mother Nature finally calmed down and I drifted off without another unexplained noise disturbing a peaceful night's rest. Until the sound of footsteps outside my door woke me.

Chapter Thirty-Seven

With my eyes wide and body frozen, I glanced at the clock. The time read 3 a.m. My breath caught in my throat as the steps echoed along the hallway. The clomp-clomp noise sounded like boots. Was someone inside with me or was it just the clattering of an old house? It sure sounded like a person. I climbed out of bed and tiptoed to the door. Of course, I didn't have a weapon. The knives were in the kitchen. If I was going to live alone, I needed to think about security. Maybe I should get a dog. Rory had a dog. But before I contemplated life with Fido further, the steps stopped.

Did I have a ghost? First the bang outside and now this. Maybe it was a burglar. Was it the person who broke into the café? Mary Jane would find me bludgeoned to death in the morning. She'd miss me and come looking. Everyone would talk about such a sad end to a young, lonely life. Grandma Imelda and my mother would be devastated.

After a couple of seconds with no noise, there was only one option: I had to find out where the noise had come from. I couldn't stay in the bedroom forever. I'd have to take my chances with the killer or ghost. I hoped it was a ghost; I could handle a spooky mist floating around. A crazed killer? Not so much. I eased the door open an inch and poked my head out enough to see down the hall. No one was in sight. When no one lunged out at me, I mouthed a silent prayer.

I opened the door the rest of the way and tiptoed out from my safe haven. In the hallway, a right turn led to the kitchen: if I turned to the left, it led into the dining and living room. I decided to check the kitchen first. The only light was from the cracked powder room door. Ray had always complained about the electric bill and me "leaving the damn lights on." Now I was thankful for my bad habit. I never had liked the dark.

I peered around the open space. Nothing seemed out of place, so I turned and walked down the hallway toward the dining room—each step calculated so as not to alert my intruder. The only sound in the room was my heavy breathing. No ghosts or predators. The same with the living room. The grandfather clock ticked in time to my heartbeat.

Easing up the stairs in the dark, I checked the upstairs rooms, looking under beds and in closets, but I didn't find a soul. My hands trembled every time I lifted a bed skirt or opened a closed door. Maybe an animal was in the house? The crazed raccoon or cat? Okay, it would have to have been a very fat cat. The noise had sounded very much like human footsteps.

Stumbling through the dark, I slipped back to the kitchen. With still trembling hands, I poured water into a glass, then leaned against the old Formica countertop. What had I heard? As I gulped my water, I studied the back door. My gaze traveled down to the knob, then to the lock. It was unlocked. I knew I'd locked it when I'd returned home. Had I been sleepwalking and unlocked it? I thought I'd checked every window and door before bed, but I must have forgotten that one. An open door was just asking someone to come into the house. I walked over and flipped the lock.

Pushing back the dread that overwhelmed me, I peeped out through the corner of the shade. A strange feeling came over me, as if eyes were watching me. The backyard was one big black blob. Darkness blanketed the trees and bushes until nothing stood out—only the golden flicker from fireflies. I couldn't have seen my hand in front of my face. I needed to get a bright light out there as soon as possible. Staring into the darkness wouldn't solve anything, so I placed my glass into the sink and wandered back to my room. Closing the door behind me, I jumped into bed and pulled the covers back up under my chin again. I prayed whatever I'd heard wouldn't come back. After a while, I'd convinced myself I'd only heard the old house settling. My constant flopping from one side of the bed to the other ceased. The tension in my muscles eased and my eyelids grew heavy.

Chapter Thirty-Eight

Something roused me from sleep. I opened my eyes in the early-morning darkness. The shades blocked out most of the light, but I knew it was morning by the sliver of sunbeam coming through the edge of the shade. My breathing was the only sound until a rustling noise caught my attention. My heart did a flip. I sat up in the bed, attempting to focus my eyes in the darkness. Somewhere a set of eyes focused on me, I just knew it. When my eyes adjusted to the darkness, I saw her.

"What the heck are you doing in my room? In my house?" I yelled.

Kim stood at the foot of my bed, staring at me with her arms crossed in front of her surgically upgraded chest.

She clutched the *Mystic Magic* book in her hands.

"You stole my book?" I couldn't believe my eyes.

"Who's to say that I didn't find it?" She scowled.

"Did you find it?" I raised an eyebrow.

"No, I stole it." She set the book on the edge of the bed, then straightened her shirt.

My voice rose. "Why would you do something like that?"

"I overheard you." She paced the length of the room, her heels clicking across the hardwood floor. That had been the sound I'd mistaken for boots clomping. "I want you to whip up some magic and make Rory love me like he used to."

"I can't do—"

She cut me off. "Listen to me. I tried the magic myself but, after reading the book, I realize you have to have some kind of silly special talent for it." She snorted. "I'm guessing you possess said talent, since you owned the book. Now get up and make some magic happen for us. I want sparks to fly." She waved her hands.

I stared at her, my mouth agape. No words formed, she'd left me speechless.

"Well, don't just sit there with that goofy look on your face, get up. I'll force you if I have to." She tapped her foot against the floor.

By the expression on her face and the fact that she broke into my home in the middle of the night, not to mention stealing the book from the café, I kind of believed her about the whole 'forcing me' spiel.

"Why did you break the window at the café?"

"Duh, how else was I going to get the book? Stupid." She rolled her eyes.

"Um, calling me stupid probably won't get me to perform the magic any faster."

She straightened her shoulders and lifted her chin. "If you don't get up out of that bed and make some f'in magic happen, I'm going to pull every single hair out of your head."

"Okay, okay. I'm up." I held my hands up in surrender.

Untangling my legs from the sheets, I stood from the bed, clutching my neck and wincing at the pain caused by the lumpy mattress. I made my movements slow so as not to rile her any more. She was acting nuttier than a family-sized bag of Snickers bars at this point, and I didn't know when she'd completely snap.

"I'm not sure I can make magic like you want. There are certain rules with this stuff, lots of rules, in fact. If a person doesn't love you, I can't make them, no matter how much magic I try."

"Bullshit," she yelled. "It says right here." She flipped open the cover of the book and fumbled through the pages. "Right here." She pointed. "Page two-forty-six. Love Spells: Helping Someone Capture The Person Of Their Dreams. I want that." She crossed her arms in front of her chest.

An ache formed in my chest knowing she had possession of *Mystic Magic*. I stared at her for a beat. "That's the thing, Kim. Don't you understand? Rory isn't the person of your dreams." I watched for a reaction. When she didn't respond, I continued. "You don't really love him. You just want him to love you so you can control him. Wouldn't it be better to have someone love you for who you are, not under false pretenses? You deserve that."

She stared back, as if the little wheel in her mind was spinning, mulling over what I'd just said. "How the hell do you know what I want? You work in a diner." She smirked. "And by the way, I don't think the food is as good as everyone raves it is."

People raved about the café? Even after Grandma Imelda left? I smiled a little on the inside.

I shrugged. "Okay, but I do know because I can see it when you're around Rory. Heck, you've even said as much."

"When did I say such a thing?" she huffed.

"Um, pretty much every time I've ever talked to you." Frustration crawled up my spine.

She shook her head. "Uh-huh, nope. You don't know what you're talking about. So much for the stalling, huh? Nice try. I know what this is about." She pointed at me. "You want Rory for yourself. I know the two of you went out. I know he kissed you and I can see the way you look at him. Now get dressed and let's go. Chop, chop."

"Where are we going?" I asked.

"I've heard the magic will work better if we do it outside. I don't want to take any chances of it not working, so we have to go." She moved a little closer. "And you can't go anywhere dressed like that. People will think you're homeless."

I rolled my eyes. My attire was hardly that hideous. The pink sweatpants were cute. "Okay, just let me put on some clothes." I slipped out of my sweats, shimmied into a pair of jeans, and pulled on a T-shirt.

"You know, Rory might be a little more interested in you if you bothered to dress up more." She examined a nail while I pulled my shirt on.

"I work in a kitchen, not really any reason to get dressed up." Who was she to tell me how to dress? Fake Barbie had no right. I had to wear skirts and heels enough when I worked the other job and I hadn't much cared for it then.

"Whatever. I'm just saying. Rory doesn't like that." She wiggled her finger in my direction. "He likes his women put together. Very polished, like me." She studied her reflection in the full-length mirror.

"Rory works on a farm. I think that's probably the opposite of what he likes."

"Oh, shut up and let's go."

I slipped on my tennis shoes. There had to be a way to stop her from carrying out this magic nonsense. I needed to get in touch with Tom, pronto. She tapped her foot as I stumbled from the chair and made my way to the bedroom door.

Kim followed on my heels as I moved into the hallway.

"Question for you," I said, traveling toward the front door. "What makes you think that this book isn't just some gag?"

"I watched you when you didn't know it. You really should pay attention to your surroundings more."

"So you were stalking me?"

"Stalking is a harsh word. I prefer to think of it as observing with great interest."

The more she talked, the crazier she sounded. How could Rory have loved someone as looney as her? Had she ever been sane? She had to have been sane once, right? She must have recently plunged off the deep end. We made our way over to Kim's shiny green car.

"Get in," she demanded.

"Are you kidnapping me? Because in case you didn't know it, that's illegal and generally frowned upon."

She chuckled. "You're funny, a real comedienne." She opened the car door. "We're just going for a ride, you do what I want you to, and you'll never be bothered by me again. Or Rory." She smirked. "We'll be out of your hair and on our way back to the city."

As soon as I got the chance, I'd call Tom. I'd slipped my cell phone into my pocket when she hadn't been looking. I climbed into the passenger seat and fastened my seat belt. I knew the first rule of evading kidnapping was never to get in the car with the perpetrator. Once they get you in their car it's as good as over, but I didn't think Kim would really hurt me, would she?

The worst that could happen was I'd do the magic and she'd go away with Rory. Not something I wanted but, like I said, that was the worst-case scenario. But I wasn't lying when I told her about the magic. I'd read the spell before the book had disappeared—out of pure curiosity, mind you—and you can't just be matched with anyone, it has to be someone you want and they have to want you too. Sure, I could do a spell that would work for a little while, but it wouldn't last. But if I was wrong and they truly wanted to be together, well, this would seal the deal. I wasn't sure I wanted to be the one who made that happen. If it happened on its own, there was nothing I could do about that, but I didn't want to be instrumental in helping their disturbing love affair along.

Chapter Thirty-Nine

Kim's car smelled like vanilla cookies and coffee, but it was spotless on the inside. Her cell phone rested on the dash on one of those sticky pad holders. A prism hung from the rearview mirror. She backed out and onto the highway.

Music blasted from the speakers. I yelled over Britney Spears singing about holding it against her or something. "Do you mind at least telling me where we're going? We could have done this magic in my backyard."

"You'll find out soon enough, don't you worry your pretty little head." She turned down the volume. "So, tell me all about your date with Rory," she said, as if we were best friends chatting about boys.

"There's nothing to tell. I don't consider it a date."

"You're just saying that so I won't be mad." She scowled.

"Somehow I don't think it would work that way, you'll be mad at me no matter what I say." I shifted in the seat.

"I won't, I promise." She steered around a curve.

"We went to the fair." I held onto the door handle. She really didn't know how to drive that car. "Don't you think you should slow down?"

"Yeah, don't tell me how to drive and I won't tell you how to cook, although you sure could stand some lessons."

I'd like to tell her what she could stand.

"Did he kiss you?" she asked.

No way was I being truthful with that one.

"No," I said.

"Liar. I know he did. I saw you two in your tongue tango." She shot a venom-laced glare at me. "Plus, Rory told me he kissed you, too."

"Rory told you he kissed me? Why would he do something like that?" My mouth hung open. She probably forced it out of him.

"Never mind. Once you work your little hocus pocus, I won't have to worry about him kissing anyone else, ever. He'll be mine for eternity." She sounded like she was about to tie him up and keep him in her closet as a pet, only allowing him food and water. Next, she'd hug him, squeeze him, and call him George.

We moved through Main Street, past the historic part of downtown, and Mystic Café. What I wouldn't do to be in there making pancakes instead of being trapped in a vehicle with this lunatic.

"So that's all you did? The county fair?"

"We went for a walk after and you came along with your broken-down car. That's it, and I can't tell you anything else, because nothing else happened."

This was getting old. I needed to change the subject before she really went berserk.

"So you want to move away, huh?" I asked.

"Yes, I can't stand small towns. I want to be where I can see the action. I like to go dancing, to the theater and I have a favorite martini bar right around the corner from my apartment. They make a delicious Appletini. My place is great too, sure it's a tad small, but Rory will love it."

"Uh-huh."

After we made it through town, we finally pulled into the local park. The same park where I'd shared that fantastic first kiss with Rory. If Kim had anything to do with it, I'd never get a chance to feel his lips pressed next to mine again.

"The park? You bring me to the public park to perform magic? I really don't feel comfortable doing this in public. Not to mention I could get in trouble for doing this in public. There's a magical organization that oversees this stuff, you know?" Okay, now I sounded like the nutty one.

"Do I look like I care if you get in trouble?" She shifted the car into park.

"No, I guess you don't."

Everything was all about her. She had the 'me, me, me' mentality down pat.

"Come on." She jumped out from the car and motioned for me to do the same.

I opened the door, but thoughts of driving off went through my mind after she got out. I wouldn't be able to slip over to the driver's seat fast enough though, so I'd have to devise another plan. The cell phone in my pocket was my only option. I patted my pants pocket to make sure it hadn't fallen out. It was still safely tucked away. I had to distract her long enough to make a call to Tom.

She reached through the rolled-down window and hoisted the book from the backseat. "This thing is heavy, why'd they make it so heavy?"

I shook my head. "I have no idea. It's not at the top of my list of questions at the moment." The item at the top of my list was simply how to get the book back.

"We'll go over to that picnic bench." She pointed.

"Fine." I followed her. The thought of running crossed my mind, but I wanted the book back, so that was out of the question. I wondered what the organization would do to Kim when they found out she had stolen the book. What kind of punishment does someone get for messing with magic?

She plopped the book down on the table. She didn't worry about damaging it. That was the least of her concerns.

"You've got a lot of nerve doing this, you know?"

A smile stretched tightly across her face. "I call it moxie."

"You can call a weed a flower, but it's still a weed."

She scowled and gave me a stern look.

"You didn't think of one thing, and this is going to throw a monkey wrench in your little love scheme...."

"Oh yeah?" She smirked. "What's that?"

"I don't have the spices. I can only perform magic while cooking. What do you want me to do out here? Roast a marshmallow? And remember, Rory has to eat the food."

"Do you think I'm that stupid?" She scoffed.

Did she really want me to answer that?

She brushed away my words with a flick of her wrist. "I thought of that. I'm not as dumb as I look."

She said it not me, but I had thought it.

"We're going to have a little picnic. When you're finished with the magic, you'll call Rory. He'll come and we'll have a picnic."

"You need me to call him because he won't come if you call." I smirked. She frowned.

"I'm right, aren't I?" I asked.

"No, of course he'd come. He loves me." She looked away.

"Apparently, he doesn't or you wouldn't need me right now."

"You think you're so smart. Why don't you shut your mouth and get on with the magic before I get really pissed and lay a beat down on you."

Hmm. She was probably all talk. I bet I could take her if I had to. But I needed to keep her calm until I had the book and the spices back in my possession. At any minute, she could go off and destroy the book. I'm guessing Tom, not to mention the higher-ups at the organization, would definitely frown upon that.

"Fine." I threw my hands up in disgust. "Where's the rest of the stuff?"

"It's in the trunk of my car."

"So why don't you go get it. I'll start getting ready."

"Oh no. I'm not leaving you here with the book. You'll take off as soon as I get my back turned."

Damn. She had me on that one. "I wouldn't do that to you. You can probably outrun me anyway. Your legs are a lot longer."

She looked down at her legs. "That's true," she said. "Regardless, I'm not letting you out of my sight for a second. You come with me. I need help carrying the stuff, anyway."

I trudged along beside her. Leaving the book back on the picnic table made me nervous. What if someone else came along and took it? Although, as I glanced around, it didn't appear that anyone was in sight. The swings were devoid of children, the basketball court empty of players and the tennis courts were deserted, too.

We reached her car and she clicked her key fob with a swift punch from her long finger, unlocking the trunk. Inside there was a wicker picnic basket, along with several other bags.

"You went all out for this, huh?"

"Grab that blanket and the other bag," she ordered.

I hated being bossed around by Miss Priss. I grabbed the red and white checkered blanket and the bag. She set her bags and basket down and closed the trunk before retrieving her items from the ground.

"Hurry up, we don't have all day."

If she didn't stop bossing me around soon, I was going to wring her neck. I fell into step beside her again.

"You do have very short legs," she said, glancing over at me. "It's hard to keep up with someone tall like me. It must suck being so short. How short are you?"

"I'm five-two. I hardly consider it an impairment." I rolled my eyes.

I let out a sigh of relief when we reached the park bench again and the book was still there. Kim placed the basket on the ground and reached for the tablecloth. "Here give me that."

I let go of the tablecloth and watched as she whipped it out in front of her, letting it cascade across the table, then smoothing it down with her hands. She grabbed the basket and placed it in the middle of the table. "What's in there?" I asked.

"I'm getting ready to show you, don't be so impatient."

"I'm just curious what I have to work with, that's all," I said.

She opened the lid and pulled out sandwiches with artisan bread, green grapes, various cheeses, chicken, and a bottle of wine. "There are glasses in the bag." She pointed to the canvas tote bag I still clutched in my hand. "I also put flatware and napkins in there." She pointed at another bag. "That one has all those spices you use for the spells."

The scent of the sandwiches, cheese, and fruit climbed upward, assaulting my nostrils and causing my stomach to churn. Normally, the food wouldn't have had this effect, but with the current situation, the aroma made me want to heave.

"Well, there isn't exactly a lot of cooking for me to do," I said.

"Don't make this any more difficult than it has to be, okay? All you need to do is sprinkle the magic on top of the food I've brought. He'll eat it just the same; what difference does it make?" She snorted.

A lot. You couldn't just throw slop at people and expect them to gobble it up. But I wouldn't tell her that. She didn't need to know. In order for the magic to work, I needed to prepare the food. That was part of the magical deal. If everything went as planned, I would cast the spell and Kim would think it had worked. And I'd be off the hook. I'd get the book and spices back, and Tom could handle Kim. Whatever punishment they handed down was none of my business as long as I got the café back. What would Rory think if he found out I was playing around with his life like this?

I prayed I wouldn't cast a spell that would leave Rory with this awful woman for the rest of his life. He was lucky he got away from her when he did. I placed the bag on the table and removed the contents, setting the napkins and forks next to the food. Kim grabbed the bag with the spices and began pulling them out, one by one. I was never so happy to see little bottles of spices in my whole life.

"Now, do you have everything you need?" She placed her hands on her hips, waiting for my response.

By the glare in her eyes, I knew my answer had better be 'yes.' "Uh-huh, everything looks hunky-dory."

"Good. Now get to work. I'm so excited, I'm ready to pee my pants."

Oh, goody gumdrops. My magic had not only gone awry, it had created a monster. A clingy, looking-for-love-in-all-the-wrong-places monster.

Chapter Forty

"Don't do that, please. Peeing in your pants isn't allowed. Mind if I have a seat?" I asked.

She waved her hands. "Yes, yes, whatever. Just do the magic."

"Now who's being an impatient little thing?"

She stuck her hands on her hips and frowned.

I took a couple deep steadying breaths. "Okay, here goes."

"Rory will be mine forever." She giggled.

She was scaring me. Kim had taken this too far. She was acting like the Wicked Witch of the West. Next thing I knew, her skin would turn green. I climbed over the bench and sat at the little wooden picnic table. Avoiding Kim's stare, I lugged the book over beside me. The familiar spicy scent tickled my nose as I opened the cover. My fingers fidgeted as I looked up the spell in the index, then turned to the correct page. I'd put on a good show for Kim. My face felt flush as I scanned the page, then I grabbed the spices listed.

"I think I'll use the sandwich, okay?"

She nodded and waved her hand. "Whatever."

"But don't forget which sandwich is his. I'd hate for you to get them mixed up. He may fall in love with me or, worse yet, you may eat it and fall in love with me." I snickered.

How she trusted me not to perform a bad spell on her, I had no idea. The thought had probably never occurred to her that anyone would have the audacity to do something bad to her.

"As if." She snorted. "Don't worry. I have everything under control. I think I can manage to give him the correct sandwich. Unlike some people I know." She rolled her eyes.

I gaped at her. She knew. Somehow, she knew about the magic spell and had never said a word until now. How long had she known?

"How do you know that?" I snapped.

"I overheard. I was stalking you, remember?" She smirked.

I stared for a beat, then returned my focus to the magic that wouldn't work. I wondered if I could get in trouble for practicing magic that I knew wouldn't work? Oh well, I was willing to take that chance. I mean, could it get any worse than it already was? I sprinkled the rosemary on top, then the oregano.

"May Rory Covington set eyes on his true love and never doubt his feelings again. So mote it be." I placed the bread back on top of the sandwich and onto the plate. "There, all done."

"That's it?" She frowned. "Are you sure it's done? Aren't there supposed to be sparks? I saw sparks when you did the magic before."

"Oh no, there aren't always sparks, just sometimes. This particular spell doesn't have sparks." I tapped the page for emphasis.

She raised a brow and I wondered if my acting skills were good enough for her to fall for my little fib.

"Okay, but if this doesn't work, you'll be sorry."

I forced a smile, but it was stretched so tightly across my face, my cheeks ached. "I'm sure I will," I muttered through gritted teeth.

"Now we have to call Rory." She clapped her hands, not noticing my forced enthusiasm.

"*We* have to call him?" My eyebrows rose.

She shrugged. "Okay, you have to call Rory. Tell him to meet you in the park for a picnic."

"Yeah, but don't mention that you're here, right?" I smirked.

"Just do it." She scowled and shoved the phone toward me.

"Won't he recognize your cell phone number?"

She grunted and grabbed the phone back from me, punching a few keys. "Here." She shoved it back at me. "He won't recognize it now."

I held the phone to my ear and listened as it rang. My stomach turned with each beep, waiting for him to answer. I was about to hang up when his sexy southern drawl came through the other end. His voice made my legs quiver. Never had I imagined a voice was capable of causing such a reaction in me. I hoped Kim couldn't read the expression of lust on my face.

"Hi, Rory," I said.

"I didn't know it was you. The phone didn't show your number."

Did he have my number memorized? Did he know whom he was talking to? Maybe he thought it was Kim?

My voice lowered. "It's Elly Blair."

Kim frowned and gave me a look as if she wanted to stab my eyes out with her nail file. I knew I'd better give my name or she'd throw a hissy fit if Rory really had recognized my voice.

"I know who you are." He chuckled. "I'd recognize your sweet voice anywhere."

I shifted on the bench. "Um, I wondered if you weren't busy if you'd like to come over to the park for a little breakfast picnic?"

I knew this sounded really weird. He'd think I'd lost my mind for sure.

Kim tapped the table with her finger.

He paused, his soft breathing drifting through the line. I pictured what it would be like to feel his breath on my neck.

"Sure, I can do that, but is everything okay? You don't sound good. Is something bothering you?"

Not something bothering me, but someone. I couldn't answer him. What could I say? Your nutty girlfriend has kidnapped me, forcing me to perform magic so you'll love her? Kim frowned and poked me in the side.

"Great. So I'll see you soon?"

He paused again. "Um, sure, I'll be there in a few minutes. It'll just take me a few seconds to finish up what I was doing and get over there. What are we having, by the way?"

I looked at Kim as she stood guard over me, then at the table.

"Sandwiches, fruit, and that sort of thing." Why had she picked these foods for morning? Not much of a meal planner, was she?

"Sounds delicious, you know I love your cooking."

Kim's face grew redder by the minute. She was pissed.

Even with Kim hovering over me with a death glare, his words still make me giddy. I held back my massive smile. "Okay, see you soon."

Rory had to know I was acting weird. Maybe he just assumed I was weird. After all, we hadn't met under the best circumstances. I shut the phone and handed it back to her.

"He's on his way, are you happy now?"

"Delighted." She pulled out a mirror and began layering gloss on her lips.

"I can't believe you want to deceive someone you claim to care so much about."

"It's not deceiving. And I didn't ask for your opinion anyway. So why don't you shut your pie trap and help me lay out the food so it looks nice. And don't you dare pretend you made this food when he gets here."

I looked down at the stale, sad sandwich, its contents oozing over the sides. "Don't worry, I won't."

"My cooking is way better than yours," she scoffed.

Talking to Mary Jane's three-year-old niece was easier than this. Mine is better than yours. Something must have snapped in her weird world to make her this crazy. Wonder if it had anything to do with my magic or if she'd always been this looney. I stood beside her and placed three plates around the table.

"Oh, and just so you know, he's sitting beside me."

I saluted. "Yes, ma'am."

"Now you're mocking me."

"I am doing no such thing. Just following my orders, that's all."

This woman needed to be arrested. Maybe a night behind bars would do her good. They'd confiscate her Louis Vuitton purse and Juicy Couture clothing. She'd be forced to wear that awful orange jumpsuit; it would serve her right. Kim placed a sandwich on each plate, cussing when mayonnaise got all over her hands. I hoped she didn't expect me to eat any of that stuff she called food. The bread was probably moldy. And no telling what the actual inside contents were. Could be chicken, could be tuna, could be...I didn't want to find out.

I shouldn't judge. Maybe it tasted okay and just didn't look appetizing. She placed the container of fruit in the middle of the table.

"Here, open this bottle of wine." She shoved the bottle at me. "I don't want to break a nail."

"Of course not. We couldn't have that now, could we?"

If looks could kill, I'd have been lying on the ground, gasping for breath. I needed to bite my tongue and try to be nice—for Grandma Imelda and Mystic Café. I'd get more with honey than vinegar. When the book was back in my hands, I wouldn't spare her feelings. I wanted to save the café more than anything. Was it too much to ask for me to get Rory, too? If I righted the wrong, maybe the organization would reconsider and let me reopen the café.

She placed the glasses around the table.

"Do you always have wine for breakfast?"

She smirked. "It's romantic, so mind your own business."

"Don't you think it's odd for me to be here? Why don't I leave and let the two of you have a romantic meal? I'll just take the book and spices and skedaddle." I gestured over my shoulder. "You don't even need to drive me, I can walk. The exercise will do me some good."

"Are you insane?" she asked, as I moved closer to the book.

Kim grabbed me by the arm. Her grip was tight and I yelped.

"Let go of my arm." I was ready to punch her lights out. What little lights she had, that is.

Chapter Forty-One

Kim released my arm. "You can't go. I need you to stay until I'm sure the spell works, then you can take your stupid book and get lost."

"How is the book stupid if it gives you what you want?"

After what seemed like an eternity, the sound of a vehicle took my attention away from the bizarre scene in front of me. I glanced over my shoulder to see Rory's truck pull up behind Kim's little car. I was surprised he didn't turn around and leave right then and there. Would he run when he spotted Kim? Heck, he might run when he saw what I looked like in the morning without a hairbrush run through my hair.

He parked and climbed out.

"Okay, zip your mouth and just leave the talking to me now."

"If you say so, it's your funeral." I couldn't resist adding that part.

She scowled and sent a venom-laced glare my way.

"What's going on here?" Rory asked as he approached. He wore jeans and a pullover shirt. His hair was a touch wet. Had he taken a shower? Was that what he needed to do before coming over here? My heart thumped and butterflies flittered in my stomach at the thought of Rory wet and in the shower. He looked gorgeous, as usual.

"Hi, sweetheart." She rushed to his side. "I'm so glad you made it."

He frowned, not responding to her term of endearment.

"I thought we'd have a little picnic. I brought a lot of fabulous food. Won't you join us? We need to all get to know each other."

He looked at me. "Why didn't you say Kim was with you?"

I gave him a sideways grin, but I avoided his gaze. Guilt consumed me. Words failed me; it didn't happen often, but I didn't know what to say. My mouth seemed glued shut. I felt the heat move from my cheeks, spreading to my chest.

Kim answered for me, looping her arm around his. "Don't worry about that. She's forgetful. Come on." She led him to the table. "Have a seat."

He hesitated, then finally sat. Kim eased down onto the bench and slipped over close to him. He looked about as uncomfortable as a guy could look. Worse than a guy who'd been caught crying while watching *The Notebook*.

I wanted to run and hide under the picnic table or go back to bed and not come out for a week. This was the most awkward situation I'd ever been in. And I've been in some awkward situations before. Like the time when I was sixteen and got caught outside in nothing but my underwear just as the cute boy next door came outside his house. But this was far worse.

"What is it you want to talk about, Kim?" Rory asked.

"Here, eat some of your sandwich. I made it." She pushed the food toward him.

He looked down at the sandwich and back at her with a frown. "But you don't cook."

"Silly, sure I do." She waved off his comment. "I don't get the chance to do it a lot, that's all." Kim gave Rory a wistful look, which he didn't seem to notice.

Rory picked up the sandwich and brought it to his mouth, as if in slow motion. He took a bite and chewed with a scowl on his face the entire time. Now I knew for sure I wouldn't eat this so-called sandwich. If a guy couldn't eat it, then I knew I couldn't; guys could eat anything. I picked up a couple of the grapes and popped one in my mouth.

"Here, have some wine." Kim poured the red liquid into Rory's glass, then set the bottle back. She didn't offer me any. The one thing I could really use at that moment, too. I grabbed the bottle and poured until my glass was full, then took a big gulp.

"This is nice and all, but I want to know what's going on."

Kim frowned at me and mouthed, "Where are the sparks?"

I shrugged my shoulders. "I need to use the ladies' room, do you mind?" If Kim said no, Rory would be suspicious. If she offered to go with me, Rory may leave. She had no choice but to let me go. I'd slip into the public restroom and call Tom. He'd come and get the book and, with any luck, bring the police.

I climbed up from the bench.

"I'll go with you," Kim said, as I made my way across the park. She fell into step beside me.

"Rory will probably leave if you go to the bathroom with me. Is that what you want?"

"Crap." She spun around and traipsed back across the park.

When she was back with Rory, I slipped into the bathroom, looking around to see if I was alone in the dark space. I pulled the cell phone from my pocket, the light from the screen illuminating just how dirty the space was, and scanned through the previous numbers until I came to Tom's. Without wasting another minute, I hit send.

After two rings, he answered. "What's going on?" he asked.

"Kim has kidnapped me." The alarm was evident in my voice.

"What?" His voice rose. "What are you talking about?"

"She has the book and the spices. She forced me to come to the park with her. I can't believe it, either. She broke into my place and was standing at the foot of my bed when I woke up."

"Well, that's slightly creepy. Okay, I'll be right there."

"Do you know how to get here?" I asked.

"It's a small town. I know how to get everywhere. It's kind of hard to get lost."

"Are you bringing the police?" I tried to slow my heavy breathing.

"Don't worry. I'll take care of everything."

I had no idea what that meant, but I guessed I'd find out soon enough. I clicked off the call and stuffed the phone back into my pocket. I hoped Rory hadn't left. I wanted to explain everything to him. Whether or not he'd listen was an entirely different story. I wanted him to know I hadn't done any of this on purpose. I hoped he wouldn't hate me for putting him in this situation, but I'd had no choice. When push came to shove, I did what I thought was best, and that was all I could do.

After checking my disheveled appearance in the mirror and attempting to tame my hair with my hands, I reemerged from the bathroom, almost afraid of what I'd see. Kim would probably come looking for me soon if I didn't get back over there. Besides, I didn't want to leave Rory out there to fend for himself any longer than he had to.

When I looked over to the table, to my surprise, Rory was still there. Kim was trying to force a grape into his mouth. I needed another gulp of that wine. The sun shone down from a blue cloudless sky, covering the area in yellow shafts of light. Birds chirped as they danced along the edge of the birdbath. The temperature hadn't become unbearable yet. The scent of the honeysuckle bush beside the pathway wafted through the air and tickled my nose. Too bad this gorgeous day had turned into something so bizarre.

I hurried across the park. "I'm back, sorry it took so long."

Rory stood. "Oh, I thought maybe you'd left."

I couldn't leave him there with her.

I glanced at Kim and she mouthed, "It's not working."

If I could stall her for a little while longer, Tom would make it and get us the heck out of there.

"Um, how do you like the wine, Rory?" I asked. "Sometimes it has a taste that doesn't kick in for a while." I wiggled my eyebrows at Kim and she seemed to take my hint. Whether or not she bought my little fib, I didn't know.

"I like it," Rory said, shifting on the bench, trying to move further away from Kim.

She already had him almost falling off the edge and there was nowhere else for him to go.

"Do you mind telling me what all this is really about? I may be a small-town hick, but I'm not really all that dumb."

"Oh, no, I don't think you're dumb," I said.

"Of course not, Rory," Kim added.

"Tell me the truth." He stared at me with his gorgeous eyes and I couldn't lie any more.

Chapter Forty-Two

Whatever the consequences, I knew I had to tell the truth. The café might be gone, but to lose the book, the spices, and Rory, was too much. At least Rory wouldn't forever think of me as a liar. Somehow, I'd make it up to Grandma Imelda. Maybe we could start a new café, minus the magic.

I took a deep breath and steadied myself for what I was about to say. Kim's expression let me know she knew what I was about to do. She read me like a book. She shook her head, her hoop earrings whipped from side to side.

"Rory, I have to tell you the truth and you're going to hate me for this." I rushed the words. "On the first day we met, I accidentally performed magic on you."

"You what? Come again?" He quirked a brow.

"I have special magic skills and the magic was on your food. You got someone else's order and that's why I rushed over and knocked the burger out of your hands."

He frowned and his eyes widened. "Magic?" he asked.

I nodded.

"See, Rory, I told you she was nuts," Kim said. "Come on, let's get out of here before she goes completely insane."

"I'm not insane and she was in on it, too." I pointed at Kim. Okay, now I sounded like a tattling five-year-old.

"She's crazy, don't listen to her." She tightened her lips, pressing them into a straight line.

"Why do you think we're both here? She made me call you. Otherwise, you wouldn't have shown up. She stole the book of magical spells from the café and my special spices, too. She wanted me to perform magic on you today in the food."

Rory looked down, not meeting my gaze.

I continued; I couldn't stop now. "She wanted her true love to want her forever. But what she fails to realize is that you're not her true love. So even if you really loved her, the magic wouldn't work because she doesn't love you. She only thinks she loves you."

"Would you listen to this rambling idiot? She's completely delusional. All this nonsense about magical spell books and spices." She grabbed Rory's arm. "She tricked me into coming out here just like she tricked you. She said she had something she wanted to tell us. I had no idea it was this crazy talk."

Rory broke free from Kim's grip and gazed at me with a heartbroken look in his eyes. There was no way for me to know if what I'd done had been the right thing, and I was second-guessing my decision right now. But I'd told him and the world didn't end. Sure, he'd probably never speak to me again, but that was something I'd have to deal with.

Without saying a word, Rory turned and hurried to his truck. Kim took off after him, stumbling in the grass to keep up with his pace. I couldn't let her leave without Tom showing up. Although as long as she left the book and spices, I'd be somewhat happy about that. If only I'd locked the book away, maybe none of this mess would have ever happened. But how was I supposed to know Kim would take it, it just looked like a weird old cookbook.

I spotted Kim's car keys on the park bench and I grabbed them, shoving them in my pocket. Where the heck was Tom? Any other time he would have been here when I didn't want him around. Rory climbed in his truck, the whole time Kim pleaded with him not to go. This was very awkward and embarrassing for all of us. And she called me the insane one. Hello, stalker. This looked like it would require a restraining order. She teetered between the clingy girlfriend and I-can't-live-without-you girlfriend line.

Rory finally managed to get Kim away from his truck. He drove off without as much as a glance back. He didn't look back at me and I didn't blame him. What I'd told him didn't make any sense. It hadn't made sense to me at first either, and I couldn't expect him to understand, but I at least wanted the opportunity to try to explain. I had a feeling I may never see him again. The knots in my stomach became even more tangled.

"You," Kim yelled as she made a dash for me.

Uh-oh. The venom in her eyes caught me off guard. It was going to be an all out catfight. Too bad I hadn't worn my hair in a ponytail; it would have been a much better style for being attacked. Kim looked like a hair puller. She was skinny, but she looked like the type who made regular visits to the gym. She was probably into yoga and would wrangle me into some kind of headlock. One thing she probably didn't count on though: I was short, which meant less of me to grab. I could slither out of almost any hold like a greasy piglet.

"This is entirely your fault," she screeched. "You messed up the magic on purpose."

"Why should I do anything for you?" I asked. "I don't owe you anything, I don't even like you. You've done nothing but insult me and be rude to everyone you've come in contact with in this town. Everyone cringes when they see you coming."

"They do not," she huffed. "I'm going to rip your hair out."

See, I knew she was a hair puller. She grabbed my arms and we both fell to the ground at the same time. I landed on my back and Kim was on top of me. She slapped me. I reached up and shoved her with both hands. She fell back and landed on the ground. I scrambled, trying to get to my feet. The sound of a car caught my attention, then I heard the sirens. Thank goodness. I was about to sucker punch this floozy.

A couple of police cars pulled up with lights flashing and sirens blaring. Two uniformed men climbed out and rushed toward us. As they approached, Tom's car drove up behind the police cars. Kim glared at me as I struggled to release her grip from my hair. She didn't let a little thing like law enforcement stop her.

"So you called the police? I should have known." She tugged my hair harder.

"Yes, you should have known. I mean really, what did you think I would do?" I panted, struggling to catch my breath. "Let you get away with this?"

"I didn't do anything to you, you stupid little bitch."

I managed to roll her over so that I was now on top. "Whatever."

"What seems to be the problem?" We remained on the ground, neither one wanting to let go first. "Can you both stand up, please?" I stumbled up, trying to keep my distance from Kim in case she started her antics again.

"She kidnapped me." I pointed.

"I did no such thing. She's crazy." She smoothed her hair down.

"Ma'am, can you put your hands behind your back, please?"

"So you're just going to believe her? Obviously, she could leave whenever she wanted, that's not kidnapping. And she was attacking me."

"That's not what we saw when we pulled up. You were on top of her."

"She stole belongings from my café and broke the window."

"We have a witness who saw her do that, ma'am."

"You do?" My eyes widened.

He nodded. "We'll sort this all out at the police station, if you'll come to make a statement?"

I nodded, still trying to catch my breath.

"You bitch. I can't believe you're doing this." She jerked her arms, trying to free herself from the policeman's grip.

Tom walked up as the police led Kim toward their vehicle.

"Whether you realize it or not, Kim, doing this is the best thing that could have happened to you." He stood in front of me, his arms folded across his chest.

I scowled, still trying to catch my breath. "What? How is that possible?"

"I felt the spell weakening when I got here. She finally realized her true feelings and Rory left, so I think that shows his true feelings, too."

"Will it matter? The café is already closed."

"I'll make some calls. But I think I can get the doors open again soon." His mouth tilted up in a grin.

"So the spell will be reversed and I can keep the café?"

"Kim's part of the spell is gone. So if you fix the other, then yes, you can keep Mystic Café open."

I leapt forward and draped my arms around his neck. "I'm so excited."

"Don't be afraid to give me a thank you kiss," he said, raising his lips into a sly grin.

I poked him in the ribs. "Stop it."

"Where's the book?" He looked around.

"It's over by the picnic table and the spices are there, too."

"I'll get them." Tom gestured for me to wait for him. I needed a moment to catch my breath anyway, so I didn't argue.

I brushed off my clothes and smoothed down my frazzled hair. I hadn't been in a fight since eighth grade when Monica Malone accused me of stealing her lip-gloss. She later found it at the bottom of her locker.

An officer approached while the other one talked to Kim. She'd been glaring at me from the back of the police car. "Are you all right, ma'am? Do you need medical assistance?"

"No, I'm fine. She doesn't have a very strong arm."

He smiled. "All right. Do you need a ride to the station?"

I pointed toward Tom. "No, I have one, thank you."

Tom walked back with the book in hand. "You two were fighting? And I missed that? Damn."

I scowled and smacked him on the shoulder.

"What? I'm just saying, it would have been nice to see two gorgeous women rolling around...oh, never mind."

"Yeah, never mind."

"Why don't we get out of here?"

"Good idea." I brushed grass from my hair. "Who saw Kim break the window?"

"Let's just say I got a magical statement from Mimi Adams."

"But I talked to her. She didn't know anything."

He shrugged. "She remembered somehow, what can I say?"

"That doesn't seem fair." I shook my head.

"She's not lying. I just helped her remember the details, that's all." He winked and slipped his arm around my shoulders. "Come on, let's get out of here."

We hurried across the park toward Tom's car. I wondered what Rory would think when he found out Kim was in jail. And that it was my fault. Would he be mad at me? Would he ever speak to me again? But after what I'd told him about the magic, it was the least of my worries.

"I've got the keys to her car. What should I do with them?" I asked.

"Hand them to me, I'll take care of it." He held out his hand.

"I'm almost afraid to let you take care of anything. I think you like to use the magic a little too much." I smirked.

"Only when necessary." He grinned.

I eyed him as he wiggled his fingers. "Okay, but make sure she gets them."

"I will, don't worry."

Tom held the car door open for me and I placed the keys in his outstretched palm. "Thanks, doll."

I climbed in Tom's sleek black BMW. The inside still had the new smell, mixed with his masculine scent. The interior was clean just like the exterior. On the car's console, he had a photo of people I assumed were his parents. They smiled for the camera, arms around one another.

As Tom came around to the driver's seat, I checked my reflection in the side mirror. I cringed, wishing I hadn't looked. My hair really needed to meet with a hairbrush. Pulling out of the parking lot, we took off toward the police station.

"Did you know that Kim knew about the mistake with the love spell?" I shifted in the leather seat.

Tom glanced over at me before looking back at the road. "No, what did she say?"

"She told me that she knew. She said she'd overheard me talking about it. I swear she must have bugged the café."

"Was she mad about it?"

"No, she didn't seem upset. I think she was coming back for Rory regardless of whether the spell had been cast or not."

"So, what happened to Rory?" Tom asked.

I had a feeling Tom was thankful that Rory wasn't there when he showed up.

"He left when I told him about the magic." I buckled my seat belt. The new car smell hung in the air. Van Halen played on the radio.

"You told him?" He gripped the wheel, not taking his eyes off the road.

I nodded. "Yeah. It didn't turn out well."

"I'm sorry," he said softly.

As we headed back toward town, I asked, "So you called the police? That's it?"

He glanced over at me.

"I could have done that."

"So why didn't you?" He smirked.

"I assumed there was some kind of special magic police. Or magical court, if you will? I mean, what do you do with the magical crimes?" I asked.

"There aren't a lot of magical crimes. There aren't as many people with magical powers as you think."

So I was one of the lucky few. Great.

Chapter Forty-Three

"We do a good job of keeping it under control. Of course, Kim will need to meet with the organization. She knows about magic now and we have to keep that under control."

He steered around a curve.

"What do you mean 'keep that under control'?"

"I mean we can't allow her to tell everyone about the magic. Right now she's probably telling the police all about your magical skills, which will probably get her a stay in the special cell away from everyone else. They'll think she's crazy."

"Well..." I laughed. But my laugh was cut short as I realized Rory would think the same thing about me. "What'll happen to Rory? Since I told him about the magic?"

"He'll have to meet with the organization, too. But it's up to you, really." Up to me? How had I become a mediator for the magic realm?

"Do you think he can handle knowing about it?" I asked.

"I think he can handle it, but I don't think he'll believe it until he sees proof positive." Tom looked over at me.

"What?" I asked.

He raised a brow.

"You mean I need to do magic in front of him?" This wasn't a task that was exactly easy to approach someone with. It was something that would possibly get me a visit on a sofa with a psychiatrist.

"It's the only way he'll believe you."

"I doubt he'll come anywhere near me now. I can't force him to watch my little magic show."

"You'd be surprised how well some people accept it." His mouth may not have shown his smile, but his eyes did.

Why was he being so understanding of Rory now?

"I guess I'll have to call him." I took a deep breath, then blew it out slowly. "Why does this have to be so difficult?"

"Maybe you need to just pay him a visit?" He gave a knowing wink.

I nodded. "I guess you're right. He might not answer my calls. It wouldn't surprise me if he never talked to me again. If I see him in person, he'll have to talk to me. So what happens with the café now?"

"Well, I don't see any reason why I shouldn't give you the keys back. Once you've completed the reversal spell on Rory, you can reopen for business."

"Oh yeah, I forgot about the reversal part." How could I have forgotten about that?

If that part of the spell was gone, then all the women in town would leave him alone. Well, not all the women, he was still a gorgeous man, at least most of the women would leave him alone now. But would I be one of them? Maybe I really was only attracted to him because of the magic.

"You know," he said, "after you do the spell, I'll be on my way. I'll be out of your hair."

A twinge pulled at my heart. "Where you headed next?"

"Wherever they send me. Who knows?" He shrugged. "Could be Boise, Idaho, could be New York City. I hope it's somewhere with food as good as yours."

My mouth released a grin.

"I'll be honest with you. I don't think I've ever had food as tasty as yours."

I found myself staring as he moved his tongue across his bottom lip, then on to the top. Avoiding his gaze, I looked down.

"Oh, you're just saying that. Stop it." I blushed.

"No, I mean it. And the pies...I'm going to miss the pies."

"You'll stop back in from time to time?" I couldn't believe I'd just asked him that.

"Sure, but make sure it's not because I've been asked by the organization to come by."

I chuckled. "I'll try my best not to let any of the food get messed up anymore."

"I knew you'd make it through this." A twitch of his lips turned into a full-on smile.

"You did?" My mouth probably hung open. "Tom Owenton had confidence in me? I'm shocked."

"You're a smart woman, Elly. You're also a little clumsy, but smart." He flashed a wicked grin.

"Thank you for the compliment, but I haven't finished the spell yet."

"It's all just a formality at this point."

"I could still mess it up, trust me."

We pulled up in front of the police station and I wanted to keep driving. I wanted all of this craziness to be over. Confronting Kim was something I didn't want to do. Her actions were self-centered, but I felt sorry for her, too. She had no idea what she really wanted, and I knew that feeling. I'd never known what I really wanted...until now. Moving away from Mystic Hollow had seemed like a glamorous thing, but now that I was back, I never wanted to leave.

"Shall we?" Tom gestured with a tilt of his head toward the building.

"If we must." I swallowed the lump in my throat. "Do we have to?"

Tom nodded. "Yes, we do."

We marched up the steps to the main entrance. Tom walked close beside me, as if he would reach out and grab me if I tried to make a run for it.

"She's in the interview room," Sheriff Jasper said when we entered the building. "Do you want to press charges?"

I stepped over to the room and looked through the window at Kim. She didn't notice me as she wiped at her tearstained cheeks. Her frazzled hair swept back from her face gave her the appearance of a vulnerable child. I knew I couldn't allow her to wear that orange jumpsuit. She'd done nothing more than the equivalent of a high school prank. Heck, she acted as if she were still in high school.

"No, I don't want to press charges."

"Are you sure?" Tom placed his hand on my arm.

I nodded.

"She wanted to talk with you, if that's okay?" Sheriff Jasper asked.
I hesitated. "Okay, I'll talk with her."
I stepped over to the room and the sheriff opened the door. When Kim saw me, she sprang from her chair. "Oh, Elly, I'm so sorry. I didn't mean to do any harm to you. I wouldn't hurt a fly."
"It's all right. We'll forget it, okay?" It had been a long day already and it had barely begun. I didn't have the energy to argue anymore. "I'm not pressing charges, if that's what you're worried about." What could I say, I was a softie.
"Well, I was worried, but thank you."
"What are you going to do now?" I leaned against the door.
"I'm going back to New York." She picked at her fingernail, looking down. "You know, I'd been thinking of coming back for Rory for a long time, then a couple days ago the desire became so strong, I had to. But that desire's gone now. I know it's over with Rory, and I'm okay with that. I never wanted to be alone, but I realize now that I'll be fine."
I nodded. "I wish you the best of luck, Kim."
"Thank you, Elly. Same to you." She still didn't know I was the reason she came back in the first place. But after what she'd told me, I wondered if the spell had even mattered. She'd have come back anyway.
After an hour, we were back out in front of the building. Even though I'd declined to press charges for the kidnapping and burglary, I knew she'd have to deal with the organization. And that probably wouldn't be easy for her. Plus, the organization would take care of the situation enough without me adding to it. Kim never meant me any harm. While inside the jail, she'd paid me for the broken window and extra for the mess she'd caused. As far as I was concerned, I never wanted to see Kim again—too many bad memories. Now that left one thing that needed to be completed.
"Shall I drop you off at home?" Tom walked beside me, our strides synchronized.
I nodded. "Yes, I need to get prepared to pay a certain guy a visit."
"He's a lucky man," Tom said, brushing a strand of hair away from my cheek.
He tilted down and pressed his lips against mine. They were soft and warm. It was nice, but a vision of Rory flashed through my mind. He leaned up from the kiss, shifting his gaze away from mine.
Tom's actions had caught me off guard and I didn't know how to react. Did I want Tom to kiss me? He was handsome, had an unassuming sensual quality and a slight cockiness, not to mention he was a part of my new magical world, but was that enough to give up on spending more time with Rory? Plus, it wouldn't be fair to Tom if my feelings weren't the same as his.
"I'm sorry if I was abrupt with you when I first came to the café. It's not every day they send me to a case with someone as beautiful as you."
My cheeks heated. "Thank you," I said softly. "You weren't that abrupt...well, just a bit. I was a little overwhelmed."

"I wanted to help you, but there's not a lot I can do in these situations. My hands were tied."

He handed me the keys to the café.

"Thank you." I wiped a tear from the edge of my eye.

"Hey, none of those tears, okay?"

I nodded.

"Let's get you home." He placed a hand on the small of my back and guided me toward his car.

Chapter Forty-Four

A short time later, I set out for Rory's place. My thoughts jumped between wondering if Rory would acknowledge the magic, or if he'd warn me never to come near him again. It was asking a lot to expect someone to understand.

Horse farms with miles of black pasture fencing spread out from each side of the road. Occasionally, moss-covered stone fences flanked the narrow country path. Long sweeping driveways sporadically popped up along the way and I barely saw the houses at the end. Horses grazed in the lush fields. I relished the ride along the curvy stretch of highway, soaking in the beautiful summer scenery. But the knot remained, the uncertainty of what Rory would say gnawed at me.

I pulled up to the long dirt road where Rory's cabin sat at the end. I'd gotten his address from Sheriff Jasper. My car bounced along the long gravel driveway. A cloud of dust twirled behind in my wake. The radio played faintly in the background and I flipped it off out of nervousness. My nerves fidgety, I tapped my fingers against the steering wheel as I navigated the path.

On my right, pine trees lined the path, blocking part of my view of the rolling pasture just beyond—only giving a glimpse every so often. Rory's house looked like a cozy place in the middle of rolling acres, shadowed by the expanse of trees. The tranquility of the country setting swept over me, easing my stress somewhat, but I still had no idea how Rory would react to seeing me again. His world was isolated, off the beaten path away from civilization.

I pulled up in front of Rory's cabin. My heart thumped. What would he say? Would he speak to me? The questions whirred through my head. I hesitated for a moment, then forced myself out of the car. Birds chirped as they played tic-tac-toe along the power lines and tree branches ruffled, but the air was peaceful in spite of the slight breeze. I took my time walking up onto the wooden porch. It creaked under my feet.

Hesitating with my fist in midair, I finally knocked on the door. The dog barked and I knew there was no turning back now. He knew someone was outside.

When Rory answered, I almost lost my breath. He only wore jeans. His bare chest glistened with beads of water and his hair was wet. He blocked his dog from stomping out the door after me.

"Did I catch you at a bad time?" I asked, trying not to stare at his chest.

"I just got out of the shower."

"I'm sorry. Should I come back?" I shouldn't have asked. This was the perfect opportunity for him to say no.

"It's okay. Do you want to come inside?"

"Thanks." I moved past him and through the door. He smelled of soap and spicy aftershave. I wanted to wrap my arms around him and pull him close. Feel his hard wet chest pressed next to me.

"Hi there, big guy." I rubbed the top of his dog's head as the golden retriever sniffed my arm. "What's his name?"

"Beau. I've got to warn you, he loves women."

I chuckled. "Well, I love him already." Beau sat and stretched his right paw out toward me. "Oh, he knows tricks. What a little charmer."

"I'm not sure I'd call them tricks, but he knows how to work a room." The little lines at the corners of his eyes appeared as he smiled. So far, so good.

I continued rubbing Beau's head, but focused my attention on Rory. "I wanted to talk to you about what happened." I'd get straight to the point. No beating around the bush. "I didn't ask you to come to the park on false pretenses on purpose. Kim was acting crazy and I didn't know what else to do."

"Please sit down." He gestured toward a spot on the dark brown leather sofa. "I'll let Beau outside while we talk, I've got a fenced-in area for him back there."

I nodded. As I waited for Rory, I perched myself on the edge of the sofa. I glanced around the room. His cabin was sparsely decorated, but it had all the essentials and appeared clean and neat. When he returned, he sat on the corner of the table in front of me. My heart beat a little faster at his nearness.

"I guess you want to know what all the talk of magic was about. Do you think I'm crazy?"

He let out a deep breath and ran a hand through his hair.

When I thought I couldn't wait a second longer for his answer, he said, "I don't think you're crazy."

I wanted to jump for joy.

"I figured Kim worked her charm on you and convinced you to say those things, or you practice witchcraft? My mom's best friend was into that, so I saw a little of what she did when I was younger."

"Well, it's not exactly witchcraft. Or, maybe it is. Heck, I don't know what I'm saying. Like I said, Kim was acting crazy."

Rory touched my hand. "I know how she can be, believe me. I dealt with her antics for far too long. Elly, I'm sorry. I was angry. I don't want to be with Kim. My relationship with her was over a long time ago. Then I saw her trying to manipulate you, and I just had to get out of there."

"I understand why you left."

"So if it isn't witchcraft, then what is it?"

"Heck, I don't know what it is. All I know is my life was normal, fine, nothing out of the ordinary, then I took over my grandmother's café and now there's nothing but chaos in my life. Some of it's bad chaos and some of it's good. You're the good." I looked down at his hand covering mine.

He squeezed my hand. I looked up and stared into his eyes.

"My grandmother did the magic to help the customers. I don't know why or how it all started. She has these spices and book of magical spells. Kim stole the book when she busted out the window of Mystic Café. Anyway, Tom Owenton isn't there to help me with accounting." I let out a deep breath, thankful to get that much off my shoulders and out into the open. No more secrets.

"He wasn't?" A crease formed between his eyebrows.

"No, he was there because I messed up the magic spell. There's an organization that keeps track of magic performed and stops anyone from doing any further damage after something goes wrong. I did damage when you got the wrong spell."

His expression was one of shock and disbelief. "So you did magic for me? To help me get my ex-girlfriend back?"

"No. I mean, yes, that's what happened, but the magic spell wasn't meant for you. It was meant for another customer, and...you accidentally got their order." I took a deep breath. "Mary Jane was talking and she set the wrong plate down."

"So it wasn't your fault?"

"Not technically, but I should have watched more carefully. Magic isn't something to mess around with. Look what happened. I almost ruined your life."

"But you didn't ruin my life."

I grinned, fighting back tears. I'd kept my feelings in for so long, my emotional dam was about to come crumbling down.

"What happened then?" He patted my hand.

"Like I said, that's why I knocked the food out of your hand. And that's why all the women were following you around. I wanted to make the other customer's girlfriend a little jealous. It backfired on me. Not that women wouldn't follow you, because I know they would." I was rambling. I wiped at the corner of my eye.

"I don't want women following me and I don't want Kim. I think I've made that clear."

"Everything happened so fast and it was so confusing. I know you said that, but I just wasn't sure."

"Well, I'm telling you now, so you're clear, I don't." He placed his index finger under my chin and lifted my face to meet his gaze.

I stared at him.

"I can tell you what I do want," he said.

Oh yes, please, tell me. Unless it was bad, then I didn't want to hear. Before the words left his lips, the front door burst open and two men stormed into the room. Rory jumped up and so did I.

Rory stood in front of me with his arms shielding my body. The men stared at us as if we were at some kind of Old Wild West shootout. The silence hung in the air as the staring showdown continued for what seemed like an awkwardly long time. They didn't have their guns pointed directly at us, but in the general vicinity, which was way too close for comfort for me. One wrong move and they'd probably fill us with bullets. Beau's barking echoed from the backyard. He wanted a piece of these men badly.

"What's going on?" Rory asked.

"Elly Blair needs to come with us." The taller of the two men moved toward me.

Kidnapped twice in one day. That must be some kind of world record. My mama always said I'd be famous, now I knew she was right. In the Book of World Records for being kidnapped multiple times in twenty-four hours. Lucky me. The two men grabbed me and dragged me off. Rory made a lunge for us. I don't know what the bigger of the two men said to him, but it made him stop in his tracks. I didn't know where they were taking me.

"I thought everything was taken care of," I said.

The men held their guns and pointed them at Rory the whole time they dragged me to their car. I kicked and screamed but it didn't have any effect on the situation.

"Where are you taking me?" I demanded.

"Be quiet and get in the car," the taller one said.

They both wore black suits with white shirts and black ties. Their black sedan had dark tinted windows. The taller one shoved me in the car and got in next to me as the other one climbed behind the wheel.

We spun out from the gravel drive and, just like that, I was gone from Rory's house. What was going through his mind? Probably the same thing that was going through mine. Who in the heck were these men?

"I demand that you tell me who you are."

The driver glanced back in the rearview mirror.

"We're saving you."

"Excuse me? Come again? What are you saving me from?"

"We had information that you'd been kidnapped."

"Had been kidnapped. Had been. That was hours ago. Where were you when I needed you? I was at that man's house because I wanted to be, not because I'd been held captive. Now turn this car around and take me back this very minute. I order you to."

"Sorry, no can do. We have to take you to the boss."

Chapter Forty-Five

"We were told to come rescue you. Although, I was told it was a woman who'd kidnapped you, not a man. Where was she?"

"I was kidnapped by a woman this morning, but not now, you big dummy. Now turn this car around, you've made a huge mistake. Huge. Do you mind telling me who your boss is?" I asked through gritted teeth. My heart pounded loudly in my ears. It was one thing to be kidnapped by Kim, but entirely another to be whisked away at gunpoint by two intimidating men. Being kidnapped by Kim was like being kidnapped by a puppy compared to these two roughnecks.

"Do I mind, she asks." He laughed, holding his stomach. "Do I mind," he whispered to the driver who glanced at us in the rearview mirror. "Mr. Wibble, of course."

"Of course. Do you mind if I call Tom Owenton and tell him about this madness? I think he'll have something to say about this."

The back of the limo had black leather seats, of course, and smelled of cigar smoke and old liquor. The last time I'd been in one of these was in New York when I dragged my drunken, half-naked boss out of the back of one and helped her inside her apartment. She had called me at two a.m. from a nightclub insisting if I didn't pick her up, she'd end up in jail. That was probably one of her more sane assumptions, which were few and far between.

The limo had a small bar stocked with a variety of liquors. I wasn't much of a drinker, but now seemed like a good time to take up the habit.

"I'll call him." He fumbled in his jacket pocket and pulled out his phone. He dialed the number and handed it to me.

Tom picked up on the first ring.

"What is going on, Tom?" I yelled into the phone.

"I'm eating a doughnut," he mumbled. I envisioned the crumbs all over the receiver.

"Can you explain to me why I'm being held against my will in the back of a black limousine?" I asked matter-of-factly.

He coughed. I assumed over the chunk of doughy goodness. "What the hell. Where are you?"

"I went to Rory's like we discussed. But in the middle of our conversation, these two scary-looking..." I cleared my throat. "Um, gentlemen stormed in and took me away." I glanced over at my backseat abductor. He frowned as if he were offended by being called creepy. I just called it like I saw it.

"What are the two goons' names?" Tom asked.

I moved the phone from my face a little, then asked, "What are your names?"

He hesitated, then finally answered. "I'm Bob and that's Charlie."

I put the phone back up to my ear. "Charlie and Bob. That's all they'll tell me."

He groaned. "Put one of them on the phone, would you?"

"No problem." I handed the phone toward Bob. "He'd like to speak with you."

He quirked a brow, then took the phone. "Hello," he said. "Uh-huh. Okay. Yeah, but I was just following orders. Whatever the boss says is what goes. Yeah, well, why don't you have the boss call me?" He hung up the phone and glared at me.

Apparently, he was upset that I'd ratted him out. I shrugged. "It's not my fault you messed up," I said.

His phone rang and he answered. "Uh-huh. Yes, sir. Yes, right away." He hung up. His face had turned a shade whiter.

"That man is following us," Charlie said.

I whipped around to look out the back window. Rory was in his truck, now tailgating the limo. He'd come for me. Aw, my hero. How he planned to rescue me from these numbskulls, I had no idea, but that was beside the point. He'd cared enough to come after me. Did that mean he was willing to accept the magic? Did he no longer think I was one pudding cup short of a six-pack? With any luck, I'd soon find out. Jumping out wasn't an option. I wasn't brave enough for that. Plus, at forty miles an hour, I'm guessing it would have been a tad painful.

"Do you mind pulling over now?" I demanded.

"No can do," Charlie said, glancing in the mirror at me, "we have to take you to the boss."

Bob cleared his throat. "Um, about that...We may have made a teensy mistake."

"What?" Charlie straightened behind the wheel, glancing back in the mirror again.

"Um, apparently I didn't listen to a voice mail that said we weren't supposed to pick her up." He shifted in the seat.

"You two are the worst rescuers in the history of rescues. Now pull over." I glanced out the back window again. Rory's truck remained inches away from the limousine's bumper.

Charlie guided the long car over to the side of the road, gravel crunching under the wheels. Rory had almost rammed us when Charlie had slowed down. He pulled his truck up behind us and jumped out, not bothering to close the door behind him. I pulled on the handle, but it didn't budge. Rory pounded on the window. I was afraid the glass would break into a million pieces he was beating so hard.

"Unlock the door now," Rory's voice boomed through the glass.

The door clicked and unlocked, but before I had a chance to grasp my fingers around the handle, Rory yanked it open. When I jumped out, Rory captured my hand, pulling me toward him. Once away from the car, he grabbed me with both arms.

"Oh my God, are you all right?" He held me at arm's length and looked me up and down.

"I'm okay." I nodded, taking in a deep breath.

He pulled me close again, hugging me tightly. My heart thumped. His chest felt so right pressed against mine.

"What the hell happened?" he asked with an edge to his voice. Rory looked as if he wanted to punch both of them.

"It was all a misunderstanding. They thought I still needed to be rescued from Kim."

Rory responded with a lift of his eyebrows. Charlie stepped from behind the wheel and Bob fumbled with the lock on the other door. He finally shoved it open and jumped out.

"Right fellas, everything is okay now?" In spite of wanting to clobber them earlier, I kind of felt sorry for them now.

"Yeah, sorry about that, man. Let us know if we need to have your front door fixed."

Rory scowled. "Don't worry, I will. Come on, let's get out of here." Rory led me by the elbow toward his truck.

He glanced back several times, frowning at Charlie and Bob. He was none too happy with those two. I hopped in his truck and he closed the door behind me, then went back to the limo where Bob was getting into the vehicle. Uh-oh. Did I need to break up a fight between these three? I wasn't sure Rory could take on these two meatheads although, as mad as he seemed, maybe he wouldn't have any problems.

The men talked and Rory pointed back at me. Bob held his hands up in surrender, then Rory stomped back to the truck and climbed in behind the wheel.

"Everything okay now?" I asked.

"I can't believe that they'd just break into someone's home like that. What if I'd had a gun? But I guess they had guns too, huh?"

"It would have been an ugly situation, I'll admit that. But they had my best interests at heart."

He let out a deep breath as he started the truck. "Yeah, I suppose they did. It was just a bit of an adrenaline rush, that's all. It'll take me a minute to get over it."

"I understand. I was freaking out, too. I'm really sorry about all this."

"It's okay now. I need a minute to calm down, that's all. It's not every day someone breaks into your home with guns."

"I'm sorry I dragged you into all this."

"You didn't drag me into anything. If I didn't want to be here, I wouldn't be."

Chapter Forty-Six

Rory turned the truck around and headed back in the direction of his place. As much as I liked the thought of going back there, spending time alone without worrying about ex-girlfriends and magic spells, there was one last thing I needed to take care of in order to reopen the café.

And one last thing needed to be settled before I continued any kind of relationship with Rory. The magic. I had to make sure the spell was reversed. Plus, I could show Rory that I wasn't a complete nut-job. Our relationship would be stuck in neutral if I didn't right my wrong. When he saw the sparks from the spell, he'd have to believe me.

"Are you hungry?" I asked. "How about some good down-home cooking?"

"Are you trying to add magic again?" He steered the truck, not taking his eyes off the wheel.

I frowned. He'd never eat another bite of my food.

"Sorry, forget I said that."

"Consider it forgotten." I pushed forward with my mission. "You must have burned up a lot of calories with that adrenaline rush. How about we go back to the café and I'll fix us some food. The picnic wasn't much."

No more secrets, I reminded myself. I didn't want to tell him what I was trying to do. Maybe he'd rush to get out from under the spell. After all, women still followed him almost everywhere he went. Two cars full of women tailed us now. I wasn't sure, but I thought I recognized one of the women behind the wheel of a gray Buick as my first grade teacher.

"No, it sure wasn't much. Kim never could even make a sandwich, although she liked to think she was a gourmet chef. I'm still trying to wrap my head around what went on today, though." He glanced over at me. I didn't think he'd noticed the women following us.

"I know it was weird and, in hindsight, perhaps I could have dealt with things differently." I looked in the side mirror and willed the women to go away. It didn't work, they continued their trek.

"No, you did what you had to do, I understand that."

"She broke into my bedroom, you know. I still can't believe she did that. I think the city smog may have gotten to her."

"Well, apparently the small-town fresh air didn't reverse it," he said.

"Do you still have feelings for Kim? I know you said you didn't love her but, deep down, I think she might have some redeeming qualities. Somewhere."

A small smile crossed his lips. "I'll always have feelings for her, but not in that way. Not the way I feel for you."

My stomach tingled against my will. I couldn't stop the smile from spreading across my face. That was the answer I'd wanted to hear.

"I stopped loving her a while back. She wasn't exactly an ideal girlfriend, if you know what I mean."

"So I've heard." I placed my hand on his shoulder.

"There's a lot of talk in this small town, huh?" Rory steered the truck onto Main Street.

"Everyone knows everyone, no way to hide much. That's the way it works."

"Yes, it does. And since it's hard to hide much, you want to share more of this magic story with me?" he asked.

"Apparently, my grandmother has been performing a little magical intervention on Mystic Café patrons for years now. She wanted to retire to sunshine and golf in Florida. Heck, knowing her, she probably wanted to find a younger boyfriend."

He chuckled.

"Anyway, as you know, she left me the café. But she didn't spring the full job description on me until she was on the way out the door. No wonder my mother didn't want to take over the business, well, that and the fact she's a terrible cook. The spells are all good, only to help people feel better—physically and mentally. A little love." I cast a glance and grinned. "Maybe something to take away the aches and pains. That sort of thing."

"Doesn't sound like black magic or witchcraft."

"Really, it's not. What made you think it was?"

"Nothing specific. It's just that a lot of people might think evil when they hear about magic spells. Especially in a small town like this. Like I said, my mom's friend used to cast spells. She used herbs and oils. As far as I know, she didn't have special powers." He gave a little shrug of his shoulders. "Maybe she did, I don't know."

"Yeah, the whole evil thing is probably why people in Mystic don't know. Not because it's bad, but because they would assume it was." I glanced in the mirror to see the carload of women still trailing us. I hoped they didn't storm the truck, toss me out, and ride off into the sunset with Rory. He still didn't seem to notice them or, if he did, he didn't mention it.

"Huh, I guess that's why it's called Mystic Hollow."

As we pulled up to the café, the two cars drove past, but pulled into a nearby parking lot. With any luck, I would reverse the rest of the spell before they formed an angry mob.

I shrugged, answering his question, but distracted by the women. "Maybe. I don't know, but there are a lot of things I don't know."

My cell phone rang. "It's Mary Jane, excuse me for a second." I held up my index finger, indicating I needed one minute for my call.

"What's going on? Where are you?" she yelled into the phone.

"Take a deep breath." I listened to her exhale, waiting for her to get a hold of her excitement. "I was going to call you, but things have been crazy." I brushed a stray strand of hair out of my eyes with one hand while holding the phone with the other.

"Sheriff Jasper told me what happened. I leave to take a test and this is what happens? Am I going to have to put you on a leash?"

I laughed. "Maybe you will. I'm with Rory now. We're having food. Why don't you come by and bring Sheriff Jasper?"

She paused. If I knew Mary Jane, she was blushing. "I'll be by soon and I want the full story. Are you working on a spell for Rory?"

"Yep."

"A reverse spell."

"Yep."

"I'll be there soon." I knew she would and, with any luck, she'd have a police escort.

When I clicked off the phone, Rory said, "She worries about you, huh?"

"She does. It's like having another mother. I have enough as it is with my mother and my grandmother."

"Speaking of your grandmother, does she know yet?"

"No, but I'll have to tell her soon. I can't put it off forever."

We made our way out of his truck and to the café without incident. The women may have followed us, but there were no signs of the limousine, Charlie or Bob. Or Kim. And for that, I was thankful.

I wondered if Kim was with Tom. For Tom's sake, I hoped Kim hadn't set her sights on him. He was annoying sometimes, but a great guy and he didn't need Kim's claws in him. Although, Tom probably wouldn't fall for any of her silly shenanigans.

My excitement level spiked when I remembered I was very close to opening the café again. A second chance, and this time I wouldn't screw it up. I'd learn to work the magic just as grandma had. After all, she'd given me a gift, not a curse.

"You're nothing but an adventure, you know that?" Rory said, as he waited for me to fish the café keys out from the deep caverns of my purse. Luckily, he'd thought to grab it from his house when he went back for his truck keys.

I shook my head. "No, I didn't know that. Isn't everyone kidnapped at least once in their lives? Don't most people inherit their grandmother's magical café?"

"No and no." He chuckled. "And you weren't just kidnapped once, but twice."

"Oh, yeah, thanks for reminding me."

"So you didn't press charges against Kim? Why's that?"

"There was no need. She didn't mean to harm me. She'll be out of my hair now."

"Out of our hair." He winked.

I didn't want to tell him she'd still have to deal with the organization. I'd probably never get used to all their magical rules.

I unlocked the café door, yanked the *Closed* sign off and we stepped into the empty space.

"The glass should be in soon, they said."

"Thanks again for taking care of that. It'll be ready for the reopening soon."

Foot in mouth. He didn't know I'd been forced to close.

"Reopening? I didn't know you were ever officially closed."

"Well, that's the thing. After the break-in, the magical organization felt it best if I closed until things were settled. Luckily, it didn't last long." He looked confused but didn't question my answer. He probably thought I was being ditzy. I didn't bother filling him in on all the details, like the fact that I'd almost lost the café for good.

"I wondered why when I drove by it looked empty and the lights were off."

Being in the café was as if I'd come home again after being away for a very long time. It hadn't even been twenty-four hours, but it felt like twenty-four days. It was strange every time I saw the café empty. I didn't like it that way, it felt right when it was packed full of Mystic Hollow residents—as if all was right with the world and everyone was safe and cozy. Of course, the world isn't really safe and cozy, but it was nice to have that feeling once in a while.

"Why don't you take a seat and look at the menu?"

"I'll trust you to make whatever you want me to have." He smiled. "As a matter of fact, why don't I help you?"

Chapter Forty-Seven

He read my mind.

I beamed. "I'd like that."

As we made our way toward the kitchen, the front door opened. We spun around and Rory let out a small groan. Apparently, he still hadn't warmed up to Tom who waved at us with a huge smile spread across his face.

"I just came to say goodbye." He winked at me as he placed his duffel bag on the counter.

"Oh, leaving so soon?" Rory deadpanned.

I knew why Tom was there, to make sure the spell was complete. The case would be marked closed and it wouldn't come soon enough for me.

"I was getting ready to fix food for us. How about a little something for the road?"

Rory probably just wanted Tom to beat it, and I wanted the café out of danger as soon as possible, so I'd make the quickest thing I could.

"How about my southern style chicken salad? It has mustard and a little bit of vinegar. Grandma and I use vinegar in a lot of food. A little bit will never hurt, she says."

"Sounds good," Tom said.

"Chicken salad it is." I clapped my hands together.

Rory followed me to the kitchen and Tom tagged along, too. One wasn't going to let the other one outdo him. I'd miss Tom when he left. He'd really started to grow on me.

"So you're leaving town, huh? Elly finally doesn't need you anymore?" Rory asked.

"I suppose she doesn't." Tom looked at me and smiled with a wink. "It's a shame because I'd like to stay around longer, if she'd have me."

"Well, I'm sure you have plenty other work to keep you busy." Rory sounded as if he'd have pushed Tom out the door right then and there if he could have.

This was awkward. I'd never felt this kind of tension in the air before.

"I almost forgot the book." Tom hurried back out to the counter and pulled the book from his bag. "You left the book and spices in my car, so I thought I'd bring them over."

That book had a way of keeping up with me and it's a good thing; I still hadn't learned to keep a better eye on it, but it had been safer with Tom than with me during my second kidnapping of the day.

"Thanks." I wrapped my arms around the large book and carried it to my workspace counter. "This is my magic spell book, Rory, the one I was telling you about."

He stepped closer and reached out, touching the cover. "It looks old."

"It is, sort of," Tom said. "Well...the content is old. We're not sure how old it is really."

I glanced at Tom and he nodded his approval at the question he knew I was getting ready to ask Rory.

"If it's okay with you, I want to show you the magic. Reverse the mistake I made."

"Are you serious?" Rory stared wide-eyed.

I shook my head. "I'm serious."

He glanced from me to Tom, then back to me. "Okay. I'm game. I'll try anything once. Shoe me what you've got."

I started grabbing food and utensils. "I'd be happy to."

After spreading the chicken salad I'd made onto the bread, I laid out all the spices in front of me. My shoulder muscles tensed and my heart pumped harder. If I screwed this up, my happy ending would crumble faster than grandma's cinnamon crumble coffee cake. Steadying my shaky hands, I flipped to the correct page in the book, then sprinkled the first spice on Rory's sandwich.

As long as he didn't get the wrong one this time, everything should work out fine. Without looking his way, I knew he was watching me. I felt his gaze. What was going through his mind? My fingers were crossed that there'd be no more mix-ups this time. As I added the second spice, a fizzing sound bubbled up from the sandwich. Sparks popped from the food, some shooting straight up, and others out to the side in a spectacular little light show. Glancing over at my audience, I waited for a reaction, but there was none. Tom watched on as an approving coach, and Rory looked captivated. Since Rory didn't ask me to stop, I turned back to the task at hand. I whirled my hand around and through the blue and red streams of sparkles, hoping this might help ease Rory's reservations and show him it wouldn't hurt anyone.

"Is this safe to eat?" he asked over the whirring sound of the mini-tornado.

"You ate it before and it didn't kill you."

"Good point," he said.

When I added the third spice, more sparks ignited, flashing up into the air.

Rory looked on wide-eyed. "I've never seen anything like it. It's like mini fireworks. Either I'm crazy, or you've rigged some kind of special effects, or you were telling the truth."

"I wanted you to know the truth." Under my breath, I spoke the words I felt would make the spell go away for good. "So mote it be," I whispered, finishing off the spell. Before adding another slice of wheat bread to the top, I dashed one last sprinkle of cilantro over the sandwich.

"Take a bite." I stretched the plate toward Rory.

"What will happen when I eat it?"

"Nothing, since it's a reverse spell," I said.

"Why do I feel like a guinea pig?" he asked.

"Because you kind of are." I laughed. "Don't worry, the only time the spells are bad is when the wrong person gets them, so you're safe now."

"Now." He smirked.

"That little mix-up you experienced rarely happens," I said, casting a glance over to Tom. "Right, Tom?"

Tom raised a brow. "Yeah, rarely." He rolled his eyes.

Rory picked up the sandwich and slowly moved it toward his mouth. I held my breath. He looked at me again, and I motioned for him to go ahead. He raised it to his mouth and took a bite. He chewed and swallowed.

Chapter Forty-Eight

"This is delicious," Rory said with a mouthful of food. "I don't know about the magic, but I never knew a sandwich could taste so good." He took another bite.

I wiggled my brows. "What can I say? I've got a magic touch."

Tom and Rory laughed, then looked at each other as if shocked they'd actually shared a moment of mutual agreement and not gotten into a fistfight yet.

"I can't argue with that," Rory said, then took another big bite.

The feeling of unease that I'd experienced since the spell slipup vanished. A heavy weight had lifted from my shoulders with the first bite Rory took. Gone was the malaise that had hung so heavy in the air. It had been replaced by a new feeling, one of exuberance and confidence. Tom smiled with a nod. He felt it, too.

With my newly acquired poise, I made a sandwich for Tom, cutting it down the middle. "You sure you can't stick around long enough to eat?" I wrapped the sandwich carefully, placing it in a bag.

"No, I'd better get started. I've got a long trip ahead."

Tom looked to Rory. "Mind if I kiss her goodbye?"

Rory seemed to tense up, as he eyed Tom up and down. "I'm timing you." He looked at his watch.

Didn't I get a say in this matter? They acted as if I wasn't even standing there.

As if reading my mind, Tom asked, "How about a kiss goodbye?"

I nodded. "I'd like that."

Tom stepped close and cupped my face with his hands. He tilted his head, then gently placed his mouth on my cheek. His warm lips whispered across my face. He lingered there for several seconds until Rory coughed.

He stepped away and said, "I'll see you around, Elly."

Tom walked toward the kitchen door, stopping just before exiting. He smiled, then winked before moving out the kitchen door and out of my life. Just like that, he was gone. Would I ever see him again? Something told me the answer to that question was yes.

I turned to Rory. "There really was nothing going on between us."

Rory moved closer. "I believe you."

"You do?"

He didn't answer my question, instead he said, "You know what's wrong with you?"

My heart rate increased. He was going to let me have it, and rightfully so, I supposed. My stomach turned, waiting for him to tell me to stay out of his life. Out of nervousness, I studied my shoes. When I looked up again, Rory stood in front of me. My emotions spiked and I swallowed the lump in my throat. Rory's gaze moved down to my lips. He leaned in, placing his hands above me against the wall. My heart pounded and my insides quivered. The heat from his body encircled me as if I'd stepped into a sauna.

"Not a damn thing." He leaned down and pressed his lips to mine, pulling me close against his chest. Rory kissed me and I let him.

His kiss was slow and sensual, sending a surge of heat rushing to my feet. With one hand, he stroked the back of my neck and caressed my cheek with the other. In that moment, the world seemed to stand still. With my fingers threaded through his hair, I pressed my chest next to his, feeling his hard muscles against me.

His lips were warm and soft and he sent a tingle down my body—a feeling that left me wanting more. Rory let out a soft moan as he traced his tongue across my bottom lip. When I didn't think I could handle any more without melting into a puddle at his feet, he lifted his lips from mine. I opened my eyes and met Rory's gaze.

After the best kiss I'd ever had, I said, "You think that's funny? You scared me."

His grin widened, then he laughed. "As a matter of fact, it was kind of funny. The expression on your face was priceless." His gaze traveled the length of my body, lingering over the cleavage provided by my black v-necked T-shirt.

My heart sped up again. He was going to cause me to need a cardiologist.

"You look beautiful," he whispered.

I glanced down at my jeans and sneakers. Obviously, he saw something I didn't. Kim had been wrong. Apparently, Rory liked my style of dress just fine.

He looked me straight in the eyes. "Elly, since the first day I saw you, I can't get you out of my head. Even after you told me about the magic and I thought you might be crazy, I didn't care."

"Hey!" I couldn't blame him. The idea of magic spells did sound outlandish.

He chuckled. "All I know is the night we went to the fair and shared ice cream was the best time I've ever had. The way your mouth curves to one side when you smile, the way you clench your fists when you're mad and the way your hazel eyes sparkle. Those are all reasons why I want to know you better."

"Did you plan that whole talk?"

Rory took my hand and lifted it to his lips. "Nope. It just came out."

I looked him straight in the eyes. "Since the first day I saw you, I can't get you out of my head. I don't know why you came with me after hearing my magic crazy talk, why you put so much ketchup on my hamburgers, or why you shuffle your feet when someone is talking to you. But I know the night at the fair was the best time I've ever had. The way your butt looks in jeans, and the way your dimples pop up when you smile doesn't hurt, either. Those are all reasons why I want to know you better."

I pulled back so I could get a better look at Rory's expression and grinned. This still didn't seem real. The café would remain open and I didn't have to worry about the messed up magic. No more Kim, and no more crazed women chasing Rory.

A knock sounded on the door, which made me jump. I was certain the spell had worked. Were the women of town back? I peeked out the kitchen window and saw Henry standing at the door.

"Oh, it's Henry. I told him to stop by anytime for coffee and pie."

"Looks like you got a customer then." Rory held the kitchen door open for me.

"You said I could stop by anytime," Henry said when I opened the door.

"Of course. Why don't you sit in this booth right here by the window?" I gestured with a sweep of my hand. "I think it's the best seat in the house."

Henry shuffled in. He looked Rory up and down while taking off his cap.

"How ya doing?" Rory asked.

"I'm fair to middlin'." Henry answered with a nod.

"Can I get you something to eat?" I asked.

The smell of whiskey around him had lessened. "I'd love a cup of coffee."

"I don't have any pie at the moment, but there are a few muffins left. It may not be as good as Imelda's, but it's a close second, I think."

Henry smiled. "I'd like that."

I placed the muffin on a plate and turned on the coffeemaker. All of this felt right—serving food and making people happy with magic. This was where I belonged. I may have had to leave Mystic Hollow before discovering it, but now I knew there was nowhere I'd rather be.

I set the muffin in front of Henry. "It'll be just a minute for the coffee."

He nodded, picking up his napkin.

When I moved back to the counter where Rory stood, he scooped me up in a hug.

Tilting his head down, he smiled and asked, "So, what do you think? Wanna make a go of it?"

I raised a brow. "It?"

"Uh-huh. Us? You and me?"

Did I ever. But there was one unanswered question.

"Do you accept my magic?"

His fingers wrapped around mine and I felt my anxiety melt away. "Just don't turn me into a toad."

"I promise. Unless you eat the wrong burger."

"Will you spray whipped cream on me?" he asked with a teasing curl of his lip.

Heat rose in my cheeks. "Only if you want me to."

"I like the sound of that."

I lifted on my toes and draped my arms around his neck, pressing my lips on his. "So do I," I murmured against his mouth.

I kissed Rory and my body tingled. But this time, I knew my feelings had nothing to do with magic. Or did they? Maybe it *was* written in the stars. After all, magic happens.

About Rose Pressey

Rose Pressey enjoys writing quirky and fun novels with a paranormal twist. She's always found the paranormal interesting. The thought of finding answers to the unexplained fascinates her.

When she's not writing about werewolves, vampires, and every other supernatural creature, she loves eating cupcakes with sprinkles, reading, spending time with family, and listening to oldies from the fifties.

Rose lives in the beautiful commonwealth of Kentucky with her husband, son and three sassy Chihuahuas.

www.rosepressey.com
rose@rosepressey.com
www.twitter.com/rosepressey
www.facebook.com/rosepressey